Praise for
Where Dreams Fall

"The romantasy book of the year! *Where Dreams Fall* is the kind of book that consumes you. Caulder is a master at transporting her readers to a lush and sexy fantasy world with a nonstop plot and hot-as-sin romance. If this is a dream, please don't wake me up." —Sara Cate, *New York Times*–bestselling author of the Salacious Players' Club and Wilde Boys series

"A fierce romantasy that's not afraid to show its claws. Pulse-pounding intrigue, delicious romance, and an ending that left me speechless! *Where Dreams Fall* is everything I want in fantasy romance."
—LJ Andrews, *USA Today*–bestselling author of the Ever Seas and Broken Souls and Bones series

"A pulse-pounding descent into a world where nightmares bleed into reality and salvation comes cloaked in starlight. R.L. Caulder weaves terror and tenderness with masterful precision. Elysia's desperate flight will leave your heart in your throat, only for a velvet-voiced dreamkeeper to steal it entirely. Dark, seductive, and utterly addictive, this is fantasy romance at its fiercest. Dive in . . . if you dare wake up."
—C.R. Jane, *USA Today*–bestselling author of the Spartan Flame and Pucking Wrong series

"R.L. Caulder delivers a sweeping tale of resistance and romance. The characters pop off the pages and make you love—or hate—them, and the deft worldbuilding, deep emotion, and poignant longing make this a series I cannot wait to continue. Fans of smart and determined FMCs, hot and capable elves, magic, and slow-burn romance will gobble this up!"
—Amanda Bouchet, *USA Today*–bestselling author of the Kingmaker Chronicles

"A dark fantasy in the realm of dreams and nightmares, with elven court politics, a brooding, possessive elf, and a strong heroine whose empathy will be both her downfall and her salvation? YES PLEASE."
—Steffanie Holmes, *USA Today*–bestselling author of *Fangs for Nothing*

"There is little I enjoy reading more than a slow burn, but when you add in tension, forbidden attraction, and soul mates, I will eat it up and that's exactly what I did with R.L. Caulder's *Where Dreams Fall.* A sweeping, fast-paced, spell-binding romantasy, I was gripped from the first page to the last."
—Elayna R. Gallea, bestselling author of the Binding Chronicles and the Giving Chronicles

"An absolutely addictive read, filled with high stakes, hot elves, and a heroine you can't help but root for. Elysia is everything you could want—cunning, protective, and determined. This is the perfect read for fans of Nisha J. Tuli and Lauren Roberts or anyone who has been aching for their next forbidden bodyguard romance. You are not going to want to miss this!"
—Vasilisa Drake, author of the Kingdom of Dark Magic and Shifted Fates series

"Caulder's strong series opener presents a dark fantasy romance with a complex, richly developed main character whose strength lies uniquely in her compassion. . . . The explosive resolution will have readers dreaming of a sequel."
—*Kirkus Reviews*

WHERE DREAMS FALL

WHERE DREAMS FALL

R.L. CAULDER

All rights reserved. No part of this publication may be reproduced, stored in a retrieval system, or transmitted in any form or by any means electronic, mechanical, photocopying, recording, or otherwise without prior written permission from Podium Publishing.

This is a work of fiction. Names, characters, places, and incidents are either products of the author's imagination or used fictitiously. Any resemblance to actual events, locales, or persons, living, dead, or undead, is entirely coincidental.

Copyright © 2026 by R.L. Caulder

Cover design by Franziska Stern

ISBN: 979-8-89539-956-9

Published in 2026 by Podium Publishing
www.podiumentertainment.com

AUTHOR'S NOTE

This story was born from a single question that wouldn't let me go: *What if I meshed Legolas and the Sandman?*

From that spark, my dream swoon-worthy elf book boyfriend was born, and an entire world bloomed around him. Yet somehow, *Where Dreams Fall* grew into something far deeper than I ever imagined. I was only four months postpartum when I began writing this book, and the tender, fierce love that blossomed inside me alongside my daughter found its way onto the page and into Elysia's soul.

This story is my love letter to the soft-hearted heroines who fight even when the world tells them they shouldn't. To every reader who sees themselves in Elysia—in her defiance, her quiet courage, or the ember of hope she refuses to let die—this book is for you. May you always remember: your dreams are worth fighting for.

B. J. Caulder

VOTHIA
NORTH
DARKETHORNE
THORNMARSH
STORMREACH
COLDFEN
AELWORTH
CAVEMIRE
VIREMOOR
FALLOWMERE
IRONREACH
WOLNBROOK
SHADEFELL
GRAVEMIRE
DUSKWATCH
EBONHOLLO
DARKHARROW
GLOOMRIDGE
VEXRUN
WHITEROOT

EMPIRE
SERINVALE
ILYRA
FALKETH
AERILON
DURIEN
THORNEVAL
NORWYNTH
TRAMIR
CELAINE
VARINHOLT
GRESSAR
RAVESS
BRAVELLE
PLITHU
MIRELIN
AVENTRA
HALLOWMERE
EDRITCH

WHERE DREAMS FALL

CHAPTER ONE

ELYSIA

The shrieks come in waves, bloodcurdling cries that pierce the air, signaling their hunt.

The hunt for *me.*

My heart races, hammering against my ribs like a caged beast, desperate for escape as I pump my arms and legs to find exactly that. There has to be a way out, a place of sanctuary.

Each of my inhaled breaths is ragged, each pulse a countdown to what feels like my end.

The sounds of my enemies sharpen as they draw closer to me, a predator homing in on their prey despite my continued race through the darkened night.

Only the moon illuminates the dead forest rushing by, full of husks and rotted trees, partially obscured by a gentle, wafting mist. My breath hitches as the ground rushes up to meet me, my foot caught in a tangle of roots. A sharp gasp escapes from my parted lips as a throbbing pain rushes through my palms and knees.

I quickly snap my mouth shut, eyes widening as the weight of my carelessness slams into me.

Strands of my dark hair brush over my eyes and cheeks as I quickly glance around for a place to hide. The air is thick with something rotting and damp earth, as if death itself festers in the mist. A tingle of familiarity runs down my spine at the scent before a deep, foreboding dread takes hold of my core and the truth crashes into me.

The Valgys? No . . . it can't be them.

Deep within my being I know this to be the truth—that they're here for me—with no explanation as to how I know it. It's like an endless

void when I try to probe within the recesses of my mind, yet I continue to push. White-hot flashes of pain bloom behind my eyes and finally I relent, re-focusing on what I can.

I need shelter and I need it now.

My eyes scan the roots of all the dead trees I can make out as my wheels turn. My tumultuous thoughts come to a halt as I realize a key detail: I've never seen a tree with such massive roots, ones that spring up from the ground like cresting waves through the mist a mere five feet away from me. I inhale sharply, that simple detail telling me all I need to know as someone who grew up frolicking in the forest surrounding our village . . . I'm nowhere close to home.

Worse, I don't remember how I got here.

A particularly large set of roots reveals itself—I may be able to take shelter beneath. I stay low as I crawl toward them, hoping the mist will aid in my attempt to stay hidden. Fresh pain blossoms on my palms and knees as they scrape against the rough, hard-packed earth, covered with splinters of broken wood.

A small, short-lived sense of relief floods my mind as I squeeze between a small gap in the roots at the edge of the rotted tree. Curling my knees up to my chest, I wrap my arms around my trembling legs where my threadbare dress rides up.

A tingling, biting cold begins to work from the tips of my extremities before settling into my limbs fully, making them feel far heavier.

Shadows coil at the edges of my vision as my eyelids droop, moving with unnatural grace, whispering their sickly promises. *Just let go.* It would be so easy . . . so painless.

A vision of my mother slips into my mind. Her standing over my grave . . . her sobs raw and broken. I can almost hear her now, furious through her grief. *"I raised you to be stronger than this, Elysia. I ought to bring you back to life just to give you a tongue-lashing for leaving your family behind like this."*

My fingers drop from my legs and curl into the ground, scraping against the hard-packed dirt as I fight for a way to center myself.

No. I will not be a name carved into stone.

The thought is a lifeline, a defiant thread I cling to in the abyss.

"I will not . . . die here." My voice wavers, barely more than a breath through the chattering of my teeth, but saying it aloud shakes the shadows away.

The shrieks rise again, shaking me from my paralysis. My body rattles with adrenaline, a welcome feeling to fight the numbing cold. The dead tree roots arch around me like skeletal fingers, my only meager wall of defense; my only chance of not being found. Moonlight slants through the gnarled roots, illuminating nothing but mist and decay, yet I know they draw closer.

I blindly feel around for anything that I can use to defend myself while keeping my eyes on my surroundings. My fingers wrap around a thick branch and I barely hold back a sigh of relief when it doesn't crumble at my touch.

I won't go down easy if they find me.

The grit and determination within me builds as a new round of shrieks echoes into the night sky, pulling my head to the left.

A snap pierces the darkness.

Every instinct screams at me to *run*, but to where? I do a quick sweep of my immediate surroundings, in case I missed something, but there's no clear path to safety.

The shrieks merge into a single, unified blast. Agony rips through my skull as if daggers are being driven into my ears, over and over. I drop the branch and instinctively clap my hands over them, barely stifling a cry. Black dots dance across my vision.

I fight through the pain sealing my eyes shut as I grope for my branch. Finding it once more, I hold on to it tightly as the barrage continues, grateful for the splinters of wood that dig into my skin, reminding me that I'm still here, that I can still fight.

Then . . . silence.

A deeper, more insidious dread coils in my stomach. The wind has stopped. No crickets. No night birds.

My head jerks at the sound of a branch snapping nearby, and I all but cease breathing to remain hidden. I can practically feel the hot, heavy breath of the creatures on my neck as they lurk in the dark, drawing ever closer.

Searing, white-hot pain explodes in a trail of fire across my back and I let out a gasp despite my best efforts to contain it. Two more branches snap in front of me, closer this time, giving me no time to discover why the muscles in my back are suddenly seizing.

I bite down onto my bottom lip hard enough to feel the warmth of my blood spilling from the split in my skin. The metallic taste fills

my mouth and the flare of pain does its job of distracting me from the unknown wound on my back.

I can't help but recoil as the smell of those hunting me assaults my senses, a rancid combination of sulfur and something sour. There is no doubt they have found me now, and that the creatures hunting me *are* the Valgys, as I feared.

Despite being hunted by these creatures, I can't help the brief second of wondering who they were before this. Before the loss of their elven origin and the lives they could have led. I'm sure they had been loved and important to someone before being tempted by evil.

Now I have to kill them, or be killed myself.

The sharp sting of their stench draws tears to my eyes and raw terror claws its way up my throat.

I'm not sure how I got here, but I'm damn sure going to get out of here and back to my family. They need me now more than ever, especially if the Valgys are in our world.

An image of my family slain in our home flashes through my mind and I attempt to shove it down, but don't succeed. Their blood, soaked into the wooden planks of our home that my father cut down and built with his own hands. My mother's fabrics for work strewn about and dipped in crimson pools. The lifeless eyes of my little sister staring up at me as I drop to my knees to cradle her body to mine.

A shadow moves in the fog, dragging me back to the present.

I press a trembling hand to my chest as if I could quiet my racing heart when the first of the creatures steps into view.

Monstrous, broken creatures that were once elves before they were twisted by a dark god's corruption. They're only supposed to exist in stories, buried with the Blood War four thousand years ago, but I know what I see, and I know what I smell.

Four more Valgys step into view.

Their heads loll at unnatural angles, and their eight glowing eyes burn like dying embers. Acid drips from their melting skin, hissing as it eats into the earth. The scent of their rotting skin hits me, choking my throat with bile.

The blinding pain on my back flares once more, and within seconds their multitudes of catlike irises are trained on my position, causing my heart to sink into my stomach.

Their mouths stretch open, unveiling rows of serrated teeth as they release their victorious shriek.

I have to get out of here. This measly branch won't be enough to defend myself from this many of them.

Adrenaline surges through me as I quickly dart through the tree roots, not caring anymore in which direction I go from here. Anywhere is better than sitting and watching my death grow ever nearer.

Just as a new wave of pain threatens to rip a scream from my throat, I'm sent to my hands and knees once more, my body locking up.

My vision dances with black dots threatening to take me under just before light explodes from the darkness. The light emanates from an unknown figure, illuminating the dying land like a fallen star.

The Valgys recoil, hissing in agony while my breaths become shallow and desperate as I struggle to understand this new development.

I squint and raise my hands to shield my eyes as I attempt to make out the shape moving within the ball of light. It causes the Valgys to shriek as if in pain, and that alone boosts my morale. An enemy of my enemy is my friend.

All I manage to make out through the brightness is the lengthened tips of their ears, and despite their towering height, that they move with such grace.

My chest tightens. *A Dromin elf.*

Could it be? We're taught from a young age that they will never appear to the human they're watching over.

Awe consumes my mind at the thought of seeing one, causing my lips to part in a soft gasp.

We revere them as guardians—elves who ensure our dreams stay blissful under their watch. In return, we offer the energy of those dreams to nourish their magic.

If one has come to my aid, then none of this is real. It's just a dream.

The sheer terror blooming through me fades, like they pulled it from my chest and replaced it with quiet contentment. This is the serene peace we're supposed to feel every night beneath the Dromins' care.

Relief floods my body and my shoulders slump as my hands fall to my sides. I'm safe now. My family is safe, tucked in their beds, still sleeping in our home.

My eyes close and a sigh of relief slips from my parted lips.

It's just a dream.

I barely register the touch on my cheek before warm, callused fingers tilt my chin up. I try to open my eyes to see the dream-keeper, but my body stills under his grip as heat seeps through my cold limbs. After a few moments of it flowing through my body, it starts to feel like more than just warmth. Something sharp and unfamiliar stirs in my chest, as if his touch has reached the depths of my soul.

The elf chuckles, a low, velvety sound that snakes down my spine and unravels my line of thought.

"Don't conjure this nightmare again, Little Dove." His voice is a lazy drawl, brushing against my senses like silk. "I'm starting to wonder if you did it just to force me into revealing myself to you."

A shiver runs through me, though not from the cold.

Little Dove.

The name settles strangely in my chest, like it belongs there.

"I . . ." My tongue feels thick, like I'm forcing my body through sludge to counteract the weight pressing down. "Nightmare? Isn't this a dream, if you are here and not a Nithrin?"

While this dreamscape was haunting and spiked fear within me, it didn't even occur to me that it could be a nightmare because it's not possible. I don't live under the Nithrins' stormy clouds, so how would they have access to my mind, to induce a nightmare to feed from?

Another husky laugh, like he finds me impossibly naive. "How do you know I'm a Dromin?"

I huff at the absurdity of it and fight to open my eyes again, but still my body won't cooperate. There is no way he is a nightmare-keeper with the pure white light emanating from him.

I don't need to see him to confirm that, but I selfishly want to lay eyes on the elf who saved me. I want to breathe in this sense of peace and his warmth while looking into his eyes.

"Wake up, Little Dove," he murmurs.

His lips graze my ear and the contact leaves a tingling trail of heat in its wake as the dream shatters.

CHAPTER TWO

ELYSIA

My eyes snap open and all I feel is loss.

Not the slow, aching kind. This is sharp—like something vital was taken from me the moment I surfaced into wakefulness. I don't know if it's the loss of his touch, or the sharp contrast from how I feel every other morning.

I should feel rested. That's how it's always been in the mornings . . . my limbs light, thoughts clear, and my mind tingling in a way that was a sign the Dromin had fed well, as the Elders had told us as kids.

Yet this morning my muscles are throbbing with exhaustion and my head feels heavy. My skin is damp with a sheen of sweat, despite the chill lingering in my limbs, as if I'd slept outside.

Even still, I feel the warm energy of the Dromin, as if his presence followed me back, burrowed into my chest. The phantom brush of fingers against my cheek still lingers, and I raise my own to trace my skin, needing confirmation his hand is no longer there.

Fractured pieces of our encounter come rushing back until every detail sharpens: every bone-deep tremor of fear as I was hunted, every sulfur-laced tendril of air, every whispered word from the stranger cloaked in light.

I clutch my worn blanket tighter around my shoulders, as if it could smother the unwanted memories of the Valgys and will them away.

It wasn't a dream. It was a nightmare.

I don't have any previous experience to know that with such certainty, but the stories from our childhood stay with us.

We were warned of the Nithrin, cloaked in shadow and silence, slipping across the Sacrum mountains to our territory to feed on the

untouched dreamers. Once they'd driven the humans on their land to the brink of insanity, they'd come for us, unable to influence their broken minds any longer and in need of new minds to feed on.

They were only cautionary tales used to frighten us into obedience when we acted up—or so I thought.

"If you ever wake up cold, with your heart racing and your mind aching," the Elders said, *"you'll know a nightmare has struck and the Nithrin are afoot."*

Exactly how I woke up.

My chest constricts, a slow, creeping tightness that coils around my ribs like my fear is trying to squeeze the breath from my lungs. Yet the more I try to push the feeling down, the more it sinks its claws in.

Maybe those stories weren't just meant to scare us.

Maybe they were meant to warn us.

I thread my fingers into my scalp and tug on the roots of my hair, just enough to ground myself. The sharp pull does nothing to ease the pressure building behind my eyes. No one I know has ever admitted to experiencing this phenomenon, but maybe someone in town can explain this. Or at least they can convince me I'm imagining it.

I press the heel of one hand against my chest, willing my heartbeat to settle. The ache of fear and confusion doesn't fade . . . it deepens, tangled with too many impossible truths.

The same way I know it was a nightmare, I also *know* he is a dreamkeeper. The two truths don't make sense together. Is it possible a Dromin and a Nithrin both touched my mind last night, but only the Dromin chose to show himself?

The confusing thought makes me drag my pillow to my face, stifling the groan building in my throat. The sound still escapes, low and strained, but it's muffled enough not to wake my parents or my sister.

If they heard me now, they'd come rushing in, and I can't explain this, not yet. Not when I don't even understand it myself. The last thing I want is to instill this same fear into them.

I throw off the blanket and sit up, scowling at the weak protest of my sore limbs.

My thoughts return to the Dromin. That inexplicable pull I felt when I saw him and the warmth in my chest that shouldn't exist now that I'm awake.

It should be the Valgys haunting my thoughts, but it's him, and I don't know what that says about me.

After tossing the pillow back to the bed, my eyes instinctively drift to the window, searching for a distraction in the soft indigo horizon. The night sky hasn't yet fully surrendered to dawn, but a faint glow signals the sun's approach.

A muscle in my jaw tightens as I pad across the room, bringing my threadbare blanket with me and wrapping it tighter around my shoulders as I stand in front of the window. I don't have long until I need to meet Pat at sunrise, but the confusion in my mind won't let me focus on getting ready for the day just yet.

I need to make some sense of this—the nightmare *and* the elf who visited me.

His blinding white light I saw couldn't be mistaken for a Nithrin—I'd stake my life on it—but to that end, why did he choose to appear and speak to me?

It breaks multiple laws we have in place.

My brow pinches with the thought that brings forth.

If a Nithrin was near enough to influence my mind, that would also be a breach of the laws.

The Vothia Empire is split in two, east and west, divided by the towering Sacrum Mountains. The elves live above us, atop massive cloud systems that mirror our own borders—Dromin in the east, Nithrin in the west. Each court feeds only on the humans beneath them. That's the agreement. That's what maintains the balance.

There are so many things we don't know about the ways of the elves, but that we know.

Why would anyone break the laws to visit *me*?

The question clings to my thoughts as I turn from the growing light of the sun rising and begrudgingly begin my morning routine. My hands move on instinct, tightening the laces of my work leathers, securing my boots, and braiding my hair. All the while, my mind drifts back to his words.

Don't conjure this nightmare again, Little Dove. I'm starting to wonder if you did it just to force me into revealing myself to you.

I can't help the scoff that escapes my mouth. He said that as if I had any say over my unconscious thoughts, considering the elves' magic is supposed to control them every night without fail and shape them into our dreams.

Yet the rumble in his tone makes a traitorous, aching part of me wonder if I have the ability to summon him . . . and if I could do it again.

I splash cold water across my face in the washbasin, hoping to chase away the thoughts swirling through my mind . . . but they cling.

That wouldn't be possible, though. An elf isn't allowed to visit the same human more than once a year, to prevent attachments on either side.

My hands tighten to the edge of the counter and I nibble on my bottom lip as part of my confusion begins to shift into fascination.

That visitation limit would only matter if the elf in question wasn't willing to break laws, and he already had in other ways. In our dreams, under no circumstance is the human or Dromin allowed to speak to the other.

Not only did he speak to me, but there had been a playful cant to his words and tone . . . not to mention the warmth in the nickname he'd murmured.

Little Dove.

A spark of intrigue and . . . desire blossoms in my core. I bite down on my bottom lip hard and take a deep breath. I don't know if his clear breach of the laws is what's drawing me to him, or if there's a connection between us that I can't place.

The absence of his presence this morning hit me hard, in a way that shouldn't be possible if he's a stranger.

A plan hatches in my mind then, offering a small sense of peace to my tumultuous thoughts since waking.

I'll quietly inquire to see if anyone else has experienced a nightmare, but the last thing I'm going to do is report these broken laws to my elders like I'm supposed to. A rebellious part of my mind wants to prove that it's not me conjuring this Dromin . . . but him returning out of desire and not duty.

I snatch up the satchel containing my tools for work and swing it over my shoulder, but pause at the door. My eyes drift to the warped floorboards of our little cottage, the scent of my mother's lavender oil lingering faintly in the air. That nightmare . . . those images of my family lying dead return with sudden panic gripping my stomach.

Breathe, Elysia. They're safe.

It was only a nightmare, and as terrifying as that is, I have to remind myself that they still aren't real.

I quickly escape from our modest cottage and run down the trampled path of grass I've taken every morning for the past twelve years. As the forest thins and wind sweeps against my bare arms and face, a chill rolls through my body. The fall cycle is nearly over, the air biting with its warning of winter and a reminder that my family will need supplies soon.

I haven't quite made enough from my work rotation to get the items on the list I've made for my parents. They give my sister and me everything, forgoing their own necessities, so it's my turn to give that same love back.

My mother's boots are threadbare and my father's coat has been patched by my mother more times than I can count. Our meals are beginning to have more vegetables and starch than meat.

I see their diminishing income every day.

Her hands aren't agile or quick enough for the seamstress business she once had, with younger women my age taking over more than half of the customers she used to have. Then there's my father and the back injury he never recovered from as a woodworker out in the surrounding forest. Forced to let his partner take over the everyday orders and help as he feels able, the majority of our family income has dissipated.

Brambles catch on my satchel, tugging me back like the world itself is trying to delay me. This cycle, the farmers left this plot of the forest to harvest the elderberries from last, allowing the bushes to run rampant.

I growl under my breath and untangle it quickly before breaking into a run. The sky is beginning to shift to lavender and I know if I don't get there soon, I will never hear the end of it.

"By the gods," a familiar voice calls out, laced with amusement as I crest the final rise. "I thought I'd have to send a search party."

"Bite me, Pat," I grumble, though the corners of my lips twitch upward.

He grins, dimples on full display. "Charming as ever, Lys."

"I have to be, in order to compete with your beauty," I quip. "Maybe save some for the rest of us."

He flips his sun-kissed blond hair over his shoulder, knowing exactly how envious I am of it changing hues throughout the cycles. Mine stays black. Predictable and boring year-round.

His laugh echoes through the valley. "I don't think you're hurting for admirers, considering your father's turned down how many suitors this year?"

My smirk fades and I can't help the eyeroll that ensues. It was a nice moment of levity while it lasted.

"Careful, Lys," he warns, "your eyes might get stuck like that."

"I wish they would," I mutter, letting the truth bleed into the joke. I toss my satchel to the ground and drop beside him with a sigh. "If they did, maybe I'd stop having to deny proposals."

In our village, a woman is expected to marry, bear children, and keep the cycle moving, just as it's always been. Each time I refuse a proposal, I delay that rhythm. I deny my family the bridal price that could ease their financial burden, and yet . . . I keep doing it.

My parents never ask me to reconsider and reassure me that I have time to find the right person. That I should wait until I find love.

Yet I feel the weight of what I'm costing them every day.

So I work twice as hard. I take every job I can and try to earn back what I've withheld from my decisions. There's very little I wouldn't give for my family, but this . . . this one thing feels like the line I can't cross.

If I gave myself away, I know exactly what I'd lose, and I'm not sure I'd ever get it back.

My spark.

I glance out at the land below us, now washed in soft gold as the sun stretches higher, and my yearning grows alongside its glow.

Maybe it's not just about marrying for love or money. Maybe the real truth is the one I never say aloud: I don't want to spend the rest of my life here.

That restless part of me—the piece that still believes there's something more beyond this village—won't go quiet. It never has.

Perhaps that's why the Dromin lingers in my mind in ways he shouldn't. He broke laws and stepped beyond the boundary of his role as a dream-keeper.

Everyone in this village just follows the rules, day in and day out, like we were made to be obedient.

What if I wasn't made the same?

For a moment, I let myself pretend everything is normal. That the hush between us is the comfort between friends and not my own avoidance.

The Dromin's voice drifts back to me, clear and unshakable.

I'm starting to wonder if you did it just to force me into revealing myself to you.

The memory of his teasing curls low in my stomach, unsettling in a way I can't explain.

It's such a stark contrast to the way Pat's banter always settles around me like the warmth of a well-worn blanket—familiar, safe, expected.

The elf's voice didn't offer comfort. It offered something sharp and untamed. It felt like being seen and challenged at the same time, and it tugged at something deep inside me.

Maybe that's why I've never looked at Pat as anything more than a friend, even when others expected me to. Why every suitor has felt like stepping into a life too small for me.

Even in the middle of a nightmare, the Dromin didn't dull my spark. He made it burn brighter.

"You look like you didn't sleep at all," Pat says, lightly bumping his shoulder against mine. "Long night?"

I nod, then swallow, trying to find the words to admit what's happened.

My voice comes out quieter than I expect. "I had a nightmare."

I feel him freeze beside me.

"You . . . mean a bad dream?" he asks slowly, breath catching slightly.

"No," I murmur, shaking my head. "I mean a nightmare. It was real, Pat. The fear. The chills and exhaustion I woke up with. I felt drained instead of rejuvenated."

He turns toward me fully now, brows drawn tight. "That's not supposed to happen. You know that."

"I *know*. That's why I'm telling you." I glance over, searching his face. "You've never had one?"

He shakes his head, slow and certain. "No. Never. Just dreams. Sometimes strange ones, sure, but never anything like you're describing."

Disappointment settles heavily in my gut, even though I knew the answer before I asked. Still, a part of me hoped I wasn't the only one.

Pat seems to sense it.

He runs a hand through his hair, then says, "Maybe . . . I don't know. You should talk to Maggie. If anyone's heard of or experienced something like this, it's her."

I let the suggestion settle between us, the weight of it heavier than I expected.

She's the only one of us who's ever interacted with the elves—chosen once for the offering, only to return weeks later with jagged memories

and a fractured mind. If she remembers anything at all, I don't know if it would bring clarity or only deepen the dread curling in my chest.

"Maybe," I say, though it comes out more like a breath than a promise.

Pat doesn't press. He just leans back beside me, arms looped loosely around his knees, and lets the silence return.

Only now, it's comforting that I've admitted this festering problem out loud.

It may not be gone, but it's no longer just my problem to carry alone.

CHAPTER THREE

ELYSIA

Instead of filling the silence with more questions, Pat just watches the sunrise a moment longer, then lets out a slow breath. He raises a brow like he's thinking of pushing me for a second, but decides not to.

When he speaks again, his voice is gentler. "I want to marry Persephone."

I blink. "Wait, *what*?"

The whiplash of it hits me fast—so much that I laugh, eyes wide and startled, the sound bubbling out before I can stop it. "Pat, that's amazing!"

A smile spreads across my face before I can stop it, real and warm. My heart and spirit genuinely lift for the first time since waking. Persephone is perfect for him. Quiet, but fierce in her own way. Steadfast, opposed to his whims. They bring the perfect balance to the other's needs.

I couldn't have picked someone better if I tried.

"She accepted," he murmurs, but his voice is heavy, tinged with a weight that doesn't belong with such good news.

My back straightens as I narrow my eyes on him. "So why do you sound like someone just stepped on your heart?"

"Her father raised the bridal price," he mutters, rubbing his temples. "I can't afford it. Not for another few cycles, but there's another suitor already knocking."

My blood ignites with fury. "What? That's not legal. The price is set by the Elders. He can't just . . ."

"He did," Pat says, defeat clear in the slump of his shoulders. "And the Elder approved it."

My hands curl into fists, my nails biting against my tender flesh. Our Elder has turned down all fathers' requests for a higher price in our lifetime.

Why now?

Anxiety and unease stir within my core. First the laws that were broken by an elf—perhaps two—while I slept, and now this.

Subtle cracks in the order of things, all widening at once.

There's something changing in our world, I just can't put my finger on it.

"Let's just enjoy the sunrise," he says quietly, squeezing my hand.

I nod, squeezing back, sure that he will let me know when he is ready to stir up a fight. For now, I breathe in the sweet air, tinged with the scent of berries, and soak in the golden light streaming down between the clouds that sustain the elves' courts atop them.

As the warmth of the morning rises, I can't shake the ache in my chest. The whisper of fate still clings to me, and I can't help but wonder if the Dromin from my nightmare is up there, looking down at our lands as I gaze up at them.

The smile that had bloomed on my face only moments ago fades, and a sour feeling blooms in my stomach.

The truth is, I fear the price of ever being able to see their world in the clouds. The only human that has is the Queen, and no queen has ever returned.

The rest of the morning passes in a blur of repetition once I'm at work—loops and pulls, thread and tension, the bite of fiber against skin. I keep my head down and my fingers moving, grateful that the work is demanding enough to distract me from the thoughts I can't seem to shake; not even a short reprieve.

Still, no matter how fast I move, I can't outrun them.

The Dromin's voice lingers like a thread woven through my mind, taut and humming. Pat's problem with the bridal price loops alongside it, gnawing at me like the raw skin beneath my nails.

By midday, I'm combing through the names of everyone I know, testing out conversations in my head—imagining reactions and weighing risks.

Who would listen?

Who could help Pat and Persephone?

Who wouldn't call me cursed or broken for the nightmare?

And who wouldn't go straight to the Elders the moment I walked away?

By the time the sun begins its slow descent beyond the hills, the pads of my fingers are sore, the skin cracked at the edges and smeared faintly with blood.

And in all that time, the only name I've managed to settle on to talk to about my problems is Maggie, just as Pat suggested. Unfortunately, that's one more name than I've thought of to help him.

A thin line of crimson streaks the side of my thumb where the bowstring fibers have worn through the budding callus that had already formed, and I hiss softly as I flex my hands.

Another full day spent crafting strings for the guards' weapons—my new post, and the highest-paying one in our village. It comes with pain, yes, but it also brings money we need to prepare for winter. I'm not about to complain when few are ever offered the task.

Bowstring crafting requires precision, patience, and speed. It's a delicate balance not all possess, but I'd leapt at the chance to prove myself halfway through the cycle when a spot had opened. My fingers are small and quick, deft enough to loop and bind at the pace the overseers demand, and I take pride in the fact that I earned this position on merit.

The ache beneath my nails pulses as I gather my things and make my way up the familiar path through the village to head home. The gentle breeze tugs at the braid that hangs over my shoulder, the scent of drying elderberry leaves filling the air in comforting waves. I breathe it in deeply, the spice of it grounding me.

Just a few more weeks, I remind myself. The harvest season will end soon, and the work will shift again for the winter cycle to give my fingers a chance to heal. For now, I need to be grateful. It's steady work and it's needed.

And it's better than accepting a proposal.

"Elysia!" Harven, the old baker, calls out from his stall as I pass the edge of the square. "You still owe me a song, you know. That voice of yours could charm the flour right from the sack."

I chuckle, pausing just long enough to wave. "You'd regret it the second I opened my mouth, if you don't have a cup of mead in your belly already. I don't sound as lovely as you think."

He laughs, eyes crinkling. "Take care, girl. Tell your mother I'll be bringing over a few items to have her patch up before winter."

"I will," I say, offering a smile. "And thank you for being patient with her needing more time now to complete orders. I know it's slower than it used to be."

Harven waves a hand, brushing off the thanks. "Elysia, she and your father have cut me more deals than I can count. I was fresh out of coin two winters ago, and your mother still mended half my clothes. Never asked for a single copper for that order, all these cycles later."

I blink at his admission, surprised, but only a little. I've seen them do that before, quiet acts of grace . . . but I always thought it was just a delayed payment or discount, not something they'd chosen to give away entirely.

"She and your father have done that for plenty of folks in this village," Harven continues, his voice low, almost reverent. "Finished work they should've been paid triple for. Fixed things for people they knew wouldn't be able to pay at all."

I'm not sure how to process that, standing here with cracked fingertips and a heart full of responsibility, trying to contribute however I can. All while carrying guilt for not accepting a proposal that would've eased our burden with the bridal price.

Maybe this is why they never made me feel like I *had* to accept. I thought they were just being kind and loving, but maybe they've made so many quiet sacrifices for others that they never expected me to sacrifice myself in return.

My chest tightens, warmth and ache mingling deep in my ribs.

"You inherited that soft heart, girl," Harven says, nodding toward me. "Don't let anyone try to harden it, and remember—there are plenty of us willing to help your family if it ever comes to that. They're the type to never ask, but they've earned it."

"I won't," I say quietly.

His words stay with me long after I've left the edge of the stall.

All this time, I've carried the weight of our struggles like they were mine alone to fix—shouldering the burden my parents never asked me to carry. They've chosen to live with less, again and again, rather than watch others go without, whether it's my sister and me, or the villagers we live among.

The thought settles over me like a balm, mending a self-inflicted wound in my heart.

Maybe I inherited more than their deft hands and their kindness . . . maybe I inherited the grace to silently carry what I can for those in need.

Farther down, a few children run past, one of them nearly barreling into me. I steady the smallest one with a hand on his shoulder.

"Careful, Kas," I say with a smile. "Your legs are faster than your eyes, it seems."

"Sorry, Elysia!" he calls, already racing to catch up with his older siblings.

A flicker of warmth rises in my chest at seeing the childlike joy, but it's fleeting, serving as a stark reminder that joy has become a rare currency in this village.

Around me, the square churns with the quiet rhythm of late-day trade. Baskets scrape against wooden stalls and shoes crunch over brittle leaves of the wilting foliage.

A woman I don't know well glances up as I pass and scowls faintly, eyes lingering a second too long before darting away. I smile anyway, a small, deliberate curve of my lips, and keep walking.

I've learned that most people don't want kindness here. They want someone to blame for the blessings we haven't received.

Our village has been caught in a long, bitter stillness with no queen chosen from our lands. The gifts the elves bestow upon the human queen's homeland—gold, enchanted artifacts, even enhanced crop yields—haven't touched our soil in many centuries. Meanwhile tales reach our border of the blessings in other villages and how the lives of all within their lands are altered and made easy. While no one dares speak their resentment aloud in public, it shows in their narrowed eyes and tightened mouths anytime Maggie is around.

The current queen was chosen when I was still an infant, and the elves' magic stretches her reign across several human generations. She could outlive us all, so most believe we've missed our chance entirely to experience the luxury and softness the blessing affords.

I shift my satchel higher on my shoulder as I weave between the merchant stalls, careful not to jostle the worn crates stacked with end-of-season produce. A cabbage rolls free near my foot, and I crouch to catch it, brushing away a smear of dirt before placing it gently back with the others.

The vendor—Rhenna, who rarely speaks unless she's shouting—grunts a sound that might be gratitude. I nod in return and keep walking.

I clench my jaw as the resentment pointed at Maggie resurfaces in my mind.

Twenty years ago, Maggie was the hope of our village . . . the one they considered our best chance at being chosen as the next queen. Yet when she returned, deposited with her parents by guards from the northern port, her mind was fractured in ways no healer could mend. She was ostracized by the village as if she were suddenly the worst we had to offer, not caring what she had sacrificed in being chosen for the selection.

We have no idea of how or why the Queen is chosen from all those offered. All we are told is to offer our brightest and most beautiful for the selection when the High Priestess requests it. The rest is up to her, when she comes down to our lands to meet the selected.

I've almost made it to the main path home when Jeren appears, tall, broad-shouldered, and wielding that ever-hopeful glint in his eyes that makes my stomach tighten. Not with excitement, but dread.

"Elysia," he says, falling into step beside me. "I was hoping to catch you."

Of course he was.

"Hello, Jeren," I respond tightly, careful to not give anything more than a polite tone.

I suppose there are still some people in this village I don't wish to bring joy to.

Mainly the ones who think I might one day belong to them.

"You know," Jeren says, keeping pace with me as we pass the butcher's stall, "I spoke with my father this morning. He's thinking of submitting a new offer to yours—especially now that Persephone's bridal price has increased. Do you think that might appeal to your family?"

Not this again.

"That's thoughtful," I say carefully, forcing my tone to remain neutral, when all I want to do is tell him to bug off and forget my existence. "But I think my father already made his stance on that clear."

His brow furrows, but he presses on. "You work so hard. You shouldn't have to do it alone."

I bite back a sigh as he reaches for my hand before I quickly reach up to brush hair out of my face to avoid it. I think he means well, but this isn't the life I want, at least not the way he imagines it.

Just as I open my mouth to excuse myself, a shout echoes from the middle of the square.

"Someone get her out of here!"

Another voice joins in, closer this time. "I swear, if she spits on my stall again—"

The irritation in the air thickens like smoke and then I hear her faintly.

Maggie.

Jeren turns toward the sound coming from behind us with a furrowed brow. "What now?"

I already know and I don't hesitate.

"I think it's Maggie," I say, already moving back toward the central square.

"She's always doing this," he mutters, falling into step behind me. "She needs someone to keep her indoors."

"She has no one," I snap without looking back.

Both of her parents had passed away in the last few years. First her mother from a winter illness, then her father from a fall when trying to repair their home. Since then, Maggie's been alone in that cottage at the edge of the woods.

My family does what we can, but I know it's not enough.

We round the edge of the fountain at the center of the square, and that's when I see her, gesturing around.

I don't consider myself particularly tall or broad, but the years alone have made Maggie even more frail than her petite frame should be. Her baggy brown smock hangs off her like it's borrowed from a woman twice her size, the hem dirty and frayed, evidence of her wandering walks. Her cheeks are a bit hollow, the bones beneath more pronounced than they should be. Fine lines mark the corners of her eyes and mouth as she squints and shouts.

They're not the deep creases of the elderly, but the subtle etchings of a woman who's carried too much in silence alone.

Her graying auburn hair is pulled back in a loose, tangled knot, and those moss-green eyes are wild with confusion and fire.

"You don't see it!" she's yelling now, pointing at nothing. "You never see it until it's too late!"

A few villagers flinch as her gaze passes over them. One man mutters something under his breath and spits into the dirt.

I pick up my pace, trying to politely push through the gathered crowd.

Beside me, Jeren slows. "She's really lost it this time . . ."

"She's not a problem to be stared at," I say under my breath, barely holding back the words I really want to yell at him.

Maggie's breath hitches when I touch her shoulder. Her eyes flick to mine, blinking fast, like she's trying to place me through a fog.

"It's alright," I murmur, gently curling my hand around her thin arm. "Let's get you home, hmm?"

She doesn't resist. The fire drains from her eyes, leaving her small and shivering.

The onlookers begin to drift off, but their muttering stays behind. One woman clutches her shawl tighter and hurries away. Another vendor shakes his head, voice low and pointed. "Someone ought to keep her out of town."

"She's not hurting anyone," I say loudly, enough to carry. My fingers tighten around Maggie's arm, my voice softening as I add, "She just needs someone to help her."

I glance back at Jeren, who still stands a few paces behind, awkward and unsure, hands stuffed into the pockets of his pants. His posture screams discomfort, but he hasn't walked away yet.

Perfect.

"Jeren," I call gently, pitching my voice just enough to turn heads and put him under scrutiny, "would you mind walking Maggie back to her cottage? I need to run home to get her something warm to eat."

He blinks. "Me?"

I keep my expression open, calm. "She knows the way, but I'd feel better if she wasn't alone. Just until I catch up. It would mean so much to me."

There's a pause of hesitation, but then he straightens, shoulders pulling back like he's being measured and might change my mind about his proposal.

"Of course," he says. "Yes. Of course."

He steps forward, carefully placing a hand on Maggie's elbow. She stares past him like he's no more solid than a shadow, and directly into my eyes.

"Be careful with your kindness, girl. It'll make them choose you next."

Jeren grimaces at me before gently guiding her away. I watch them for a few moments as they start down the road toward the edge of

the woods. Maggie walks slowly as her head turns slightly toward the clouds.

I try to shake off her words, but her voice lingers as I make the trek home.

It shouldn't mean anything, and yet with the Dromin's voice still lingering in the back of my mind, and the fear from the nightmare's echo still etched into my memory, it doesn't feel like nonsense.

It feels like a warning *and* a reminder.

I was thinking of speaking to Maggie anyway. Now, I'm sure of it.

CHAPTER FOUR

ELYSIA

By the time I reach the edge of the village again, the lanterns have begun to flicker to life, casting soft pools of light on the worn cobbled paths. I make my way home with quiet purpose, my steps brisk with new resolve.

Maybe madness remembers what clarity forgets.

Maggie might be the only person who's ever come close to that world. If anyone could recognize the thoughts, sensations, and fear that still linger in my chest . . . it would be her. Maybe all it would take is someone to speak the right words, paint the right memory, for something in her fractured mind to spark back to life.

Even if it doesn't . . . at least she won't repeat what I say. No one would believe her anyway. That fact stings more than it should.

The moment I step inside our little cottage, the scent of roasted root vegetables and warm broth greets me. My mother hums softly by the hearth, ladling stew into wooden bowls while my father tends to a loose hinge on the window frame with a furrowed brow.

"You're back late," my mother says without turning, but there's no reprimand in her tone, only warmth.

"Work ran long," I answer, slipping off my boots by the door. "But I was wondering . . . do we have any extra dinner to spare tonight? I want to bring something to Maggie."

My mother turns, a smile blooming across her face. "Of course we do, sweetheart. Take as much as she'll eat, and more. I don't know how often she eats anymore, she has become so frail."

She ladles a generous portion of the stew into one of our clay crocks, covering it carefully with a tight-fitting lid and wrapping it in a woven

wool cloth to help retain the heat. "I'll never understand how this village could turn their back on her after she returned from the selection."

It's entirely cruel, the way this village treats her like a plague they could get sick from.

My father pauses in his work, his gaze sharp as he watches me. "Just don't stay out too late," he says, voice low and protective. "You know how the cold settles in fast this time of season."

I nod as my heart warms with his concern. "I won't. I promise."

From across the room, my younger sister looks up from her stitching and grins. "Will you be back in time to braid my hair the way I like for tomorrow? You know, with the ribbon twist?"

I laugh softly and walk over to brush a kiss across the top of her head. "Of course I will. I'd never leave you to your own tragic braiding skills."

"Rude," she teases, but there's love in her voice.

With the warm parcel tucked into my satchel, I step back out into the cooling night, heart a little steadier, breath a little fuller. The stars begin to blink to life overhead, and the weight of what I'm about to do presses against my chest, but it's not heavy. Instead it's thrumming, alive with something unspoken, something stirring just beneath the surface of the world.

Because something is changing. I can feel it in the way the wind shifts, in the way my pulse quickens.

As I head toward the crooked path that leads to Maggie's tiny, vine-covered cottage at the village edge, I know one thing for certain: Tonight, I'll start asking the right questions.

The twinkling stars have taken their rightful place in the sky by the time I reach the northern edge of the village opposite from my home. The night air is crisp, settling over the land like a hushed whisper as the bustling town square quiets.

Ahead of me, Maggie's cottage looms and my steps falter. I swallow a lump of unease choking my throat as I stare, feeling like there is an invisible barrier I'm about to cross that I won't be able to come back from.

"Take the step," I whisper to myself as my hand tightens on the well-worn satchel strap at my shoulder.

All of my previous determination seems to have withered away in the face of actually implementing my plan.

What if the answers I get aren't the ones I want? What if they are the kind that twist thorns into my stomach with nerves and lead shadows of doubt into my already tumultuous thoughts?

My brow pinches at the overload.

Should I even be this worried? I could be unnecessarily building up this strange thing that happened to me.

I take a few moments to breathe in and out, slow and controlled, as I focus on Maggie's home. Ivy crawls all over the battered fence posts lining her crooked yard, and the shutters creak softly in the wind, one of them hanging loosely on rusted hinges. Shame fills me that no one, including myself, has thought to come help repair her home, since her dad passed attempting to do just that.

I add it to my mental list to ask my father to stop by before the winter cycle comes.

With a huff I force myself over the line between the village path and into her private residence. I can't daydream about all that is out there, thinking I'm meant for more, and then shy away from taking a step in that exact direction.

A single candle flickers behind the dirty glass of her window, casting distorted shadows across the door. It's the kind of light that feels more like a warning than a welcome, but I push the thought from my mind. Maggie has never been anything but warm to me, even amidst her confusion. I don't think there is a drop of malice in her soul.

The cobblestone path narrows as I continue, wild with thistle in the cracks. I raise a hand and knock softly. At first, there's nothing. No footsteps and no greeting called out from within. Only the faint sound of a low hum, drifting through the door like the echo of a lullaby I just barely recognize. I knock again, firmer this time.

Suddenly, soft footsteps sound just before the door creaks open a breath, just wide enough for Maggie's pale face to appear in the gap.

"Hello?" she says, soft green eyes unfocused as she gazes up at my face.

"It's Elysia," I say gently, taking a small step back, in case I'm intimidating her at all. "I brought you dinner, like I promised you earlier. My mother made stew and it's still warm."

I hope she lets me in, even if she doesn't feel well enough to talk. She needs to get some food in her belly.

She blinks slowly, her gaze roving over my face. For a flicker of a moment, something sharp cuts through the fog of her mind as her eyes widen and lips part.

"Still whole," she whispers, almost to herself as her fingers run through the loose strands of hair hanging around her face. "Not yet frayed at the edges."

Is she implying she needs help cutting her hair?

I smile at her before asking, "May I come in?"

She nods absently and steps aside. I quickly enter and hear the door creak closed behind me. The interior is dim and cluttered. Dried herbs hang in bundles from the rafters, their scent mingling with dust and old earth. Bits of parchment and broken trinkets are scattered across every surface, like she's stopped halfway through a copious number of projects. I set the crock down on the nearest table, unwrapping the wool and letting the heat rise in gentle steam.

Maggie doesn't seem to notice. She shuffles toward a worn rocking chair and lowers herself into it, her gaze fixed on a point far beyond the walls of her cottage.

I hesitate, unsure how to begin. "I wanted to ask you a few questions, if you feel up to it. About what you experienced being chosen."

Her body stills. The air in the room instantly seems to be sucked out.

"The orb," she mutters suddenly as her chair begins to rock back and forth, almost as if it helps her focus. "It hums. Sings. Burns."

I swallow at the last word. That sounds decidedly unpleasant. She's spoken of the orb before in ramblings, but never anything understandable.

"What was meeting an elf in person like?" I push gently as I prepare her meal and breathe a sigh of relief that my mother included a spoon. I wouldn't know the first place to look to find one here.

She doesn't answer and I press on, "Was the High Priestess a Dromin? One visited me in my dreams last night."

She turns her head slowly as I approach her with the stew, eyes flicking toward mine but not truly meeting them. "It knew me. Unmade me. Made me again, but not all of me came back."

Unease presses down on my chest. *Is this still about the orb?* I steady my voice. "And the elven High Priestess? What was she like?"

Maggie's fingers trace patterns on the armrest as I offer the food to her. "White-fire eyes. Tongue of silk and sharp teeth beneath. She speaks with shadows. Calls it devotion."

I shiver as the sharp teeth of the Valgys in my nightmare surface.

A grimace tugs at my lips at her disinterest in the food. I place it on the side table near her chair before taking a seat on the floor in front of her. I'll ensure she takes a few bites before I leave.

Maggie laughs then, low and hollow, but shocking me down to the tips of my toes. I could never recall a time I heard her laugh. The chair creaks sharply as the pace of her rocking increases. "She chooses what bends. Not what breaks."

We sit in silence as I struggle to process her words. I knew they would be confusing, but I wasn't expecting for her answers to inspire such dread within me. We're speaking of the High Priestess, after all. If anyone should inspire tranquility and peace in someone, it would be her.

"Maggie . . . do you remember anything else? Anything about the Nithrin or nightmares, maybe?"

She tilts her head as if listening to something I can't hear. "History repeating. A name spoken over and over until it forgets itself. A crown and no head to wear it now."

My hands clench slightly. "But the crown is on the Queen's head, right?"

Maggie is quiet for a beat too long as her rocking stops. "It comes in threes, but the middle one never saw it coming."

I fear I'm losing any clarity from her mind. "Earlier, when you told me my kindness will make them choose me next, what did you mean?"

Her eyes shift and settle on mine, clear and focused for one devastating heartbeat. "You're next."

Silence swallows the room whole as she doubles down on the sentiment with no added explanation.

Then, as quickly as it came, the clarity drains from her face. She hums again, low and tuneless, her fingers twitching in her lap.

I push to my feet, my thoughts warping under the weight of her words, but I don't leave.

My gaze falls to the untouched crock of stew, the steam nearly gone now. I pick it up, settle back beside her, and gently scoop up a spoonful. "Maggie," I say softly, "you need to eat. Just a little, please."

She doesn't resist when I lift the spoon to her lips, she only blinks slowly and opens her mouth as if it's a reflex. I offer another, then another, in silence. The rhythm of it soothes some of the unease inside me.

When the bowl is nearly empty, I set it aside and take her hand in mine. Her skin is paper-thin and cold, her fingers feather-light in my grasp.

"Let's get you to bed," I whisper, helping her stand. She leans heavily on me, her body lighter than I imagined, like a collection of bones held together by sheer will.

I guide her across the room to the small cot tucked in the corner, its quilt askew and faded with age. She sinks onto it without protest, and I help ease her beneath the covers, tucking the edges snug around her frame.

She hums again, softer now, like she is content to drift away to her dreams.

My thoughts drift to the Dromin and I make a silent prayer. *Please ensure she always dreams of happy memories and a time before her mind was fractured.*

I linger for a moment, brushing stray strands of hair from her forehead. "Rest well, Maggie," I murmur.

I turn and quickly stoke the fire in her hearth before stepping quietly back into the night, the door clicking shut behind me.

The wind is colder now, the shadows deeper, and my heart heavier.

Deep in my bones, something begins to stir, a truth I don't yet understand, but one that's already watching me from the shadows.

I make it home faster than I expected, my feet seemingly carrying me instinctually through the quiet village paths. The house is quiet now, dimly lit by the last embers of the hearth. My family must have gone to bed.

I push the door open softly, careful not to disturb the lingering silence. My satchel slips from my shoulder with a quiet thud, and I make my way toward my sister's room, where she lies curled beneath her patchwork quilt, already fast asleep.

I sit on the edge of her bed, smiling down at her peaceful expression. The purple ribbon she loves so much is clutched loosely in her hand, tangled slightly from where she must have tried to braid her hair herself before sleep claimed her.

Gently, I take it and begin weaving her hair into the braid she loves, careful not to wake her. The familiar motion calms my fraying nerves. Each twist of her dark strands pulls me back from the fog Maggie's words left behind.

Once I finish, I kiss her forehead and slip away, padding softly toward my own room. I close the door behind me, leaning against it for a long moment before finally crawling beneath my covers.

Yet sleep doesn't come. My mind is too scattered with thoughts and questions to quiet. I stare at the ceiling, my breath shallow and pulse frantic. The weight of Maggie's words echo in my mind.

You're next.

My body remains still, but my thoughts refuse to rest. I don't know if I'll dream tonight. I don't know if it'll be a dream at all, or another nightmare.

I keep my eyes wide open, suddenly terrified to drift away as it hits me that I could experience another one, and without *him*.

Fates help me, I hope he's okay with breaking another law, because it's starting to feel like something isn't wrong with me . . . more like something is coming *for* me.

CHAPTER FIVE

ELYSIA

The bells wake me, a low, mournful tolling that cuts through the early dawn, rolling across the village. The last remnants of sleep evaporate, replaced by a strange, hollow unease.

I sit up in a rush, breath caught in my throat as a thought hits me squarely in the chest.

I didn't dream . . . not even a nightmare. Just a void.

There's no tingle in my mind that any Dromin visited and fed off my dreams, reaffirming that I simply slept. Before the nightmare I had the previous night, I had never experienced sleeping without a Dromin to spin my thoughts into dreams.

That along with the tolling of the bells is a combination that doesn't sit right within me. It's the kind of sound that means something terrible has happened.

I swing my legs over the side of the bed and toss on a simple dress before tugging on my boots. My fingers tremble slightly as I lace them, the sound of the bell echoing again, raising the hairs on my arms.

I hurry to the front room, where my parents are already gathering cloaks and their own boots. My mother's face is pale, lips pressed in a firm line as she stares at my sister's still-closed door. My father's eyes are narrowed as he fastens his cloak.

The door opens and my sister peers out, rubbing her eyes. "Why are the bells ringing? Did something happen?"

"No one knows yet," my mother answers, her voice soft but tight. "But we need to get going, Penelope, please get dressed."

I pull on my own cloak, glancing toward the window.

"It feels wrong," I murmur to myself as her door closes softly. "Terribly wrong."

My father pauses to look at me, something unreadable in his eyes. "There's always a solution, no matter the issue. We will get through it together, as a family and a village."

"That's not comforting," my sister mumbles as she emerges and tugs a scarf around her neck. "The last time the bells rang was when the locusts came and destroyed our farmland, right?"

I'm not sure how she even knows that, unless they taught it in school. It was before she was born, when I was a baby.

"Yes," he replies gently, patting her head as she walks toward us. "We did get through that, despite the hardships it brought."

We were still paying off our debts to those who offered us provisions to rebuild—villages that had been blessed by recent queens, our survival solely on their shoulders as they allotted rations to those of us impacted.

We step outside and the brisk air hits my cheeks with a particularly heavy gust of wind. The streets are already beginning to fill with other villagers. We move as one, footsteps quiet, heads low, and hearts bracing for whatever news waits ahead.

My mother walks closely beside me, whispering loudly enough for my ears only. "I don't like this, Lys. There's something off in the air. I felt it the moment I woke up."

Her hand falls heavily on my shoulder and I instantly lift my own to squeeze it. I wish I had words of reassurance for her, but I have the same eerie dread trailing down my spine.

"Maybe it was a raid from bandits?" my sister asks next to me, her voice quieter now, eyes wide as she scans the gathering crowd as we arrive at the town square.

"No," my father says without hesitation. "The guard would've been mobilized, yet they're all here. This is something else."

I take note of the guards lined up behind the center stage and count twenty of them in total. My dad is right.

As we near the square, I catch snippets of whispered speculation.

"Maybe one of our Council members died."

"I heard that a woman ran away after her father accepted a bridal price."

That makes my brain spark with alarm and I quickly scan the crowd for Pat or Persephone.

Relief floods through me when I spot them near the far edge of the square, standing close with their parents. Persephone looks pale, her hands clasped tightly in front of her, but Pat catches my gaze and gives me a small, reassuring nod. The kind that says, *I'm here, you're not alone.*

I nod back, clinging to that silent promise of friendship as my pulse continues to race. The old stage at the center—the one only used for official decrees—stands empty, but lanterns have been lit along its edges, and the village Council members pace behind it, speaking quietly with the Elder.

We find a spot near the edge of the crowd on the opposite side from Pat and Persephone, letting the majority of the population push in as close to the platform as they want. My mother clutches my arm lightly and it only adds to my unease. She is the pillar of composing oneself in the face of any adversity.

The Elder steps forward, his hands clasped behind his back, his expression somber.

He's older than most make it to, well into his seventies, with a stooped frame that speaks of a life bent under the weight of responsibility. His silver hair is neatly tied at the nape of his neck, though a few strands have slipped loose in the morning breeze. Deep lines crease his weathered face, every furrow etched with the decisions of decades past. He clears his throat, and the murmurs hush to silence.

"My friends," he begins, "today I bring words none of us are prepared to hear."

He pauses, gaze sweeping across the gathered crowd.

"The Queen is dead."

Gasps ripple through the square, and for a moment, I think I've misheard. I glance back at my mother, finding her mouth slightly parted and eyes wide with disbelief.

"She was young," my dad whispers behind me. "The elves give them longevity . . . so, how?"

The Elder continues. "She passed in her sleep. The elves have confirmed her death. No further details were given."

A stunned silence follows, broken only by scattered murmurs of confusion and fear. It feels like my brain has completely stopped functioning, only a dull buzz rolling through my head.

"She should've lived another hundred years at least," a woman near the front says loudly, her voice shaking.

"It's not natural," another mutters.

The Elder raises a hand, quieting the crowd again.

"As you all know, when a queen passes, the selection must begin anew. The High Priestess has called for another selection. Though it has not been long since our last, we must answer."

My mother's hand tightens on my arm. "Why now?"

I hear the dread in those two words so deeply that it snaps me from my own stupor. I know why she feels that way, but I refuse to acknowledge it myself.

"We will begin the nomination process today," he says. "As tradition dictates, any woman between the ages of eighteen and twenty-five may be put forward. She must be someone we believe to be the very best of us. The brightest, the strongest, and the most beautiful. She will represent this village to the elven High Priestess as our chosen."

A hush falls over the crowd. Some women shift uncomfortably while others straighten their posture, trying to look confident. I watch Persephone all but hide in Pat's shadow.

There aren't that many in our village who fulfill that age requirement, substantially increasing the odds for both of us.

My sister looks up, worry for me clear in her bright blue eyes. "You don't think . . ."

"I don't know, Penelope," I whisper, a bit harsher than I intended, before pulling her in for a tight hug. My fingers absently play with her braid as she leans into me. "I'm sorry, that was rude of me. I'm just a little scared, if I'm being honest."

Her arms tighten around my waist. "It's okay to be scared."

My mother turns toward me slowly, her gaze unreadable. "You are strong, Elysia."

I hear the words left unsaid: *If it's you . . . you can handle this.*

A line begins to form, as all villagers are required to submit nominations. At the platform, the Elder pulls out parchments and quills as a Council member pulls forth a table.

We begin to shuffle into the line and I stand still, arms folded, trying not to look like I'm watching the face of each person walking away after casting their nomination. I can't help noticing the way some of them glance at me as they walk away.

Not all of them, but enough to make my skin itch and my feet feel like boulders as we shuffle closer.

Another sideways glance, this time from Harven the baker. A hesitant flick of the eyes in my direction from Stella, who I saw two days ago in our home as my mother repaired one of her dresses. Jeren passes me, his gaze lingering a beat too long before he lowers his head.

My pulse quickens. I don't need to ask who many of them have chosen.

When it's our turn, my family and I step toward the platform one at a time. My father is first, moving forward with the quiet dignity that always surrounds him. He scribbles his nomination with a steady hand and returns to our side without a word, though I catch the small frown tugging at the corner of his mouth.

My mother follows, her movements more fluid, but no less solemn. Her face betrays nothing as she presses her parchment into the box. Penelope hesitates briefly, looking up at me before moving forward and casting hers with the same timid grace that defines her.

Then it's my turn.

I step forward, heart pounding. The quill feels heavier than it should in my hand. I stare at the blank parchment before me, the ink glistening like a dark omen.

Who do I choose?

Names flicker through my mind—women I admire and trust. Each option lands like a stone in my gut as I see their smiles morphing into Maggie's broken stare.

I've clung to the sliver of freedom I possess by not marrying, and this choice erases any semblance of freedom for the person chosen.

But this is different . . . I can't just work hard to make up for a decision that serves me.

Willingly choosing someone to walk into Maggie's fate . . .

No.

I can't carry that. I can't let someone else fall into irrevocable mental ruin for my own freedom.

My freedom wouldn't taste free if I did.

My hand trembles, and before I can think myself into more torment, I write my own name. The quill scratches softly against the parchment, sealing something that feels irreversible.

The ink bleeds slowly into the page as a quiet offering I never wanted to make.

I place the nomination into the box and step away, joining my family once more.

We return to the edge of the square, where the crowd has grown silent again. The Council has begun to tally the selections, parchment after parchment unfolding in careful hands. It doesn't take long for a pattern to form, one stack of parchment beginning to grow steadily, unmistakably larger than the others.

A hush falls, rippling out as the truth becomes undeniable. There is a distinct winner.

My breath hitches, and the sound of the crowd fades beneath the roar of blood rushing in my ears. My fingers curl into my cloak, nails biting into my palms.

The Elder steps forward once more, lifting the final slip of parchment from the now lopsided stack and reading aloud the name etched across its surface.

"Elysia Virellan."

The square falls into a heavy, eerie silence. The sound of my name spoken aloud feels like it cleaves something in me wide open.

My mother gasps beside me, her hand flying to her mouth. Tears well in her eyes, spilling silently down her cheeks. My father closes his eyes, shoulders visibly shaking, and turns his face slightly away, as if trying to mask the emotion that clutches at him. Penelope clings to my arm, trembling, her wide eyes glassy.

I wrap an arm around her tightly, squeezing back just as fiercely. I force myself to breathe, to be their strength in the moment, even as my own world tilts off its axis. I swallow down the rising knot in my throat and lift my chin, refusing to crumble.

I dig my heels into the ground, anchoring myself against the storm rising inside me. Because even as the weight of the village's choice bears down on me, even as dread coils tighter around my lungs, I will not fall apart. Not here. Not yet.

The crowd begins to disperse with everyone going back to their daily lives, unchanged, as if they didn't just alter mine forever.

My eyes catch on a lone figure standing at the edge of the town square. The same brown smock from yesterday.

Maggie.

Her green eyes are locked on mine, unblinking and sharp, more lucid than I've ever seen them. A shiver travels down my back, cold and certain.

She doesn't speak or move, and suddenly her words from yesterday don't feel like madness at all.

I stand taller, though my legs feel brittle beneath me, like branches threatening to snap beneath the strain. A storm brews beneath my skin, a mix of dread and resolve.

No matter what awaits me with the High Priestess, I want to believe that I won't break.

But, fates help me, I'm already cracking.

CHAPTER SIX

ELYSIA

Council members approach my family and me, their mouths moving with words I barely register. There are nods, murmured instructions, and scattered phrases that pass through me like wind through grass. All I retain is this: Tomorrow morning, I'm to meet with two of our guards. They will escort me to the northern port of the Vothia Empire, where the Sacrum Mountains taper off, allowing the humans from both the Nithrin and Dromin sides to gather.

That's where the High Priestess will be waiting.

Waiting for the chosen.

Waiting . . . for me.

My legs feel unsteady beneath me, but I force myself to move, to not be frozen in this moment, because life will go on with or without me. My fingers twitch at my sides, brushing the coarse fabric of my dress just before my mother's hand settles gently against my back, warm through the layers of my cloak. My father walks beside me, quiet and steady. Penelope clings to my sleeve, her fingers trembling.

The walk home is too quiet. Even the usual morning sounds—the distant chatter of merchants, birdsong in the hedgerows, and the creak of shutters opening—feel strangely dulled beneath the haze in my head. The wind has turned colder, carrying with it the scent of dried leaves and early frost.

When our home comes into view, I move toward the door, but something inside me resists the comfort waiting there. I'm sure they expect me to rest now. To cry. Maybe even to collapse beneath the weight of it all.

I can't.

"I'm going to work," I say quietly, slipping inside to grab my satchel.

My mother stills. "Elysia, no. You don't have to."

"I do." My voice is firmer now, the first edge of steel beneath the grief. "Just one more day. I need to feel useful. I need to feel . . . normal."

I sling the satchel over my shoulder and step back outside.

My father's brows draw together, but I lift my chin before he can speak. "No one would blame me for staying home," I add. "But I'd blame myself if I didn't go."

Penelope tugs at our mother's sleeve. "Please don't let her go," she whispers.

I kneel beside her, smoothing a curl behind her ear. "I'll be back before dinner," I promise. "You'll still have time to make me braid your hair."

Her lips wobble, but she nods.

I don't look back as I head toward the bowstring post. Every step presses into the dirt like a slow farewell, the weight of tomorrow heavy in my bones.

When I arrive, the scent of oiled leather and weathered wood hits me first. It's familiar and grounding. The creak of ropes, the snap of finished strings being tested, the low murmur of workers beneath the awnings . . . it all feels unchanged. Steady. Predictable.

Just one more day of normalcy.

The overseer glances up from his ledger, eyes narrowing beneath his weathered brow.

"You shouldn't be here today," he says, arms folding across his chest. "But I knew you'd come anyway. Don't think I'll find a worker like you again anytime soon. Too bad they didn't have you start here earlier in the cycle."

I manage a small nod, though my throat is tight.

He disappears into the supply shed and returns with a cloth pouch, pressing it into my hand.

"Your pay for the fall cycle," he mutters. "Every copper. You've earned it."

I stare at the pouch too long, the weight pressing into my palm harder than it should.

"Thank you," I whisper, but my voice cracks. "It feels like more than I'm owed with not getting this position until halfway through."

His eyes flick away from mine, jaw tightening. "Take it to your family," he says. "They'll need it more than we need bowstrings today."

The words sting with the reminder. He's always been fair, distant, a man of simple routines and blunt expectations. Not the sort to offer pity or softness.

I open my mouth to protest, but he cuts me off with a raised hand.

"I've worked my life away trying to forget things that hurt. Don't make the same mistake. Tomorrow isn't promised, and you don't get this time back. Not with them."

My heart sinks, heavy as stone.

He's right and I offer him my thanks again before departing for home.

When I step through the door of our cottage, the scent of root stew and simmering herbs wraps around me like a memory. It's familiar, safe, and it nearly undoes me on the spot, thinking that I may never smell it again.

I hang my cloak by the door, trying to keep my hands from shaking.

The fire in the hearth crackles softly, casting golden light across the worn floorboards. I pause in the center of the room, letting the warmth press against my skin, soaking into the cold I hadn't realized was buried in my bones.

My father turns as I reach into my satchel, pulling the coin pouch free and pressing it into his hand. His fingers close over it slowly, reverently, like it's more than coins—like it's a piece of me I'm giving away. I guess in a way, it is.

He says nothing, just pulls me into his arms, holding me with a tender strength that shakes something loose in my chest.

My mother steps closer, laying a hand gently on my shoulder. I see the shine in her eyes, but she says nothing. She doesn't have to.

Penelope wraps her arms around my waist, resting her head against my side. Her breath is warm through the fabric of my dress.

"You'll braid it tonight?" she asks softly, voice wobbling.

The knot in my throat thickens. Possibly the last braid I'll ever do for her.

I kiss the top of her head, inhaling the familiar scent of lavender oil clinging to her hair. "Yes," I whisper. "Always."

We both know that's a lie.

I feel the weight of it sitting beneath my ribs.

I can't take more of this softness. This warmth. This love that feels too big for the room and far too breakable now. It's too much.

So I retreat to my room before the grief spills over.

Many in our village would consider this status an honor, and once upon a time I thought the same. If only I could claw back that childlike wonder and innocence I once felt. My nightmare and Maggie's words have rattled me too much to believe that this will be a journey to look forward to now.

My knees hit the floor before I've fully registered the motion. My hands sink into the rug, coarse threads biting my palms, grounding me in a physical world, when my mind begins to spiral.

My name echoes again in my mind, louder than the tolling bells.

Elysia Virellan.

It doesn't sound like a name anymore. It sounds like a death sentence.

The sobs take me before I can resist. They shake through me—deep, ragged, and unrelenting. My breath stutters and my arms tremble with the weight of everything I can't hold inside anymore. I cry until my voice is hoarse and I taste iron on my tongue from clenching down too hard with my teeth. Until I'm left hollow and ragged.

When I'm done, the suffocating silence returns, heavy and unforgiving.

I rise on unsteady legs and move to the washbasin. The water is cold as mountain stone, and I splash it over my face again and again until the sting replaces the ache.

I reach for sections of my hair and begin to twist, pull, and loop. Over and over until I tie off the end.

My fingers tremble as I reach for the cracked shard of a mirror on the shelf. My reflection meets me—flushed, damp, rimmed in red, but not permanently shattered.

I may not feel like tomorrow will lead to my happy ending, but I will not go into it afraid.

Not tonight.

Not ever.

I have to remain strong for my family and myself. I can choose to feel like a victim of fate, or I can choose to weave my own threads into that fate.

I stare at my door for a long moment, feeling like there are too many unfinished issues weighing on my heart and mind. I can't leave here tomorrow without knowing I attempted to fix them.

Tonight I right the wrongs that others will not.

Breezing through to the main living space, I call out a quick goodbye and promise to be home before dinner. I pull my cloak around my shoulders again.

If this village wants me to walk into the unknown of the selection, I will, but not without ensuring those I love will be okay in my absence.

The cool air wraps its fingers around my throat as I walk, curling through the trees and tugging at the ends of my braid. Each step crunches over brittle leaves, the scent of woodsmoke and damp earth clinging to the path beneath my boots. My pulse thuds beneath my ribs, belying my nerves.

Never before have I stood up for my beliefs in such a way.

My palms are damp and my warm breath puffs in the air.

My mind spins, fighting against my fragile confidence.

Turn back, it whispers.

What if they laugh? What if they remind you, too sharply, that you're still just a girl?

I keep walking because this isn't just about me anymore.

The Council building rises at the edge of the square, slate-roofed and ivy-cloaked, its shutters always closed.

It always feels unwelcoming, but today I push the door open without knocking.

Inside, lantern light flickers against worn stone. The Elder sits at the head of the long table, two scribes murmuring beside him. They share looks of surprise before turning wary, as if my presence here breaks some unspoken rule.

The Elder leans forward slightly, brow arched. "Elysia Virellan. I assumed you'd be home, preparing for your departure. This isn't the time for—"

"I didn't come for pleasantries," I say, voice low but even. "I came to ensure my family receives the full bridal price they're owed. Tonight."

He scoffs, a sharp and dismissive sound meant to cut. "If your father has concerns, he knows the proper channels. Besides, if you're chosen to be Queen, your family will be rewarded then."

The words sting more than they should. For a moment, my certainty wavers, but then I remember my mother's tired eyes. My father's quiet strength. Penelope's hand curled around my cloak.

I straighten my spine and snap back. "You mean the entire village will be rewarded, then. If not, my family will never receive the bridal price they are owed, unless I ensure it now." I swallow and wet my lips, standing firm in my words. "You chose me. This village chose me to *sacrifice*. That means you are choosing to offer my hand in a potential marriage. That makes my father the father-of-the-bride under village law. Payment is due the same night the proposal is made and accepted."

"You presume much," he snaps. "This is not a market stall in which you can barter. You forget your place, girl."

My hands curl around the edges of my cloak. "No," I say softly. "I'm just finally stepping into my place."

His expression twists. "You'd dare walk in here and speak as if you have authority?"

"I don't," I reply calmly. "I have leverage, though, and I won't be sent off quietly while my family is left with empty hands and broken promises."

His mouth presses into a thin line. The flickering lantern casts deeper shadows across his face.

"I'm protecting them," I continue. "While I'll go where you've chosen to send me, I will not try to win the elves' favor unless these requests are honored. Now."

"So this is a threat," he growls.

"No," I say. "It's a bargain. One you'd be wise to accept."

A hush settles in the room. The scribes shift in their chairs, casting glances between us.

"I also demand that Persephone's original bridal price be honored and that Patrick Mullen's proposal be accepted tonight," I add. "No more games. No more delays."

The Elder's face darkens. "You'd really risk all of our futures for sentimental gestures?"

My answer is immediate as a fire roars within my heart. "I'd rather risk everything than abandon those I love."

Another long pause.

"Your father will be paid before dawn and the bridal match will be approved tonight."

I nod once, the tremble in my chest easing. "Then I'll leave without resistance and I'll do my best to be chosen."

I turn to leave, but his voice trails behind me, cold and bitter.

"You're playing at a role that you don't have. As if you truly stand a chance of wearing that crown."

I pause at the threshold, one hand on the door.

"That's interesting," I say softly, glancing back with narrowed eyes. "Because for this village's sake, you'd better hope that I do."

Then I step into the light, letting the door close hard behind me.

CHAPTER SEVEN

ELYSIA

I'm running again.

This time, the mist is thicker, heavier, and clinging to my skin like wet silk. My boots slip on the bloodied ground as I tear through the familiar paths of the village. The cottages are dark, windows shattered, and the scent of copper and death lingers in every sharp intake of breath.

I round a corner and see black tendrils of smoke billowing from the thatched roof of my home. The door hangs off its hinges, smashed to pieces.

"No, no, please," I murmur, tears brimming in my eyes.

I stumble through the doorway, choking on ash, while the heat of the flames licks against my skin. Inside, everything is wrong.

My father lies slumped against the hearth, blood seeping through the patchwork of his coat. My mother's weaving is strewn across the floor, soaked with crimson. Penelope's doll lies near the doorway, its head snapped sideways. A single ribbon dangles from the little hand that still clutches it.

My breath catches as I see Maggie standing in the center of the room. Her thin frame seems even more fragile beneath the flickering light of the fire, her eyes glassy and distant.

She stares straight at me and speaks in a voice that isn't hers.

"You came back just like me," she says, voice hollow. "Broken and defeated."

I stagger backward. Her voice cuts deeper than the fire's heat.

"You weren't enough," she whispers. "Now we all pay the price for that."

The shame is immediate. I try to deny it, to push it down, but it's already blooming in the hollow space beneath my ribs.

"No," I whisper, "No, I . . . I tried, I—"

I want to scream, I want to beg for another chance, but no words come. I drop to my knees, my palms scraping the floor. The weight of it all presses down, smothering me.

Then everything shatters.

The fire fractures like glass, its light collapsing in on itself, and the smoke peels away in curling ribbons, vanishing into the ether. The walls, the blood, the grief . . . they all fall away, until there's nothing left but a strange and endless stillness.

I'm not in my home anymore.

A cool mist pools across the smooth stone beneath my bare feet, faintly luminous beneath some unseen light. The air vibrates softly against my skin, like the world itself is exhaling. The pressure in my chest lessens, though it doesn't fade entirely, and something within me still clings to the terror from before.

Until a subtle shift prickles across the back of my neck.

I'm being watched.

Not in the threatening, sinister way that once clawed at my spine, but in a way that feels strangely familiar.

I turn, slow and deliberate, already half certain of what I'll find.

He stands veiled in shadow, a stark contrast from the blinding light that had once kept me from seeing him. There is no magical paralysis this time, no external force weighing down my limbs or keeping my eyes from opening.

Only a stillness between us, suspended and pulsing, waiting for one of us to reach out and break it.

I can't see his face, but I don't need to.

His presence alone quietly disarms the lingering fear from the nightmare.

He shouldn't be able to do that without a word or lifting a finger.

Why does it feel like he holds so much power over me? My feet shift uncomfortably beneath me, feeling the weight of a stare I can't even see.

Is this how all humans feel in the elves' presence?

"You ran toward your fear this time," he says, voice low and threaded with curiosity. "You've never done that before."

The remark lands with more weight than it should, not because it surprises me but because of the certainty in his tone. There's an unspoken truth layered behind those words . . . that he's watched me longer than I realized. That I've possibly had more nightmares or dreams with him in them than I know of.

I wrap my arms around myself, not out of fear, but instinct. It's an unconscious attempt to shield a piece of me that still isn't sure I should trust this deep sense of security he instills.

"I suppose I'm just finding a new strength within," I say quietly, the words falling from my lips before I can think better of them.

He tilts his head slightly, a motion so subtle it feels more like studying me than a reaction. It's like he's considering how the pieces of me have shifted since the last time we met.

"That kind of change doesn't happen without reason," he finally responds, calm and certain. "Care to elaborate?"

The mist at our feet ripples, disturbed by a current I can't see.

I thought I wasn't ready to explain to anyone the weight pressing down on me, the truth of what the village asked of me, or what I'm about to give up. I convinced myself it was better carried in silence, safer if no one else could see it.

Yet my mouth opens, ready to share it with this elf anyway. Just before the words can escape, I stop myself.

Maybe it's the subtle influence of his magic . . . this ease and trust that shouldn't exist between strangers. Maybe it's just me, aching for someone to see the burden of what I'm carrying. Either way, I can't let it slip. Not yet. I want answers before I offer any more of myself.

"Where are we?" I ask, my voice hushed, unable to shake the stillness pressing in on all sides. "Shouldn't I be in a nightmare? Or a dream?"

"This is your mind," he says softly, and somehow the simplicity of the truth takes me off guard. "There's a heaviness lingering in it that is entirely of your own creation."

I shift slightly, but I don't step back.

The shadows begin to waft and I turn with them, not wanting to take my eyes off his figure as he moves behind them.

"You act like you know me," I murmur, turning on my heel. "Intimately."

The words leave me before I can stop them, and my cheeks flush with heat. It sounds ridiculous, saying something like that to a stranger, but it doesn't make it any less true.

"I wish I could understand my mind and why I'm having these nightmares." The admission falls from my mouth as I tuck a strand of hair behind my ear and stare directly into where I assume his eyes are. "And why do you keep appearing in them?"

He halts as I drag my bottom lip between my teeth.

"You're the one calling out to me," he says, a flicker of amusement threading through his tone. "I merely answer, Little Dove."

The nickname shouldn't make my stomach flutter, but it does.

I find the edges of my lips lifting, drawn by the soft weight of his tease. A rare spark of levity in a world that's only felt heavy since the first nightmare struck my life.

"Yet I know you're breaking laws to be here," I whisper, the words soft but sure. "And by speaking to me."

He steps closer, the mist and shadows shifting around his form. I search for a glimpse of his face, but the shadows wrap around him in swirling, deliberate protection.

"I also want to know why you're having nightmares. You're an anomaly in a carefully crafted system that never has variances," he admits, exhaling sharply. "What is it about you?"

The genuine concern in his voice startles me, but more so, the way he breathed out those last five words like a whispered prayer.

A truth lodges itself deep within my chest, dangerous and undeniable. I don't know who he is, or what he wants, but I trust him in a way that is beginning to frighten me more than it comforts me.

I shift my weight, heart pounding harder than it should while asleep. "This nightmare you interrupted felt different than the other night. It felt like . . . a warning."

His form doesn't move, but the air itself seems to tighten around my skin.

"It felt like I failed everyone," I say quietly, my voice catching as the words start to tumble out. "I came back like Maggie. Empty. Broken. Everyone else paid the price for that."

I don't know why I'm admitting any of this to him, as if he knows Maggie or cares to hear my thoughts.

He seems to stiffen, his fingers flattening to his side.

"You've been taught to fear nightmares," he says eventually. "But they're just dreams in a darker mirror. Some think nightmares are made-up fears, but often they merely reflect an ugly truth you don't want to face."

An uncomfortable itch crawls down my neck, beneath my skin, and I shiver at his words.

"There weren't any dreams at all last night," I murmur, glancing toward the far edges of the mist. "Not even a nightmare. Just . . . nothing. A void."

My unspoken question lingers, waiting to see if he will trust me with information the way I have him.

It's what I need from him, if I'm to believe that whatever this pull to him is might be my own feelings, not influenced by his magic or a deception of some kind.

I need something real from him.

His silence lasts longer this time and I wonder if he's reached the limit of what he will discuss, but he doesn't disappear or even move. So I wait, feeling like we're at an impasse that he has to decide to cross or not.

When he finally speaks, his voice is quieter. "The elven courts were called to assemble. Dromin and Nithrin both, for an emergency gathering."

My spine stiffens. "Because of the Queen's death?"

"Yes." His reply is slightly clipped and hesitant, but he continues after a breath. "She was honored beneath the Goddess's light."

I try to study him, but there's nothing to study. Just that same shifting silhouette, veiled in shadows that never quite settle. Light moves strangely near him, never touching, never revealing. It's driving me quietly mad not to see his face—every expression, every emotion hidden behind a shifting shadow.

His continuous visits and now the information he's revealed tell me he feels the same ease between us that I do. Maybe I'm not crazy for finding comfort in his presence and sharing pieces of my life.

"That's why there were no dreams?" I press on, uncertain whether I'm pushing for too much . . . but I'm too scared that I'll never have a chance to ask these questions again.

"When both courts are called to assembly, the dream and nightmare flow halts." He pauses and shifts around, as if unsure about continuing,

or worried someone can hear him. "All humans alive in this time have grown used to our magic and influence, your minds unable to create either escape without our magic now. That's why you experienced a void."

I blink rapidly, trying my best to absorb that information quickly. "So without the Nithrin and Dromin, they stop altogether. Dreams. Nightmares. All of it."

The thought is unnerving. We were led to believe that our thoughts were our own and they were merely visitors, feeding off of the energy of our dreams and ensuring they stayed pleasant.

"It wasn't always that way," he admits with an edge of hesitation before taking a step toward me. "I don't want you to fear me now."

The tender statement lands heavily in my bones.

Suddenly his form is gone and a prickle at my neck is the only alert I get before sparks light up along my neck. His breath fans across my skin, just barely.

"You're right. I am breaking laws to be here," he admits, a thread of intrigue clear in his rumbling voice. "Tell me you want me to stop and I will, but I've found myself drawn to your soul and I intend to figure out why that is. I didn't mean for this to matter, but it does."

My mouth is suddenly parched and the part of my brain that is supposed to supply words ceases to work.

I lean back, desperately wanting to feel a part of him that reminds me he's real and not a figment of my imagination. I half expect to fall back into a swirl of shadows or for him to move, but a solid chest greets me.

The warmth from his body flows into me, making my breath hitch at the nearness.

"I'm leaving tomorrow," I say in a rush, unsure why I offer that piece of myself now. "North. To the High Priestess."

My tongue darts out to wet my suddenly dry lips as a breath passes, waiting for his answer.

A tremor runs through his body as I feel it tighten.

"To be . . . offered in the selection?" he asks slowly, like he's being deliberate with his choice of words.

I force my answer out, barely managing to accept it. "Yes."

His head tilts slightly as he suddenly whirls to my front again, the shadows still dutiful in their job of concealment.

My lips part as a sigh puffs across them with the disappointment I feel in his withdrawal and the sudden tension I feel emanating between us with my admission.

Maybe he's worried about being caught visiting me anymore if I'm going to be considered by the High Priestess to become the Queen. It would be a fair concern, but the thought of his presence halting stings more than I'd like to admit.

Or could it be that he thinks I'm already claimed by the King just by being in the selection?

"I know what you're thinking," I say quickly, trying to fill the silence that's suddenly too heavy. "That you won't be able to visit anymore and maybe you'll be punished if they find out you've broken the laws."

"I wasn't thinking of punishment," he says, so quietly I almost miss it. "I've covered my tracks well."

I blink, taken aback by that truth. My heartbeat quickens as I whisper back, "Then what is bothering you suddenly?"

Yet he doesn't answer, just continues to stand there, half consumed by mist and shadow. The change in his demeanor and tone was so harsh that I'm struggling to catch up to it, when my traitorous body is still thinking of how nice his quiet strength felt pressed against my back.

Why did I have to ruin the moment by admitting where I'm heading tomorrow?

I don't know why it matters so much to him, but even without words, it's clear that a wall has been thrown up between us.

My chest tightens with an ache I can't place, unsure whether it's hurt or confusion. "I don't even know your name," I admit. "I hope that this isn't goodbye. I hope I'll see you again."

I catch the briefest hint of motion, his hand lifting and reaching. Just as the dream begins to dissolve, I feel it, a whisper of touch, a featherlight brush of his fingertips along my jaw.

It sears into me, a deep warmth and ache simmering beneath my skin.

"You will see me again," he says gently. "I'm sure of it."

There's a fragility beneath the certainty in those words, like a promise wrapped in sorrow that he's not happy to make.

The space around us begins to fade. The cool floor beneath my feet dissolves into mist and his presence starts to unravel from the edges inward, slipping away into the shadows.

His voice echoes through my waking consciousness, low and steady. "When you're tested, think of me. Only me."

His words are a quiet plea, inspiring panic to unfurl within my chest.

What does that even mean? What does he know?

I can't shake the sense of absence—like something important just slipped through my fingers before I had a chance to understand it.

"No, wait!" I call out, but it's already too late.

My breath catches in my throat as I sit upright in my bed, pulse racing so hard it feels like it might break through my ribs. The room is dim, shadows stretched thin across the walls.

My fingers drift up, finding the end of my braid, clutching it tight in my fist. I curl up, drawing my knees to my chest beneath the worn covers, holding on to this last moment of my life as I know it, before the weight of the world crashes in again.

Today, everything changes.

Today, I leave everything I've ever known behind.

The sun will rise, and I will follow it, uncertain where I'll rest my head when it sets again.

CHAPTER EIGHT

ELYSIA

Dawn seeps through the cottage shutters, catching on the dust motes in the air and casting warm patterns across the worn floorboards. For one last moment I lie still beneath the covers, breathing in the scent of woodsmoke and dried lavender, listening to the quiet sounds of home—my mother's low humming from the hearth, the soft thud of a wooden spoon against a clay pot, and Penelope's light footsteps padding across the floorboards in search of breakfast.

Everything feels too normal, too unchanged, and yet today could be the last time I'll ever wake in this bed. My fingers curl into the edge of the quilt, anchoring myself for one last moment before I rise.

When I finally bring myself into the kitchen, the scent of spiced stew and dried meat clings to the air, thick and familiar. My mother stands by the table, hands moving with quiet purpose as she wraps bundles in cloth with careful intent.

"I packed a lot of your favorite dried apples," she says softly, not looking up yet, maybe because she can't bring herself to. I swallow hard. "And cured meat, a loaf of barley bread, and I tucked a new, thick scarf in, in case the wind turns with the winter cycle coming."

Her voice is steady, but I can feel the strain beneath it. Like each word is a thread pulled taut, threatening to fray. In this moment, as she buries herself in tasks, I see myself reflecting back so brightly. I learned to put others before myself from her, to choose to be kind when others are not, and to fight for our family.

"Thank you," I whisper, though the words feel too small for all that they carry.

It feels like I'm searching for a way to thank her for the past twenty-three years of life instead of the supplies she packed. For every kiss to my self-inflicted injuries from playing too hard with Pat, for the hugs that wrapped around me so tightly it felt like she could single-handedly hold me together, for protecting my heart and dreams at the sacrifice of her own at times.

My gaze drops to the large new satchel on the table, leather with a shining buckle fastened tight. I step closer and brush my fingers over it as she says, "Thald made that. It's his highest-quality leather and much bigger than your worn satchel. Your father went early this morning to buy it."

I pause my inspection of the fine leather to glance up at her, torn between frustration and gratitude. "You shouldn't waste the money on me with winter coming. You won't have my income for future cycles and—"

She closes the short distance between us and grabs my hands, cutting me off with her words. "Elysia, we will be fine, honey." Her grip tightens before letting go to cradle my face. "*You* will be fine."

My lip wobbles and I blink back tears welling up.

Penelope appears beside us suddenly, clutching something in her hands. Her eyes are puffy from crying, though she's trying not to let me see. She swallows hard and offers me a length of ribbon—her favorite one. Deep purple with faint silver embroidery running along the edges.

"For your braid," she says, her voice wobbling. "So you don't forget us on your journey. So you don't forget me."

Emotion lodges in my throat and I can't hold back the few stray tears that cascade down my cheeks. I take the ribbon with reverence, fingers trembling as I smooth it between my palms.

"I could never forget you," I say, and then I open my arms.

She falls into them, clinging to me so tightly it nearly breaks me. I rock her gently, burying my nose in her hair. She smells like the lavender oil our mother rubs into her scalp at night, soft and floral and heartbreakingly familiar.

"You'll wear it?" she whispers into my shoulder.

I nod, even though my voice won't come. I don't trust it not to crack, along with my heart.

My father steps into the room then, silent as ever, as my mother draws Penelope back into her arms. He holds something wrapped in a dark wool cloth, fingers working nervously along the corners.

"This was meant for your wedding," he says after a pause, voice rasped and quiet. "But life had other plans."

He unwraps it carefully and reveals a pendant—slender and simple. A polished piece of river stone, cool gray streaked with white, encased in a delicate twist of silver. The chain glints faintly in the morning light.

His heavy steps thud against the floorboards as he approaches and offers it to me. "It belonged to your grandmother."

The moment stings deeper than I expect. My hand closes around the pendant like it might disappear if I don't hold it tight enough.

"I'll carry her strength with me," I swear, "and yours."

He nods once, his soft brown eyes shining with love and pride. Then suddenly I'm wrapped in his large arms. This hug is longer and tighter than usual, his arms wrapped around me like he's trying to protect me from everything to come that he can't control. His chin rests against the top of my head, and I feel the slow rise and fall of his chest.

"My brave girl," he says softly, so low I almost miss it. "You've always been the strongest soul I've known, ever since your first breath and cry in this world."

A fresh wave of tears burns hot behind my eyes, and I hold him tighter, burying my face in his shoulder.

My mother joins us a moment later, wrapping her arms around both of us, and then Penelope squeezes in between, forming a knot of warmth and breath, all of our hearts breaking in unison. We stand there for a long time, wrapped in each other, not speaking—just existing in the only kind of goodbye we know how to give, one full of love.

A knock at the door snaps us out of the moment and we step back as my father walks to the door. He opens it and two guards wait outside, horses pawing the dirt behind them. One man is tall and weathered, his expression unreadable beneath the shadow of his hood. The other is younger, a flicker of softness in his eyes as they brush over me.

"We're here for the chosen," the older one says flatly.

No name. No acknowledgment. Just . . . the chosen.

I guess it's time.

I grab the satchel off the table and drape it over my shoulder before moving toward the door. I hear my family's steps follow quickly behind me as I reach the doorstep and look out. A wooden wagon is hitched behind the horses, modest and bare, its boards worn and splintering.

My home for the next however many days it will take to journey to the northern port.

I glance back at my family one last time. My mother presses a kiss to my forehead, her lips warm and trembling. My father takes the pendant from my hand, securing it around my neck, his touch lingering on the stone as he tries to muster a smile. Penelope slips her hand into mine and whispers, "Don't forget to braid it in."

"I won't," I promise before I attempt to force myself to let go of her hand. Our fingers slide apart, the tips lingering a brief second before I turn over my shoulder toward my unknown fate, my hand falling flat to my side.

Take the step.

I let the tears fall freely as I walk toward the wagon, afraid that if I look back I'll lose the small bit of strength and courage I'm clinging to. The younger guard silently helps me up, steadying me with a nod that feels almost like an apology as I wipe the tears from my cheeks and settle onto the sideboard.

My eyes look down at the ribbon in my hand, my tears quickly falling onto it, seeping into the soft fabric. I take in a deep breath as I thread the ribbon into the end of my braid.

The reins snap and the wagon lurches forward, the wheels creaking beneath me as the village begins to pass by in a blur. People have gathered in silence. Some nod solemnly. Some avert their eyes. A few children wave hesitantly before their mothers pull them back. No cheers. No happy farewells.

Just a somber quietness.

I swallow the lump rising in my throat and keep my chin high. Someone had to be sent, at the end of the day. There was always going to be a woman in this wagon riding off and a village full of people expecting her to come back broken and a shell of their former self like Maggie, if they aren't chosen as queen.

I know some of them feel shame for being a part of writing my name down and I wish I could tell them to believe in me now, that I will fight for myself, for all of us. That I won't let this journey break me. But my words would sound hollow to them, and I vowed then to let my actions speak for themselves.

We're halfway through the square when I hear someone shouting.

"Wait!"

The wagon continues on as I turn my head toward the voice, heart catching in my throat at the streak heading toward us.

Pat.

He's sprinting down the road, cloak flapping, golden hair tousled from sleep. He reaches the wagon in seconds and slaps his palm against the side.

"Stop the damn wagon!" he yells.

I don't wait for permission; I jump down and meet him halfway. He crashes into me with a breathless hug, arms clenching so tightly it knocks the air from my lungs.

I hear the guard yell and the wagon creak to a halt.

"I almost missed you," he says, voice thick with emotion. "I'm so sorry. I thought I had more time."

"It's okay," I whisper, holding him just as fiercely. "You made it."

He pulls back and presses something into my hand, and I quickly glance down. My eyes roam over the leather sheath around what I presume to be a dagger.

"You always think of everyone else," he says before pausing and wrapping my hand around the weapon. "Not everyone will be as kind-hearted as you and they will take advantage of it, Lys. Promise me you'll protect yourself."

I blink a few times, processing his words and the weight of them. I may find the ways of our village to be outdated and suffocating, but I always knew I was safe. Beyond my home, I'm not naive enough to think that will be the same, yet it never occurred to me that I may have to bloody my own hands to ensure it.

"I promise," I whisper.

We stare at each other a moment longer before I step away and climb back onto the wagon. There's so much I could say, but only a few words come to the tip of my tongue as I gaze down at him.

"Marry Persephone and love her deeply, check in on my family every once in a while, and keep our spot on the hill warm for me when I return."

I watch his throat bob as his lips thin. He nods over and over, seeming to get choked up before brushing his hand over his face harshly.

"I know it's you who convinced the Elder," he whispers back. "Thank you."

I nod, clutching his gift in my lap as the wagon lurches forward again. I watch until the village begins to blur behind us. The twisted ivy

around our fence posts, the uneven slats of the roof, the fields that fed us, the faces of the only people I've ever known and cared for.

There, at the edge of the square, I see Penelope. Still standing, still watching, her cheeks blotched with red patches and tears streaming down them.

The wind rises, brushing against my cheeks, tugging gently at the end of my braid and the ends of the ribbon, and I wonder whether I'll ever see home again.

CHAPTER NINE

ELYSIA

The wagon rocks gently beneath me, wheels creaking as we roll along a narrow dirt road that cuts through the open countryside. The sun hangs low now, its light slanting across the open plains. My fingers brush the smooth leather of my satchel as I put away the remaining apples, and my thoughts drift to the few villages we've passed.

Each one told its own story.

Some, like mine, clung to dignity in small ways: tidy fences, modest fields, children laughing despite patched clothing. Others were worse. Cracked stone walls. Shoes stitched with twine. Eyes dulled by the ache of hunger. All of them shared one thing in common: the absence of abundance that spoke to no queens being produced in their lands.

Yet each village had something that marked it as distinct. Gressar was known for its sturdy clay craftsmanship. Beautiful, utilitarian pottery lined their markets, even in poverty. Plithu, which we passed shortly after leaving my village, boasted deep dyeing vats with brilliant fabrics hung in vibrant rows, colors so rich they felt misplaced against their bleak landscape. Mine, of course, is known for its elderberries. The rows of thorny bushes, the tart smell in the air during harvest season, and the wine that was our singular pride.

None of our individualities mattered when compared to those who lived under a queen's blessing, though. My jaw had remained unhinged as we passed through Tramir. According to my guard, they had been granted a steady stream of magical rainfall over their crops for over a century when their chosen became Queen. That land still glowed with enchantment all these years later despite the magic dissipating without renewal. Their trees heavy with golden fruit, streets lined with

enchanted lanterns that lit without oil, fields that bloomed out of season due to the rain.

My stomach had twisted as we passed it, full of guilt, envy, disbelief. I hadn't realized how much we'd been left to rot until I saw what the elves' goddess could give the chosen's lands.

We've been traveling since morning, and as dusk falls, we finally crest a small ridge, revealing a village nestled in a shallow valley below. The inn is visible from here, a sturdy stone structure with a smoke plume curling from the chimney and a flickering lantern over the door.

The older guard, Luan, is hunched slightly in his saddle, his jaw locked tight with the stoic silence he's worn all day. The younger one, Berrin, looks back at me, offering a brief glance as we slow.

"We'll stay here tonight," he says, voice low. "Roads beyond here grow narrow, and bandits favor the dark."

I nod, grateful for the chance to rest somewhere other than a jostling wagon bed. My bones ache more than I care to admit.

We roll into the village square just as the sun dips behind the hills. The light slants low, casting long shadows over the cobblestones. Evening vendors are packing up their carts, and candles flicker in windows. Life is still moving here, unbothered by the weight pressing down on my shoulders.

All movement stills when they see us, I'm sure because of who accompanies me. The guards are what they see first, two mounted escorts in ceremonial leather, with weapons strapped to their backs. A clear sign to anyone who's ever heard of the selection process.

The villagers' eyes flick to me next. No gasps. No awe. Just a shift in the air . . . a quiet tension and a recognition laced with guarded interest. They know I'm one of the chosen and they don't like it. I'm just someone standing in the way of their own chosen and this village's possible glory.

The wagon halts in front of an inn with a timbered frame and freshly painted shutters. A swinging sign creaks above the door, depicting a horse leaping over a crescent moon. The smell of fresh bread and roasting meat curls into the air from within.

An innkeeper steps out with a towel slung over one shoulder and a mug in hand. He squints against the setting sun, his gaze scanning the guards before settling on me.

"Another one," he mutters, not unkindly, but with no warmth either. "A chosen?"

Luan dismounts first and gives a curt nod. "She'll need a warm meal and a room. We'll head north again at first light."

The innkeeper nods, jerking his chin toward the door. "You'll want the upstairs corner room for her safety. You're not the only ones traveling this road."

I stiffen. "There are others?"

"Two arrived earlier today," the innkeeper replies. "One came through a few hours ago, a girl from Gressar, and another that has been here since midday, from Celaine."

My stomach tightens slightly at the latter.

Gressar had been similar in status to my own as we passed by it, but Celaine is a name I've heard many times. It's the village of the recently deceased Queen. . . . Their village was the main one to loan supplies to villages struck by the locusts. They are rumored to be wealthy, refined, well-fed. If they've sent someone, I have a feeling she won't be like the rest of us.

I follow the innkeeper inside, keeping my eyes low, the weight of the villagers' stares still crawling across my back.

Inside, the inn is warm and softly lit. A hearth glows on one side of the room, and the scent of roasted meat and baked leeks drifts through the air. The innkeeper's wife gestures toward a table near the fire, where a tray has already been laid out with a meal.

"Eat," Luan grunts as he follows behind me. "Then get some rest."

I nod, too tired to argue. He lingers long enough to ensure the room is safe before retreating, letting me know they'll sleep in the stables tonight, alternating watch shifts, both wary of bandits or townsfolk wanting to stop us from reaching our destination.

I settle into the chair, hands trembling slightly as I begin to eat, mostly to give them something to do. My throat feels too tight to swallow much, but I manage a few bites before footsteps creak down the stairs.

A girl appears in the entryway, her cloak tossed over one arm, auburn curls spilling from a thick braid over her shoulder. She's slender and soft-looking, her features gentle and eyes wide with curiosity.

She sees me and freezes briefly before offering a tentative smile. "Are you one of the chosen, too?"

I nod, unsure how much to say, but something in her expression is warm and unthreatening.

"I'm Thalia," she says, stepping closer. "From Gressar. Just stopped here for the night before heading on."

"Elysia," I reply, still a bit wary of anyone's motives outside of my village. "From Edritch."

She brightens at my response with wide brown eyes. "I passed through there once as a child. Your elderberry wine is well-known."

I smile faintly. "That's all we have."

She pulls out a chair and sits across from me as soon as I answer, folding her hands neatly in her lap. Her eyes roam the room briefly before she leans forward and whispers, "I've never been this far from home before."

"Me neither," I admit, startled by how easily the truth comes.

Perhaps I should be less forthcoming, but my chest aches with the need to have a friendly face in the midst of all the unknown.

We fall into quiet, safe conversation about the same road we took to get here, the strange looks, the ache of leaving family behind. She's soft-spoken yet filled with a warmth that exudes from her without trying. I find myself smiling gently at her as she carries the weight of our conversation.

Another figure descends the stairs, interrupting our focus. She walks like she owns the floor beneath her feet with her chin high, spine straight, hair arranged in elaborate coils pinned by silver combs. Her cloak is made of fine velvet, the hem embroidered with silver thread.

Her eyes skim over me with cool disinterest, then land briefly on Thalia before flicking back to the hearth.

"That's Lisbeth. She's from Celaine," Thalia whispers quietly once the newcomer has gone to the far side of the room. "I overheard the innkeeper talking."

Of course she is. She fits the arrogant picture I procured in my mind earlier.

She takes a seat alone at a table near the window and signals for a drink with the kind of ease that tells me she's used to being waited on. She hasn't looked at us again, but I feel her gaze as it travels across the rest of the room, as if she's assigning value to everything she sees.

"I heard she was a unanimous choice," Thalia continues, her voice hushed as she leans in. "They think she's destined to be Queen, as she's related to the one who just passed."

After receiving a cup of what I presume to be wine, Lisbeth's gaze finally lands on me again with quiet calculation. Assessing, judging, measuring. She pushes to her feet and walks over to us, choosing to

remain standing over us despite the open seat at my side. Clearly she prefers to feel imposing to others.

"Another chosen . . ." she muses with a haughty tone as her eyes dance over my features. "And where is it that you are from?"

My jaw tenses at her tone, as if she believes I'm beneath her without even knowing who I am.

The presumption that she doesn't need to introduce herself ignites a fire within me. Thalia may have told me, but it doesn't excuse someone from introducing themselves before prying into my life.

"You are?" I counter with an uncharacteristic edge to my tone. My chin tilts back as I glance up at her, unblinking as I wait for her answer.

She offers a tight smile, the kind that hides her teeth and true emotions. "Lisbeth, from Celaine."

I nod in greeting, my voice tight as I answer, "Elysia, from Edritch."

She steps closer, her eyes flicking over my worn cloak, the ribbon in my braid, the faint calluses on my hands. She doesn't say anything cruel and she doesn't have to. Her silence is condescension enough.

"Well," she says, tone polite and cutting all at once as she places her untouched wine down on our table. "At least you'll make for an interesting comparison."

She sweeps past me and disappears back up the stairs, leaving the scent of rose oil in her wake.

I don't respond. I can't. The words I want to say burn my tongue, but I swallow them down, hating the bitterness that she inspires in me. That's not who I am.

My eyes flutter closed as I take a few deep breaths and think of home. Warmth fills the center of my chest and I smile, feeling the wild storm of emotions calming within me as I recenter and ground myself.

Thalia and I fall into silence, both of us seeming to retreat internally. Eventually she clears her throat and looks into my eyes, curling her hands into her lap. "I'm scared," she admits in a whisper. "I thought I was ready, but the closer we get to the port . . ."

I offer a quiet nod of support as that sinking feeling of dread reappears in my core. "Me too."

As patrons leave and the room becomes quiet, still we sit together, as if neither of us wants to be alone with our thoughts. The silence that wraps around us isn't awkward, but comforting. A shared space to let the weight of the journey waiting for us be distributed equally between us.

"Alright, ladies, off to bed with you," the innkeeper's wife instructs gently from behind the bar top. "We're going to be locking up the doors down here, but I suggest you lock the ones in your rooms as well."

Her words bring Thalia and me back to the present, jolting slightly and blinking as we refocus. With a nod and our thanks for the hospitality, we head up the stairs to our respective rooms.

"We'll be okay, right?" Thalia asks as she comes to a stop at her door.

Her question feels so heavy, despite being so simple.

My lips curl into a soft, reflexive smile, though it's forced. "Of course we will."

She gives a shaky nod and turns toward her door, fingers lingering on the latch for a moment longer than necessary.

As I watch her, something catches in my chest, an echo of familiarity in the way her shoulders hunch slightly inward, like she's trying to make herself smaller beneath the weight of her nerves. It's the same thing Penelope does when she's frightened, when she's pretending she's brave and hoping no one notices how much she's shaking inside.

My heart aches unexpectedly, a soft twist of homesickness blooming beneath my ribs.

Without thinking, my fingers drift up to the end of my braid, finding the smooth ribbon wound through it. I run it between my fingers absently. Penelope's ribbon. The fabric is soft and cool beneath my fingertips, grounding me, reminding me who I am and what I carry with me.

For a moment, I let myself believe that maybe I was meant to meet Thalia, that our interactions continue to guide my heart toward kindness even when the world feels colder by the day.

"Sleep well," I say softly, lingering at the hallway's edge.

Thalia turns back to smile faintly. "You too, Elysia."

She disappears behind the door with a quiet click, leaving me alone in the flickering lantern light of our hall, fingers still curled around that silver-edged ribbon.

If there's trouble ahead, I'll make sure Thalia doesn't face it alone, because not everyone gets to be born in a village with gold, magic, and blessings. Some of us were forged in quiet places, with nothing but grit, heart, and stubborn hope.

We deserve to stand just as tall as anyone else, even if we have to fight for every inch of it.

CHAPTER TEN

ELYSIA

Morning breaks over the inn with a soft haze of light filtering through the heavy clouds, washing the square in a pale glow. The air is damp, still holding the remnants of a night chill, and dew clings to every surface.

The square has come alive with movement and I feel like I'm in a fog as I take it in. Impatient hooves striking cobblestone, leather buckles clinking, murmured commands between guards. It all passes by in a blur, my eyes heavy with exhaustion. All night I tossed and turned, thinking of home and what is yet to come.

If I'm being honest with myself, I was also afraid to close my eyes and have an answer to whether the Dromin elf would still visit me or not. The thought of having a nightmare grip me in its claws for the entirety of the night was most unwelcome, preventing me from getting a minute of sleep.

We're gathered in the square, the three chosen, each marked by circumstance that brought us together, but even within this shared fate, the divide between us gapes wide.

Lisbeth's carriage stands polished and elegant, pulled by two sleek, dapple-gray horses that snort impatiently, their reins adorned with braided silver tassels. Her guards wear matching dark cloaks with a glint of silver embroidery. She steps off the porch of the inn, wrapped in a deep plum cloak trimmed with fur as one of her guards rushes to place her bag delicately into the carriage before helping her inside.

Thalia and I exchange glances and I barely hold back the eyeroll that leaves my face twitching with the effort.

We stand beside two nearly identical, simple and sturdy wagons, with the only difference being a cloth cover on hers and the absence of

one on mine. Our horses are older, with patchy white-and-brown coats, and old tack. Luan and Berrin ready our harness lines, checking the bolts and wagon wheels with practiced efficiency.

Lisbeth is the first to set off, her carriage wheels crunching softly over the cobblestone path as her horses trot forward. As her carriage disappears down the road ahead, Thalia glances over at me, her expression uncertain.

"Do you think . . ." She hesitates, her brow pinched for a moment before smoothing. "Would it be alright if I rode with you today? Just for a while. I . . . I'd rather not sit in silence."

Before I can answer, Luan interjects, blunt and dismissive. "That's not protocol. Each chosen travels with her assigned guards. It's not up for discussion."

Thalia's shoulders sag slightly, and her mouth closes again before another word can escape. I see the disappointment flicker across her face and something rises in me, sharp and hot. I've been silent too many times and let others make choices around me, for me.

Not today.

"She can ride with me," I say, stepping forward and drawing my guard's eyes. "There's enough space, and it's hardly dangerous to share a wagon with another chosen without her guard."

Luan's jaw tightens, dark stubble beginning to poke through his skin, but I meet his gaze, unflinching. He says nothing for a moment, eyes narrowing slightly in reluctant acknowledgment. Then he turns with a grunt and returns to his work, muttering under his breath. "Don't get paid enough for this."

Thalia's eyes go wide with relief and gratitude as I glance back at her. I offer her a small smile and tilt my head toward the wagon.

"Come on," I say, nodding toward the seat beside mine.

Thalia nods, then turns to her guards, who immediately begin to protest.

"Your wagon has already been prepared—"

"I'm riding with her today," she says, cutting them off, voice soft and slightly wobbling. "That's my decision."

I don't miss the pride that swells in my chest at her bravery. Small, yes, but brave nonetheless.

The moment we're settled and the guards give the all-clear after talking together, the wagon lurches forward, wheels groaning beneath us.

The hours pass with quiet conversation and stretches of silence. We share the food from our satchels at midday, her eyes lighting up at the taste of the apples from our village. Likewise, I'm shocked by the rich flavor of the cheese she brought.

After our lunch, we stare up at the fluffy white clouds above our lands.

"Do you think we'll get a chance to see their world even if we aren't chosen?" she asks, a note of wistfulness that I entirely relate to in her voice. "Or will only the chosen return with the High Priestess?"

I narrow my eyes as something gleams brightly from a small opening between the clouds. My heart jumps at the chance to know what their world looks like. Just as quickly as it came, it's covered with drifting clouds and my excitement plummets back to reality.

Maggie's face comes to mind as I choose my words carefully, not wanting to alarm Thalia. The majority of her broken thoughts seemed to revolve around the Priestess, and despite her confusion, I felt certain she didn't see the elven courts.

"I think that perhaps it will be better if we just return home without seeing a glimpse of their world."

If we do, there's likely a price neither of us wants to pay, is what I want to say at the end.

Her lips thin and turn down before she begins to nibble on her bottom one.

Drawing her thoughts back to ones that inspire happiness within her, I ask, "But what do you think they look like? I want to picture your version of it."

The day grows warmer, chasing off the worst of the chill, allowing me to put my thick scarf back in my satchel in the height of the afternoon sun. Tall fields of wheat blur by until the sun begins to dip toward the horizon behind the approaching forest.

Just as the trees thicken around us, a strange scent catches on the wind and I take a deep inhale. *Burnt wood.*

"There's something ahead," Berrin says grimly. "Smoke."

The wagon rolls forward cautiously now, hooves muffled by leaf-strewn ground. I sit straighter, my pulse rising as we follow the narrow path through the forest.

Flames flicker ahead in the fading light. A carriage, or what's left of one, lies half overturned, one wheel split, its ornate side scorched black.

Smoke curls from the wreckage, stinging the air, the scent thick and acrid. The horses that once pulled it are missing entirely.

My stomach churns as recollection slams into it.

Lisbeth's carriage.

"No," I breathe, heart slamming against my ribs. I glance at Thalia, who sits frozen beside me, her face pale, eyes wide with horror. Her lips move silently, mouthing prayers to gods I'm not sure are listening.

"Stay in the wagon," Luan barks as he and Berrin leap down, weapons drawn. The steel sings in the open air, a sharp, decisive sound that cuts through the fog of fear.

I'm already moving, my body reacting before my thoughts can catch up.

The wagon bed thuds beneath my feet as I leap to the ground, sprinting across the uneven terrain. Embers scatter beneath my boots. The heat from the smoldering wood singes my skin. Ash clings to my clothes, my lungs rasping as I breathe it in.

"Elysia!" Berrin shouts, but I don't stop. I can't.

His voice is a dull afterthought as my heart hammers in my chest, eyes scanning the wreckage for bodies. Two guards, crumpled near the trees, come into view, blood darkening the leaves beneath them. I don't need to move any closer to know their stillness isn't by choice, but by the absence of such.

My guards flank me as I run to the other side of the broken carriage. My eyes find her barely visible, half-hidden beneath the wreckage.

"Lisbeth!" I drop to my knees beside her. "She's alive!"

Her cloak is singed, her hair disheveled, a trail of blood seeping from a deep gash on her forehead. She's unconscious, face pale and slack.

Berrin rushes forward, helping me pull her free, careful not to jostle her head. I lower my ear to her chest, the beat of her heart steady and strong—for now.

"We need to get her into the wagon," I say, voice rising with urgency. I know nothing of the ways of healing, but I know that as long as her heart still beats, I won't give up on her. "There might be a healer in the next village."

Luan doesn't hesitate. He lifts her with little effort and brings her toward the wagon, while I clear a space beside our supplies.

That's when the arrows fly. Resounding thuds into the side of the wagon with vicious cracks.

Chaos erupts.

Four men emerge from the trees, faces half-covered in cloth, blades drawn. With no armor or signifying emblems, it's clear they must be bandits.

Berrin charges the nearest one, blades clashing with a screech that makes my teeth ache. The other bandits fan out, surrounding us with feral grins and eyes glittering with something close to hunger.

Thalia screams and ducks low, curling herself beneath the wagon bench, her hands over her head.

I freeze. My entire body locks in place, breath caught in my throat, muscles stiff with panic. I've never seen a real battle, never felt the bone-deep terror of knowing someone is trying to kill you.

The screams, the clash of metal, the feral roar of a bandit charging at Luan as he gently drops Lisbeth into the space I cleared.

A blur of movement catches my eye.

Another bandit, smaller and wiry, is slipping around the front of the wagon where Thalia is hiding.

I don't think, I don't weigh my odds, I just take a step, and then another.

My hand dives into my satchel and I yank out the dagger Pat gave me. The metal is cool against my palm, the weight unfamiliar but anchoring. My legs move before my mind can scream at me not to.

The bandit is almost to her. He crouches low, creeping toward her trembling form.

I run.

I reach him just as he grabs at her. My scream rips from my throat as I throw myself forward, the dagger plunging outward on instinct, slamming into his side just beneath the ribs.

The world seems to suddenly move in slow motion as the bandit gasps, a wet wheeze coming from his throat as he releases Thalia's screaming form. He turns, staring at me with eyes wide, stumbling back until the ground slopes down away from the road. He loses his footing and collapses in the piles of leaves at the bottom without another word.

My eyes race back and forth between his prone form and my hands.

There's blood on my hand, the once silver dagger stained with crimson within my grasp.

Someone else's blood.

The fight rages behind me with shouts and the clash of metal, but it feels distant now . . . Muted. All I can hear is the rush of my own blood in my ears as my eyes stay glued to the dying one's staring up at me.

I stare at him, my legs suddenly shaking uncontrollably as my grip on the dagger turns my knuckles white. The blade trembles in my hand. I want to let go, but my fingers won't obey.

My heart pounds in my chest as I take deep, gasping breaths. There's blood on my dress. Blood on my skin.

Not mine, but his.

I watch as the alert focus on me fades from the bandit's eyes, leaving them empty and unfocused.

I don't need to check his pulse to know he's gone.

I killed someone.

The realization hits like a blow, knocking the air from my lungs. It's too much. Too fast. The world sways on its axis.

I drop to my knees in the dirt, staring at the blade still in my hand as it glistens in the light of the dying fire.

This isn't a nightmare or a dream.

This is real, and it's only day two.

CHAPTER ELEVEN

ELYSIA

Danger isn't distant or abstract anymore. It's close, ugly, and lethal. It's blood on my hands and the memory of a man's dying breath and the hollow drop of his body hitting the leaves, never to get up again.

The road stretches long and silent beneath the slow-turning wheels of our wagon.

No one speaks.

The only sounds that live in my head are the wet rasp of a dying breath, the scream Thalia made when the bandit lunged, the sickening crunch of metal against bone as Luan split a man's head open beside the wagon.

Every time I blink, I see it again . . . the blood on my hands, the dagger in my palm, the vacant stare of the bandit whose life I ended.

I don't know how I'm still sitting upright. I haven't slept since I left my home and my eyes burn with fatigue, but I can't lie down. I can't close my eyes. Every time I try, the memory comes rushing back, vivid and violent. The nausea coils low in my stomach again and again, curling tighter with each inhale.

Lisbeth's unconscious body lies beside me in the wagon, her head cushioned on folded fabric from our supplies. The gash at her temple stopped bleeding hours ago, but her skin still holds a pale look that has me on edge. She hasn't stirred once.

The ache behind my eyes has turned sharp, like shards of glass buried in my skull. I press my fingers against my temples, hoping pressure will drive it all away, but nothing helps.

I can still feel the resistance of his bones, cartilage, and flesh beneath my blade.

I still see the way his mouth opened in shock . . . not rage, not even pain . . . just surprise. Like he couldn't believe it either. Like he wasn't supposed to die there, by my hand. As if the universe had made a mistake.

Maybe it did, because something inside me died today. Something innocent, something soft.

A low, involuntary sound escapes my throat, somewhere between a sob and a breath I can't quite finish inhaling. My eyes burn as my vision blurs with unshed tears.

Berrin glances back from his spot at the front of the wagon, but says nothing. He's been glancing back at me occasionally, as if he wants to comfort me, but always returns his focus back to the road, lips pressed tightly together.

There were two other villages after the ambush, both too small to have a healer. We didn't stop long, just asked, checked, and kept moving. Hours passed in silence, the world blurring beyond the trees, dusk slipping into night, night slipping into something deeper and colder.

The ache in my joints has settled into something worse, a numbness that comes from more than just a lack of sleep. The kind that comes from witnessing something that will never fully leave you.

I lean my head against the wooden sideboard, closing my eyes just for a breath. Hot streaks of tears trail down my cheeks silently.

I'm not in the wagon anymore, I'm back in the forest. The bandit's eyes are wide and glassy, staring up at me from a bed of leaves. My hand is still wrapped around the dagger, his blood still warm, the color so dark it looks black under the trees.

Thalia is screaming again. The bandits are shouting. Clashing steel sings.

I jolt upright seconds later, gasping, heart slamming in my chest like it's trying to escape me entirely. My hands are shaking again and I rub them on my dress, but it's no use. The blood's gone, but I can still feel it . . . It's soaked into my soul. No amount of water will wash it away.

How does anyone ever forget that?

Lisbeth's fingers twitch slightly, drawing my attention to her prone form, and a sharp ache settles behind my ribs.

Why her? Why am I carrying the weight of this fear for her well-being when she's someone who wouldn't have lifted a finger for me if the roles were reversed?

My mother's voice rolls through my head. *Because that's who you are.*

I swallow hard and reach out to adjust the blanket around Lisbeth's shoulders. My fingers brush her temple and come away tacky with sweat. She's still burning up.

The trees close in tighter on either side, and the wind begins to sound like an eerie howl floating through the forest. It's haunting and mournful.

I don't know how long we've been riding when the wagons finally slow. Berrin says something ahead of us but I don't hear the words. I only hear the hum of exhaustion droning behind my eardrums.

The wagon creaks to a stop in the square of a small village tucked beneath a ridge. Lanterns flicker in low stone windows, and a few faces peek out from doorways. A man in green healer's robes steps into the center of the road, flanked by two others carrying wooden stretchers.

They reach for Lisbeth and something feral within me comes to life.

"No!" I lurch forward, clutching her arm, trying to shield her from them with my own body.

The men stop, startled. One even raises his hands back like he's been burned by touching her.

"You can't just take her!" I snap, my voice cracked and wild as I stare wide-eyed at them. "She's going to wake up alone and confused with strangers around her. She needs someone she knows."

Luan frowns from their side, exhaustion heavy and clear on his weathered face. "You need rest."

"I'm not sleeping," I bite back, eyes blazing. "I'm going with her."

"She doesn't need you anymore," he counters, crossing his arms.

"She will," I growl, heart hammering. "I'm not leaving her."

The healer glances at me for a long moment, then nods slowly. "Let her stay."

I exhale shakily as they lift Lisbeth carefully between them and carry her toward the healer's cottage. Thalia climbs out of her wagon and stares with wide-open eyes at me before inclining her head in a single nod of acknowledgment, that she knows I need to give my attention to Lisbeth and that it's okay. I follow close behind the men, my boots dragging and my entire body aching.

Inside, the cottage is warm, the heat instantly seeping into the depths of my bones. The air smells like crushed herbs and something

acidic. I glance around and take in the shelves lining the walls, filled with bottles, salves, dried flowers, bundles of root and leaf.

They lay Lisbeth on a cot with a clean wool blanket and remove her ruined cloak before leaving Lisbeth and me alone with the healer. I stand in the corner, arms wrapped around myself. My hands tremble, yet I can't make it stop.

The healer inspects Lisbeth with practiced care, murmuring to himself as he checks her head, limbs, pulse. He stitches her wound with deft hands and coats it in a thick golden salve with a heavy floral scent.

"She's lucky," he mutters. "The blow missed her temple. Another inch or so and the skull thins out there. It could have caused a brain bleed or cracked her skull completely."

I don't respond, trying to hold off the images of Luan doing exactly that to a bandit. I just nod vaguely and sink down into a stool nearby, every bone in my body groaning with the weight of the day.

"As is, she might be concussed. We won't know until she wakes."

When the wound dressing is secured, the healer rubs a different salve into her temples and lays a fresh compress across her forehead. "She'll wake when her body's ready," he says, voice gentler now. "She's in no danger. You should sleep."

He dims the lantern, leaving only the flicker of firelight from the hearth before the door clicks shut behind him.

I sit and watch Lisbeth breathe. That's all I do for what feels like hours.

My eyelids droop and my chin dips. I jerk awake every time my head slips sideways toward my shoulder.

Then . . . a twitch in her fingers. A flutter in her lashes.

My heart all but leaps into my throat as she gasps and sits up violently, eyes wild, hands clawing the edge of the cot.

"No!" she screams so violently that her voice cracks.

A wail of unmistakable fear and certainty that death is coming for her. A sound I'm coming to know intimately.

"Shh!" I scramble to her side and grab her hands, trying to get her to focus on my face. "You're safe. You're alright. It's over."

Her chest heaves as her eyes dart to the walls, to the flickering shadows, to the blanket tangled around her legs. Anywhere but me.

"My guards . . ." Her voice is cracked and broken as she continues her search. "Where are they?"

"They're gone," I answer softly, "but you're here. You're safe."

She yanks one of her hands from mine, moving it to the wound on her head, wincing at the pain. "I . . . I don't remember . . ."

"You hit your head in the wreckage," I explain gently, settling on the edge of the cot next to her. I focus on dampening a cloth from the basin and dabbing her brow. "You passed out. I pulled you out of the wreckage. You're safe now."

For a moment, she just blinks at me, disoriented and vulnerable.

"You're safe now." I repeat myself, knowing she needs to keep hearing the words.

Her eyes shine with tears, and for the first time, she looks human, not untouchable and arrogant. Just a girl trying not to break, much like me and Thalia.

"Don't touch me," she says faintly, her old fire flickering as I feel her forehead with the back of my hand to check her fever.

A chuckle falls from my lips as my hand falls to my lap. "Don't worry, it's not a new hobby of mine."

That earns me a faint, broken laugh. A weak one, but real, and for a moment, it's as if she forgets herself and leans into the care.

Then she blinks, eyes sharpening again, the wall rebuilding between us piece by piece. Her expression shifts closer to the Lisbeth I met before—the distant, polished version of herself.

"Well," she says, eyes narrowing, "I suppose your odds of being chosen have gone up. I'm hardly the face the elven courts will want anymore."

I huff out a quick breath of air as my eyes widen. "You'd be surprised. The universe seems to favor women with a bit of blood on them lately."

Where would we all be if I hadn't bloodied mine by killing that man?

Lisbeth hums, a low sound that might have been amusement.

"I'd hate to lose to you," she says after a moment, eyes scanning my face. "But if I had to lose to someone . . . it'd better be someone who'd drag my body to safety."

My brows lift slightly as the corners of my lips tug up. I huff, "That's the closest thing to a compliment I've heard from you."

"I'm concussed," she mutters dryly before pursing her lips. "Don't expect it again."

We lapse into silence, but this time it's slightly companionable.

She shifts, pressing a hand to her bruised ribs and wincing. "You look worse than me somehow."

"I feel worse than you, I think."

She squints at me, her brow creasing with her inspection. "Lie down before you fall over."

"I'm fine," I argue, dropping the cloth into the fresh water before pushing to my feet.

"You're swaying."

"You're bossy," I observe, grinning faintly as I lean against the wall.

"You're half-asleep on your feet."

"Still less obnoxious than you," I mumble as my head falls back.

I stare at her out of the corner of my eye and she smiles, likely thinking I can't see her well.

For once, it doesn't feel like rivalry between us. It feels like survival.

Her voice fades as she closes her eyes. "Rest, Elysia."

I grunt at her command and collapse into the chair. She slips into sleep quickly and I'm left awake, wondering if I'll ever be hardened enough to sleep restfully ever again.

For now, I'm just haunted.

CHAPTER TWELVE

ELYSIA

The world dissolves.

One moment I'm sitting upright in the healer's cottage, trying to keep my eyes open, the next I'm falling under. At first, there's only darkness and the echo of exhaustion humming through my bones. A hollowness within me that I didn't know existed before I left my village.

My eyes open and I instantly recognize the void of my mind where I last saw my nightly visitor. The floor beneath me is smooth stone and faintly luminous. Mist coils low around my ankles, drifting in slow, lazy waves.

Then, I feel him.

His presence is immediate, wrapping around me before I see him. The air carries a quiet hum and smells like the world before a storm. The scent settles into me, curling at the back of my throat, grounding me.

"You finally sleep," he says, voice a deep murmur from behind me.

I turn toward his voice, my breath catching at the way my core tightens seeing him. It's then that I admit to myself just how worried I was at never seeing him again. Yet there he stands, shrouded in shadow.

Still hidden. Still distant. Still *him*.

My brow pinches as I notice there's something different in his stance despite the shadows swirling and obscuring. There's a tension beneath the stillness, the way storms gather pressure before releasing drops of rain into the soil beneath. His fingers are straight and pressed tightly to his side.

"I didn't think you'd come again," I admit, taking a few steps closer without even meaning to.

I'm helpless against this unnatural pull that my body has already given in to, while my mind struggles to understand it still.

"You didn't dream for two nights," he says, tone clipped with what sounds like concern. "I couldn't find you. I tried."

He tried . . .

My voice is uneven as I breathe out. "Why did you seek me out if I didn't call out to you? That's why you said you came before."

My stomach coils in anticipation of his answer. I know instantly that it will change everything, yet I fear the ramifications of it. My focus needs to remain on my own survival and ensuring I'm not fractured indefinitely if I do survive. Already I'm fraying at the seams and altered forever.

A long pause drifts between us. His specialty, I'm coming to realize.

"Because your absence felt wrong."

His words sink into me, but I don't know how to respond. A warmth blooms in my chest and I press my hand against it instinctively, as if I could gather it in my palm and hold it forever.

He moves a little closer and my eyes narrow, desperate for a glimpse of him. The mist and shadows never dare rise enough to give it to me, though.

His head and the shadows tilt to the side before his voice floats through the air, a hint of fear in it that makes my skin pebble. "What happened, Little Dove?"

That nickname again. It slides over my skin like a balm to wounds not even visible to the eye. Yet somehow in his presence, the injuries crack open, wanting to be seen and nurtured despite my best efforts to conceal them.

"I . . ." I fail to get the words out and grimace as images resurface in my mind, sharp and biting. Wetting my lips, I try again. "I killed a man."

The words scrape out of my throat like broken glass.

His head snaps straight up and I avert my gaze as I struggle to find the words to explain. To defend my actions so that he doesn't think me a monster . . . the way I see myself in the aftermath.

"I didn't mean to. I didn't think . . . I just moved. He was going to hurt Thalia, and I didn't even think, I just—" My voice breaks off into air as my throat begins to constrict and my lungs all but cease to work.

Heat flushes my cheeks as my eyes sting. My head swings back and forth, and my lips thin, trying to hold back the soul-wrenching sobs threatening to escape.

Tears begin their journey down my cheeks to collect at the edge of my jaw as I stare at him and admit with a trembling whisper, "I didn't want to take his life."

But I did.

I don't remember my knees giving way, I only know that I'm falling and that my breath won't come. I'm unraveling from the inside out.

The floor rushes toward me, but he's there first.

Arms wrap around me, strong and sure. I'm lifted gently, pressed against the solid heat of his body, my face buried in the curve of his shoulder. He sinks down with me, kneeling on the mist-drenched floor, holding me tightly.

My breath hitches as everything I've been holding back rips its way out as my eyes squeeze shut, trying to escape the memories. The unbidden sobs I didn't cry in the real world escaping now. I choke on them as I try to speak.

"I didn't want to do it," I say again, over and over, like saying it might make it true. "He looked so shocked. Like he couldn't believe it. I don't think I'll ever forget his eyes."

I curl into him instinctively, my hands clutching the fabric of his shirt, softer than anything I've felt before. My cheek presses to the hollow of his neck as my tears slip freely now, hot trails down my face that soak into his shoulder and neck. He doesn't flinch, doesn't move, just holds me tighter as I unleash everything I've held in so tightly.

His hand cradles the back of my head, and I feel his breath against my temple, even and steady. His chest rises and falls in steady rhythm beneath me, the cadence of his breath syncing slowly with mine until my lungs remember how to inhale fully again.

We sit like that in the mist and silence, his arms wrapped around me while I tremble. I don't know how much time passes. Minutes. Hours. Time doesn't exist here, only this stillness between us.

Eventually, my breathing slows. The weight in my chest eases, the sobs fading into silence. Only then do I become aware of the way I'm curled into him, how his hand strokes my back in slow, circular motions.

I shift slightly, wiping my hand across my damp cheeks before my eyes drift open, and I finally allow myself to look at the pieces of him that the fleeting shadows allow me to see.

His skin is dusky gray, with a soft purple undertone illuminated by the soft glow of the ground. His forearms are corded with

muscle, faint silver veins raised slightly beneath the surface in delicate ridges. The texture of his skin is impossibly smooth, like the river-polished stone my father gifted me, and I find my head drawing back to look up.

"Don't look," he says suddenly, the words sharp with panic. His voice is a command—but not angry, just afraid.

"I . . ." I start, but he tightens his grip subtly, pulling me back against him, burying my face into the hollow of his neck again.

"Promise me," he breathes, quieter now. "Don't look. Not yet."

I close my eyes again, heart still thudding in the cage of my chest. "I promise."

After a moment, I whisper, "Can I at least know your name?"

His grip tightens imperceptibly.

"No," he says, barely audible. "I'm sorry."

Disappointment churns in my gut, but I nod anyway. I don't want to push him away, not when I'm only just realizing how much I've needed someone to hold me in the chaos of my life.

We sit in silence again before I offer, "I'm sorry you had to witness me falling apart."

His voice comes again, soft against my temple, the warmth of his breath tickling. "You didn't fall apart," he says. "You just broke open. That's how new things are discovered."

I say nothing in response . . . I just breathe in his words, trying to infuse the clarity and resonance it brings me into my core. Because no matter what happens when I wake, I don't want to forget his words or this moment of peace within the storm.

Already, I feel the edges of the dream unraveling, the hum of waking and the pull of the real world.

"Don't go," I whisper.

The warmth of his body against mine begins to fade. His arms remain until the last possible moment, and then even they disappear into fog.

His voice follows me, faint and raw.

"We'll find each other again."

The warmth of his arms is replaced by a gentle sway and a jostle beneath me. I blink into the pale light above me, eyes adjusting slowly to the soft hues of dusk cascading across the horizon. The dream slips

from my fingertips like the mist that engulfed us, but the ache in my chest remains.

The rhythmic creak of wagon wheels and the soft clop of hooves on the hardened trail ground me back into reality. The scent of frost and pine replaces his scent of fresh rain that I'd clung to.

"About time," a voice murmurs nearby, startling me slightly.

I shift groggily and turn my head toward Lisbeth, who's sitting across from me, her arms folded tightly across her chest. She's watching me with a vague look of amusement.

"I didn't think you were ever going to wake," she says, brushing a curl behind her ear. "Luan came to collect us this morning. You didn't so much as twitch when he tried to rouse you. He was fuming about it but ended up muttering something about dead weight and carrying you into the wagon himself."

I let out a light chuckle at the image rippling through my mind. That sounds like Luan.

I push upright, groaning slightly as my muscles protest from being prone against the hard wooden floor of the wagon. My head spins with bleariness from a deep slumber I'd desperately needed.

"I slept . . . all day?" I rasp, the sound of my voice scratchy and dry.

She nods, passing me a canteen of water. "The sun's already starting to dip again. We're crossing into the northern port territory now."

I blink, trying to make sense of how much time has passed. As I move to sit straighter, something shifts across my legs, a thick wool cloak that's been draped across them. I reach toward my collar, surprised to find my scarf, the thick one my mother had packed, tucked securely around my neck. The ends are wrapped and knotted tightly beneath my chin, the way only a careful hand could achieve.

Someone had ensured I'd be warm with the growing coldness. I glance at Lisbeth. Her eyes immediately flick away, her jaw tightening slightly.

"You didn't have to," I murmur softly, fingers brushing the wool near my throat.

She shrugs one shoulder. "It was cold. You were shivering. I didn't want to listen to you coughing the rest of the way north."

Her voice lacks the sharpness it usually carries. There's something gentler there, buried beneath the armor she so often seems to wear. I

don't press her for more. I just tuck the cloak tighter around my legs and let gratitude settle quietly into my chest.

She lets out a heavy sigh and looks away from me. "Also, Thalia told me I *had* to tell you when you woke up that if you need anything she will be in her wagon."

I smile and let the conversation fade, sensing Lisbeth's discomfort.

The landscape has changed while I slept. The fields and sparse forests of our journey have given way to peaks of mountains that stretch upward like jagged teeth into the sky. The Sacrum mountain range looms close, cutting across the Vothia Empire lands like a line drawn in stone. Snow clings to the craggy cliffs, melting only in small patches where sunlight touches.

Ahead, the path twists, leading us toward whatever outcome the High Priestess has waiting for us. The sight of the mountain makes a quiet, looming unease settle deep within my chest. It whispers to my mind, signaling the drawing conclusion of one journey, while another is yet to begin.

I press a hand to my chest where my pendant rests beneath my cloak. The stone is cool against my palm, grounding my nerves as it reminds me of both home and the elf now.

The road is narrowing now, curling higher along the base of the cliffs, every breath I take growing colder and thinner. The air stings against my cheeks and lungs, but it's the sky that steals my breath.

For the first time in my life, I can truly see where the two opposing cloud systems converge in the middle.

The bright, soft white clouds that I have always lived beneath are beginning to thin and stretch, blending with the darker formations gathering near the mountaintops. Clouds that churn with various gray tones, lightning flickering within them like silver veins that remind me of my elf. The clouds darken and the storms within them seem to grow more volatile as they disappear on the other side.

They belong to the Nithrin side of the empire. The realization settles cold and heavy in my gut.

The northern port is truly at the center of it all, the place where both elven courts are suspended in the sky, anchored high above, tethered invisibly to the ground below.

I shift in my seat, fingers brushing the pendant beneath my cloak again as a strange truth settles into me: I'm about to meet humans from

the other side of the Sacrum Mountains. Those raised beneath Nithrin dominion. People who grew up with nightmares instead of dreams.

I wonder what differences lie between us, shaped by what we dreamed, or didn't. Would they be more volatile and on alert?

Time will tell.

The path narrows further as the wagon lurches up another slope, flurries of snow beginning to dance in the wind.

A chill runs down my spine, not due to the plummeting temperature, but for the fact that I'm about to face the exact moment that fractured Maggie forever.

CHAPTER THIRTEEN

ELYSIA

The wind is sharper now, cutting through the seams of my cloak, stinging against my cheeks as the wagon rounds the final bend. Snow dusts the edges of the trail, clinging to the branches of thinning trees and making the dirt road begin to turn to a muddy slush for the horses to clop through. I tug the scarf tighter beneath my chin, but it does little to shield against the rising chill.

The northern port comes into view. Stone buildings rise in jagged clusters against the icy backdrop, rooftops dusted white, chimneys already exhaling smoke into the sharp sky.

The sun is beginning to slip behind the edge of the mountains as we reach the port city square, casting long shadows across the cobbled plaza. Wagons and carriages already line the wide expanse, reminding me just how many chosen there will be. Some are plain and worn, others refined, similar to the stark differences we'd seen between Lisbeth and us. What really steals my attention is seeing the fabric-draped carriages in soft shades of cream and sage turn into black leather and ash-colored wood. Those must be from the humans in the western lands beneath the Nithrin clouds.

It's a strange contrast of wealth and need, of eastern and western lands colliding in one place. No two look the same, but all have arrived for the same purpose.

Thalia's guard lets out a low whistle from behind us. "Twenty chosen here already."

"If there's one chosen per transport," he adds, glancing around, "we'd bring the total to twenty-three."

"Should be thirty-six," Lisbeth says sharply, lifting her hood slightly. "Eighteen from the Dromin east, eighteen from the Nithrin west."

Her voice holds the steady confidence of someone who's studied this . . . who's learned these numbers like scripture. Perhaps the wealth and blessings in her territory allowed her an advantage with studies as well. There wasn't time for that in ours, past learning the basics in school.

Her eyes flick to the edge of the plaza, lips tightening. "That is . . . if they all made it here."

A silence lingers after her words, colder than the wind. A reminder that she almost didn't and a harsh reality that we likely weren't the only ones to face trouble on their way here.

A group of port guards approaches, draped in dark gray cloaks and black armor beneath. One steps forward, scroll in hand.

"Names and territories?"

"Elysia from Edritch," I answer first, voice low but steady. "Thalia from Gressar. Lisbeth from Celaine."

The guard nods, marking down the identifications, providing instructions as he does. "You'll be housed in the offering quarter. The High Priestess will arrive at first light tomorrow for selection rites and inspection."

Offering . . . not chosen.

Lisbeth mutters something beneath her breath about failing her inspection because she's "hideous now" that I choose to ignore.

Another guard joins him, stepping toward Luan and Berrin. "Your escort is dismissed. The offering transition ends here."

Once again the use of the term "offering" has my brow pinching. It's a stark change from "chosen," which felt like a special title. Already the perception of our value and place in this world is changing, and it's been mere minutes since we arrived.

My stomach twists. I knew this moment would come, but still, it feels like the last thread that is tethering me to home is now being cut loose. I lift my hand and close it around my pendant before lifting my other hand to ensure the ribbon is still safe in my braid.

I still have these.

Luan stiffens, his mouth tightening as if to argue, but I raise a hand gently to stop him.

"I'll be alright," I say quietly, but with a firm edge as I jump down from the wagon with my satchel on my shoulder. "You've brought me this far."

He looks unconvinced, his eyes scanning my face for a long beat. "You sure?"

Lisbeth gingerly lowers herself to the ground as Thalia's soft footfalls approach.

I nod, shocked by the warmth I feel by having those two women at my side. I'd known them for mere days, yet with everything that occurred, it felt like a lifetime.

"Thank you for everything," I say to my guards, truly meaning it. They had saved our lives.

Luan's jaw shifts as his lips thin, like he's not used to kindness. "Be smart. Be safe."

Berrin offers a small nod, the faintest glint of something warmer behind his stern expression. "Try not to cause too much trouble."

"No more than usual," I murmur with a tight, forced smile.

They don't linger, but I watch them until I can't anymore, a hollow ache spreading in my chest. I hadn't realized how safe I'd felt with them until now. Not until I watched that safety walk away.

The port guards direct us to a large, heavy-beamed inn near the far end of the plaza, just past a stone archway marked with the cloud and lightning bolt crest of the empire. The sun dips lower, painting the sky in deep pinks and dark lavender as the inn doors swing open.

Warm light spills out from within and I force myself to take a deep, grounding breath. This is where the chosen are being kept. All of them.

As we step inside, we're greeted with our new reality. Dozens of women gathered in clusters near the hearth or seated at long tables, voices murmuring, eyes shifting up as we enter. The room goes quiet for a beat.

I know from a quick glance that the room is divided by our homelands.

On one side are those I presume are from the western villages. Their skin is fairer, almost like a pearl with a shine that reminds me of the moon. Their hair is darker, sleeker, and their eyes have different hues of storm-gray, shadowed blue, and deep violet. A few glance our way with veiled curiosity.

A strange buzz settles in my chest, like a hum of unfamiliarity in my bones. I'm seeing the other side of the empire for the first time, and I wonder what they've grown up being told of our lands, like we have theirs. I expected them to seem more broken, fractured by living with nightmares every night, but they appear . . . normal. Just like those from our lands.

My elf's words circle back through my mind.

"You've been taught to fear nightmares, but they're just dreams in a darker mirror. Some think nightmares are a made-up fear, but often they reflect a truth you fear facing."

Perhaps we don't understand their lands at all.

The divide is clear in the room, unspoken but absolute. The chosen from the eastern lands sit on the left side of the room, clustered and whispering excitedly. The chosen from the west are gathered on the right, quieter and more watchful. No one sits at the center tables. No one dares to bridge the space between.

Lisbeth tugs gently on my cloak, her voice low. "Let's go to our side, Elysia."

Thalia hovers at my side, clearly intending to follow without hesitation, and my heart hums with the warmth of her loyalty. I don't move . . . not yet.

I stare at the empty table in the middle, where no one has dared to sit. My heart pounds, and for a long moment, I don't breathe.

Then I step forward toward that table.

Lisbeth falters. "Elysia, seriously?"

"This is fine," I say softly, looking back at her as I slide onto the bench. My voice carries just enough for all tables to hear.

A few heads turn. A few eyes narrow. Yet I don't flinch.

Thalia follows without a word, settling across from me with quiet resolve. A soft smile tugs at her lips and I return it.

Lisbeth lingers, arms crossed, her expression pinched. "You always have to be the better person, don't you?" she mutters, more sass than malice in her tone.

After a beat, she sighs and drops onto the bench beside me, grumbling under her breath about inconvenient morals and self-righteous choices.

It may be a small act of good faith, a quiet gesture from us, but it's an invitation that shows I'm willing to know both sides.

A shift of energy in the air occurs as I glance around.

From the corner of my vision, I notice several women from the Nithrin side glancing toward us. One stands slowly, tall and composed, with an unmistakable elegance in the way she moves. Her eyes are the color of storm clouds, her expression unreadable.

A large shadow moves beside her, shocking me that I didn't notice it until now. It's a hound, massive and sleek, its coat ink-black,

eyes pale silver and gleaming. Its presence is immediate and slightly unnerving.

Lisbeth tenses, her voice sharp as she exclaims, "Gods, what is that?!" Her eyes narrow, calculating, already analyzing the hound like a threat to be assessed, with slight disgust.

Thalia nearly recoils, pressing closer to the edge of the bench. "Is it safe?" Her voice is breathy, laced with genuine fear. Her hand trembles slightly where it clutches the edge of the table, and her gaze flicks anxiously between the hound's eyes and its large paws. No doubt there are some vicious claws hidden in the thick, wiry hair.

"I think he's beautiful," I say truthfully, unable to take my eyes off him.

The girl stops before our table, a faint smile curling her lips. "This is Thayus," she introduces. "A night-hound. Bred to hunt and guard in the darkest reaches of our lands. Perfect vision in blackness. Fierce when needed. Loyal always."

I smile at the hound and the woman, appreciating her approaching us so quickly.

She reaches down to run her fingers across the thick fur of his neck. "I'm Virelle. From the territory of Shadefell. We're known for breeding these pups."

I lean forward slightly and lift my hand, but halt and ask. "Can I pet him?"

Virelle chuckles, crossing her arms against her chest. "Thayus makes his own decisions, but you can try."

I extend my hand slowly, fingers open, letting him choose. Thayus sniffs, his breath warm against my skin, and then to my astonishment, he leans into me, a low rumble of contentment vibrating in his chest.

Lisbeth's mouth parts slightly in disbelief. Even Thalia stares.

"I knew it," Virelle says, settling onto the bench beside me. "I knew there was something good in you. Thayus confirmed it. He doesn't take to strangers easily."

For a moment, a soft thread of hope unfurls in my chest. Perhaps our two sides can coexist while here.

Thayus pads closer and leans his large body against our bench, setting his head on it between Virelle and me. My fingers thread through his fur, appreciating his warmth and the silky texture.

Virelle's voice lowers, drawing my eyes to hers as they narrow. "I thought I should tell you . . . there's been whispers. That not all the chosen made it. That a fellow chosen was responsible for their deaths."

We all fall still.

"There are fewer from the Dromin side than there should be," she adds, gaze flicking across the room to where the ten women are hunched together. "The others think it means the threat came from your half of the empire, since our eighteen are here."

Her words settle like ice between us.

"Be careful tonight when you sleep," she says simply before pushing back to her feet. "There's danger here . . . and it might already be sitting at one of these tables."

Just like that, the warmth of the fire doesn't feel so comforting anymore.

Thalia's and Lisbeth's gazes settle on me and there's an unspoken question lingering in the air as Virelle goes back to her table with Thayus at her side: *What do we do now?*

I take a deep breath before blowing it out gently. My voice is a whisper as I lean in toward the only people I trust here. "I don't know what the sleeping situation will be, but how do you all feel about sharing a room if they try to split us up?"

A chill runs down the back of my neck and I quickly turn toward the women from our lands, spying a pair of gleaming green eyes settled on me for the briefest of moments before flickering back to the others at her table.

"I think that's for the best," Thalia answers with a slight tremble to her voice. "I didn't expect that we'd have to watch our backs against the other chosen."

I glance back and find Lisbeth's eyes trained on the same woman I'd locked onto. Her voice is flat as she answers, "The first rule that I was taught before coming here is that everyone is in this for themselves and their village. You both defy that rule, but I'm not gullible enough to believe it extends past that."

Perhaps I'd misunderstood her originally. Maybe she was just the one among the three of us that had been mentally prepared for the true perils of this journey, and fortified herself with the knowledge that anyone could be an enemy—even us.

I'm not sure who I'll be facing tomorrow—the Priestess, the selection . . . or something far darker already sitting across the room.

CHAPTER FOURTEEN

ELYSIA

Everyone had been assigned their own room, but it didn't last long. By the time the moon rose high in the small window of my room, Thalia and Lisbeth had dragged their blankets, cloaks, and pillows into mine. My room was at the end of the hall, nestled in the corner where fewer footsteps pass. It felt safer, tucked away from the main corridor, and none of us liked the idea of sleeping alone, not after the whispers Virelle shared.

We'd made a nest of mismatched fabrics and soft layers across the floor, curling in together like children at a sleepover. I'd woken at least twice in the night to see Thalia's fingers holding my own and noticed Lisbeth sleeping with her boots still on like she was ready to run at a moment's notice. We hadn't talked about it throughout the late hours, but it was clear none of us had expected a peaceful night.

The sound of a guard's voice echoed up the stairwell, breaking the stillness of the early morning. "Chosen! Rise and prepare. Inspection begins at first light!"

A groan escapes from somewhere in the pile of blankets beside me. "Tell me that guard's voice was a bad dream and we don't have to get up now," Lisbeth mutters, voice thick with sleep.

"No such luck," I grunt, pushing off the blanket that is tangled around my legs.

Thalia yawns beside me, blinking blearily, looking like a sweet kitten waking from a nap. "Is it morning already?"

"Apparently," Lisbeth mumbles, sitting up and rubbing her eyes. "I'm happy to report that nothing killed us in our sleep, though I'm still suspicious."

"Same," Thalia agrees while stretching her arms above her head. "I barely closed my eyes. Every sound felt like it was coming for us."

I nod in agreement, too tired to voice words yet. My limbs ache with fatigue, not from strain but from the half-sleep state I'd hovered in all night. Even with Thalia and Lisbeth in the room with me, the shadows in the corners and near the door had me on edge every time I caught sight of them.

Though what haunts me more than anything this morning is that my elf didn't come.

No familiar pull. No comforting weight of his presence.

Only flickers of images had rolled through my mind throughout the few moments of sleep I got. A glimpse of a crown. Fingers brushing the edge of silver filigree. Cold metal settling against my forehead.

Just a whisper of what could happen now that we are here.

We descend quietly to the common area, the chill of the stone floor seeping through the soles of my boots with every step. The hearth still burns low, but the room has already begun to stir with activity. Guards move between tables, checking notes and glancing toward the entrance, their voices low and clipped.

All eighteen women from the western lands are already present and seated together in their same arrangement from the night before. They look well-rested, their hair neatly braided or pinned, cloaks hanging straight without wrinkles as if they didn't need them for the cold. Not a single one appears groggy or disheveled.

It hits me then that they're likely used to a more frigid temperature, living beneath the gray-and-black clouds of the Nithrin that block out the majority of the sun their lands could get.

Lisbeth steps closer and lowers her voice to a whisper. "Only ten of us are here."

I turn to her sharply. Her eyes are narrowed and guarded, while the edge of her voice is tinged with alarm.

"What do you mean?"

"I counted," she says quietly, glancing toward the remaining women from our lands. "There were thirteen women from our half last night. Only ten showed up this morning."

Thalia's face pinches slightly. "Maybe the others decided to leave early? Went home with their guards? Maybe . . . maybe they got scared."

Her voice falters near the end, like she doesn't believe her own theory.

I don't either.

As the guards move to the center of the room, calling for silence, I angle my body toward the woman with green eyes and vibrant red hair. The same one whose stare lingered too long on me last night.

She's already seated near the edge of the table, posture relaxed and expression neutral . . . too neutral. There's no trace of any emotion, unlike everyone else who shares concern.

The guards begin to speak, asking us if we know where the remaining offerings from the east are. Their tone isn't concerned. It's expectant, as though they already know they won't get an answer but have to do their job anyway.

Still, the woman with red hair says nothing.

I keep my eyes on her, not wanting to miss even a flicker of anything malicious in her eyes or expression.

The guards exchange a glance and turn without another word, heading upstairs. I presume to check the rooms of the missing women themselves. The heavy thud of boots on steps echoes up the stairwell as silence settles uneasily among us.

A voice breaks that silence, a trembling shout from the far side of the room that draws my attention despite not wanting to take my eyes off the redhead.

"How dare you take the life of a fellow offering whose fate was decided for her to come here! How dare you kill her for that!"

It comes from a small woman with delicate features and bright lavender eyes. Her voice cracks under the weight of her despair and several others flinch at the sound.

Virelle is on her feet in a breath, pulling the girl gently but firmly back down into her seat.

"Enough," she murmurs to her, a hand on her shoulder. "You don't know what happened yet. We don't know anything for certain."

The tension has already ignited, with eyes from both sides of the room narrow and accusatory. A low hum of whispers ripples through the chosen.

Thayus lets out a deep warning growl as his hackles rise and he takes a step toward the grouping of women with my suspect in it. Virelle calls for him to sit, but he remains fixated on the group, clearly warning them if they try anything with him around, they'll pay dearly.

The guards return a moment later, their footsteps heavy and purposeful.

"That dog has to stay here in your room today. The Priestess won't allow it," one of them barks out in Virelle's direction, but doesn't make a move to try to ensure it happens. His eyes remain fixated on the growling hound as his neck moves with a purposeful swallow.

I can't help but smirk at his open fear of Thayus. So they were all too afraid to tell Virelle he wasn't allowed in the building to begin with.

Another guard steps forward and speaks clearly. "Virea from Tramir, Sylvette from Norwynth, and Ceryn from Varinholt are confirmed deceased."

The words drop like heavy stones in the room. No ceremony. No sorrow. Just a matter-of-fact announcement, as though death is merely part of the process.

The guards move on, already calling for lines to be formed in preparation for us to leave the building.

As if nothing at all is out of place and there isn't a murderer amongst us.

Lisbeth lets out a soft, audible gasp beside me, one hand rising to her mouth. Her eyes widen in a flash of realization, and she leans in quickly, her voice sharp and urgent. "Elysia . . . all three of those villages—Tramir, Norwynth, and Varinholt—those are all eastern territories that had queens chosen from them after the Blood War. I remember it from the records in the archives."

Thalia's breath catches. "Lisbeth . . . what are you saying?"

"That someone's killing off the chosen from territories tied to past queens," Lisbeth finishes grimly. "I'd bet that whoever is doing this killed whoever they came into contact with on the way, but their targets changed when they got here. When they met each chosen and learned where they were from."

A chill slides down my spine.

Her voice trembles slightly now as she allows her confident mask to drop for a brief second. "There's only one chosen left from a territory that has had a chosen queen on our side of the mountains. Me."

A target has been painted on her back, clear as ink.

I take a long look at her, noting the tension in her jaw, the flicker of fear she tries to mask, and resolve blossoms within me.

No matter what this selection turns into, no matter how many secrets these walls hold, I won't let her fall next.

A hush falls over the room as the guards begin moving with renewed purpose after Virelle takes Thayus upstairs and returns. One by one,

they order us into two lines, the scrape of boots and whispered orders breaking the thick tension that's taken hold of the room.

We follow, falling into place as we're led out of the inn and down a winding path that curves toward the northern starting point of the Sacrum Mountains, just shy of the coastline, where a thin strip of land between the western and eastern lands isn't blocked off.

The air grows colder as we descend the slope, the scent of salty water carried on the wind as we approach the base of the mountain. Up ahead, something glimmers in the distance.

A barrier, perhaps. Not made of stone or wood, but something . . . otherworldly. Ethereal.

Is this magic?

It shimmers like glass bathed in moonlight, casting fractured light across the grass. At first glance, it seems like nothing more than a mirage, but as we near, it pulses softly. No doubt a veil of magic that conceals whatever lies beyond it.

I blink and squint, trying to see through it, but it reveals nothing. Just light and shadow and the faint hum of energy teasing my skin as we approach.

My mouth opens as I take in a deep breath, preparing to run smack into it, but then we simply pass through it, one by one.

The world shifts and the cold air vanishes. The scent of salt and frost is replaced by blooming flowers and the heady aroma of rich soil. My head swivels, taking in the forest we stand in now. Far different than the dense, wild woods we traveled through to get here. I've never seen colors as vivid as the ones in this grove. The trees glow faintly with magical energy flowing through their silver trunks like veins, while their leaves are a radiant blend of lavender and a light emerald.

Shared looks of awe are on our faces as we take in the otherworldly beauty.

Light filters down from no visible source, dappling the mossy pink earth in intricate patterns. The air itself thrums with power and, as I finish my exploratory search, my eyes land at the base of a tall, curved altar wrapped in white flowering vines.

Beside it is the woman I've feared meeting since Maggie's broken recollection of her.

The High Priestess.

She wears robes of shimmering white and deep gray, flowing like the clouds of the Dromin and storms of the Nithrin. Her presence is commanding, ethereal, and breathtaking. Her skin has the same gray tone as my nightly visitor, but the purple hue is more vibrant and warm. Long, pin-straight hair flows down over her shoulder to her waist.

My eyes are drawn to the sharp angles of her jaw and cheekbones before settling on her cold, silver-white eyes that glow with power. It's a stark difference from the forced smile pulling her full lips up as we come to a stop in front of her.

I wonder if anyone here feels warmth from the forced expression, or if I'm just jaded from Maggie's words.

"Welcome, offerings," the High Priestess says, her voice smooth and echoing, somehow both gentle and cold.

Tongue of silk and sharp teeth beneath.

Thalia's hand slides into mine without a word as I tremble with Maggie's words in my mind.

"Why are you afraid all of a sudden?" Lisbeth murmurs near my ear. "I've seen you stare down worse things than a priestess."

I don't have an answer. Not one I can put into words.

It feels like standing outside of my body and watching the inevitable, dire fate that is coming, helpless to intervene.

The High Priestess begins to slowly descend the altar steps, her eyes scanning over us one by one. Her gaze is unreadable, but sharp in her examination.

She stops at the edge of the platform, her hands moving forward as her sleeves pull back over her wrists. In her hands, cradled, is an orb.

Black and white energy chase each other in slow, endless spirals across the surface.

Maggie's voice echoes unbidden in my mind again. *It hums. Sings. Burns.*

A shiver crawls down my spine.

I've faced fear before, but never like this. Never with such a terrible sense of inevitability curling in my gut.

The orb gleams, its spirals turning slowly in the Priestess's grasp, and I can't shake the dread that it will strip me bare the moment it touches my mind.

"There are far fewer of you than there should be," she announces.

For a heartbeat, hope flickers in my chest. Maybe she'll demand answers. Maybe she'll right the wrongs. Maybe those women didn't die in vain.

Her voice hardens, cold and final. "Clearly, they were not strong enough to stand here and be tested as the next queen."

The words strike harder than any physical blow could. My stomach twists and that flicker of hope sputters and dies.

The Priestess turns away, already moving toward the altar again as if their deaths are nothing more than a blemish on her ledger, not lives lost or futures stolen. Just weakness, weeded out.

We really aren't *chosen*, just offerings.

"Isn't she supposed to be soft and kind," Lisbeth whispers beside me, her voice barely audible over the hush of the forest grove, "if she's the direct connection to the elves' goddess?"

The High Priestess's gaze snaps toward us—toward Lisbeth specifically—like she's heard the whisper as clearly as if it had been shouted. A slow, deliberate step forward brings her closer, the orb still nestled in her hands.

"You misunderstand my role," she says, her tone perfectly level but laced with quiet disdain. "I am not here to offer softness, nor sentiment. I am the neutral vessel tasked with identifying the one among you who bears the qualities required of a queen."

Her glowing eyes scan our group again, cool and detached. "I will not weep for the human lives lost. They were fleeting. Fragile, as they always are. It is expected that some fall before they ever reach these grounds, each selection."

Her words slice through the silence, a chilling reminder that compassion holds no place in this, and that we are seen not as the best our villages have to offer to this elf, but as vessels to be sifted and sorted.

Offerings.

"We will waste no further time," she announces, her voice ringing across the grove, final and absolute. "We will begin the testing."

My breath catches, a cold bolt of panic rooting me in place as the guards disappear back through the shining barrier.

The Dromin's words and the plea in them come hurtling back to the forefront of my memory.

When you're tested, think of me. Only me.

Why does he know anything about the selection, and what will thinking of him do for me?

CHAPTER FIFTEEN

ELYSIA

I try to breathe slowly and compose myself enough to keep my hands from shaking, but it's no use.

The dread curls tighter with every passing second, threading through my chest like thorny vines that dig deeper with each breath.

I know what's coming.

I feel it in the air . . . the way the orb pulses in the High Priestess's hands like a living heart seeking a new host. The trees around us seem to lean inward, their leaves rustling not from wind but from anticipation. It feels like the entire grove is holding its breath for the new queen to be found.

I want to speak. I want to warn the women. Gods, I want to tell them everything Maggie said, but I can't.

The High Priestess stands only steps away, her head slightly tilted in that eerie way, as if listening to a song no one else can hear. I know better after seeing how she reacted to Lisbeth. She can hear every whisper, every heartbeat, every breath.

If I speak now, if I even try to tell them what I fear is coming, I'll bring her wrath upon us.

So I stay silent and the guilt devours me.

Thalia shifts in front of me. Her fingers brush mine again, this time not for comfort, but a question of what's suddenly wrong with me.

Lisbeth's gaze flicks toward me and I know she sees it too. My shallow breathing, the tight line of my mouth, the way my fingers curl involuntarily.

"You're shaking," she whispers so quietly I barely hear it over the rustle of the wind in the glowing leaves.

I don't respond. I just give her a faint nod, hoping it's enough to make her stop looking at me like that. I don't know how to explain it.

The Priestess lifts her head and calls the first name.

A woman from the western lands steps forward. Her long silver cloak drifts behind her like smoke, boots silent against the mossy floor. The orb pulses brighter now, casting shadows across her face in slow, flickering waves.

She reaches the altar and faces the Priestess, giving us her side profile. Her palms tremble slightly as she places them against the smooth, glowing surface.

The world stills.

The light breeze stops and the glow of the trees dims.

Her lips part, but no sound escapes.

A low keening begins, so faint I think it's just in my head, but the others must hear it too as Thalia stiffens and Lisbeth leans in as if trying to understand the sound's source.

The woman's body begins to convulse. Her fingers twitch against the orb. Her pupils dilate wide until her eyes look entirely black.

Then she drops to her knees, her head lolling to the side.

Foam trails from the corner of her lips. Her limbs spasm once, then again, before going still. A strange whimper escapes her lips, low and wet and broken. Drool pools beneath her chin. Her mouth moves like she's trying to form words, but only garbled nonsense slips free. Nonsense and spit and silence.

I hadn't shared Maggie's vague words that seemed like warnings wrapped in delusions, not wanting to startle anyone if there was no reason, but now guilt is sinking deep within my stomach.

Her words weren't the ramblings of a broken woman, but those of a survivor.

A girl in the line ahead of me screams.

Another stumbles back, knocking into Thalia. My breath catches as one of the offerings at the back of the western territory's line breaks. She turns and runs full speed toward the shimmering veil we passed through to enter the grove.

"No, Threnn!" someone cries out.

She slams into it, hard.

A sickening thud echoes through the grove as her body hits the barrier and rebounds off it, crumpling to the ground. The shimmering veil

flickers. It is no longer fluid, but hardened. A wall to contain us now that the guards have left.

There is no escape.

Whispers rise. Fear thickens the air like smoke. Several women step away from the altar, edging back and breaking the orderly line, not wanting to be next.

The High Priestess's expression darkens. Her voice cuts across the panic with steel.

"Compose yourselves."

This only sends more panic through the group.

A muffled sob builds behind me.

The Priestess steps forward again, her robes billowing, the orb raised high.

"There will be order!" she says, voice cold and controlled. "You were brought here to be tested. You were never promised safety."

Her gaze sweeps over the crowd. For a moment, her eyes seem to land directly on mine and I wilt beneath her heavy gaze, wanting to shrink inward.

A beat of silence follows before the testing continues.

The High Priestess turns back toward us with sharp precision.

"Remain in your lines," she snaps, her voice slicing through the air. "Those that lived beneath the Dromin to the left. Nithrin to the right."

Women shuffle quickly, realigning their positions, fear and uncertainty clear from trembling forms and wide eyes.

At the far end of the Nithrin line, I spot Virelle. Her shoulders are rigid, her mouth parted in stunned silence. The strength she carried in every movement yesterday is gone. She looks like she's seeing a nightmare with open eyes.

For some reason, that breaks what little resolve I was holding onto for myself.

Maybe there is no hope of surviving this. Maybe Maggie is the rare exception.

Thalia begins to crumble in front of me. Her breaths come shallow and quick, her fingers trembling at her sides. Her knuckles go white where she clutches her cloak so tightly.

"This is going to kill us," she whispers under her breath, voice barely audible.

I reach for her hand again, squeezing tight.

Behind us, Lisbeth mutters low, her tone dry and acidic. "Some selection this turned out to be. Maybe they should've called it a culling and saved us the suspense."

Lisbeth's bitter sarcasm feels strained, like she's trying to provide levity for us despite not feeling any herself.

Thalia turns back to me with tears streaming down her face. Her voice wobbles and cracks as she whispers, "Elysia, what are we supposed to do?"

Her question splinters something in my chest. Because for once, I don't have an answer. There is nothing I can do to stop what's coming for us.

Before I can even try to speak, Lisbeth's voice rises with firm clarity behind us.

"We do what we've always done," she says, voice steadier than I expected. "We stay strong. We face it head-on, and when this is over, we go home tomorrow. Back to our families. If we're not chosen."

I glance at her, grateful for the steel in her words, even if we all know the cracks forming beneath them.

The words settle uneasily in my mind, because a thought rises in me that I can't shake.

What if the only way to survive this with our minds intact . . . is to be the Queen?

If the High Priestess is this awful—if this is what the embodiment of a connection to their goddess looks like—what horrors wait among the rest of the elves for the Queen?

The grove seems to pulse around me, like it knows what I'm thinking.

My mind reaches for the one moment I felt safe with an elf. The one moment I didn't feel like prey. The memory of storm-charged air and silver-veined arms holding me as I fell apart.

My Dromin elf. His arms around me. His silence and strength.

I wonder, just for a moment, if he knew I was going to be broken and if that's why he wanted me to think of him now. So that I could remember his strength in a moment he couldn't be with me.

I close my eyes tightly as another scream tears through the grove.

Then another, and another.

Each one more shrill, more guttural, more agonizing than the last. The line of women from the Nithrin lands is slowly, methodically

pulled apart by whatever horror lies within that orb. The testing is no trial. It is a war of will . . . and most are losing it.

Thalia's hand finds mine again. Lisbeth's slides in on the other side. None of us speak. We just hold on. Silent and trembling. Three broken breaths threaded together by desperation.

Each of us squeezes the others' hands with the same unspoken plea: *Hold steady. Don't fall apart yet.*

In the darkness behind my closed lids, I reach for him again. His hands on my skin. The soothing, circular motion from his hand on my back.

I replay the memory over and over again, clinging to it like a lifeline.

It's not enough to silence the screams.

Maggie's words coil tighter in my skull. *She chooses what bends. Not what breaks.*

Yet that's all I hear . . . the breaking of one mind after another, unraveling.

I've been strong for so long. For my village. For my family. For Thalia. For Lisbeth. Even for myself.

What if strength of will means nothing here?

What if all I can do now is wait and hope I don't break too?

A new sound rips through the grove—a guttural, unhinged scream that cuts sharper than any before it.

My eyes snap open.

One of the women from the Nithrin lands breaks from the line, her face twisted in anguish and madness. It's instantly clear she's already been broken by the orb. She shrieks again and lunges toward the High Priestess, who is just past her in the line. Her hands claw at the air, fingers curled like talons, her body convulsing with raw, frenzied energy. There's no recognition left in her gaze, only wild terror and fury.

Gasps echo through the grove as women stumble back, some crying out, others frozen in place.

The High Priestess doesn't flinch.

With a single flick of her fingers, light flashes, sharp and silver. A pulse of magic shoots from her hand.

The woman's body snaps mid-lunge. Her neck twists violently, a sickening crunch ringing through the trees before she crumples to the ground, lifeless.

The Priestess steps over her fallen body without a glance.

She doesn't speak . . . she doesn't even pause. She simply walks toward the next girl in line. The last one untouched from their lands.

Toward Virelle.

The High Priestess pauses in front of her, studying her with unnerving stillness. Her gaze sweeps over Virelle as if assessing something beyond her posture, beyond her physical form.

"You're different from the others," she says, her voice smooth and detached. "There is steel beneath the surface."

Virelle doesn't flinch. Her chin remains high, determination blazing in her eyes, that confidence I'd seen in her yesterday back in full force.

"You're right," she replies, her voice steady. "But the difference between me and the others from my lands is that I won't go down without drawing your blood."

Her eyes flick briefly toward me, just a glance, but it feels like a goodbye. A silent thank-you and a final farewell all wrapped into one look.

Then she turns back to the Priestess. I see it then, a glint of silver in her hand. My heart lurches as the dagger slides fully into her palm.

She's going to try to kill the High Priestess. She's going to try to save us all.

I take a step forward, the panic rising like bile in my throat. "Virelle!"

Lisbeth yanks me back, hard. Her grip digs into my arm.

"Don't," she hisses, her voice full of warning. "You'll get yourself killed."

I can't look away. My heart hammers, and my throat aches from the scream I can't release. Tears slip down my cheeks, silent and unrelenting. I don't even try to wipe them away. I'm utterly torn between wanting to shut my eyes and turn away from what's about to happen and needing to witness it. To honor Virelle's sacrifice with my eyes open.

She is fearless, she is fire, and she deserves to be remembered as more than just another fallen offering in a cruel selection.

I don't want to see her die, but I also don't want her to face it alone.

So I watch and I break in silence for the woman who refused to bend.

CHAPTER SIXTEEN

ELYSIA

The dagger flashes in a clean, defiant arc, aimed straight for the High Priestess's throat.

She moves quickly. Too fast for Virelle.

The blade doesn't land where Virelle intended, instead skimming the curve of her neck just beneath her jaw, carving a thin but visible line into that impossibly smooth skin.

Her blood shimmers like starlight caught in ink, dark and shimmering.

The High Priestess touches it with two fingers, smearing the line like paint across her skin. She blinks once, like she can't process that a human wounded her.

Virelle doesn't flinch and I clench my hands at my sides. She stands her ground, jaw set and unyielding, her stance firm as if she's not just bracing for death, but inviting it. Her chin lifts higher, and though her breath comes in short, tight bursts, her eyes burn with something furious and free, like she has no regrets.

Then the Priestess strikes.

No words. Just a violent wave of energy that erupts from her like a thunderclap.

Virelle's body lifts from the mossy ground and is thrown backward as if snatched by the wind. Her limbs flail, the dagger spinning from her hand, and her body slams into the ground with a crack that seems to echo too long in the air.

She doesn't move again, her eyes reflecting the shimmer of the barrier as if she's staring at the sky, but she isn't seeing anything anymore.

The moment swallows me whole.

I can't move. My legs feel disconnected, as if the ground beneath them has vanished. My lungs won't work and my chest caves inward as panic clamps down.

Thalia makes a wounded sound beside me and drops to her knees, reaching for me blindly. Her hand tangles with mine at my side, ice-cold and shaking.

Lisbeth doesn't speak, but I feel her hand on my back, bracing me. Her breath shudders out slowly, as if she's trying to control the fear building inside her.

When I glance at her, my chest fractures. Tears trail down her face, quiet and steady. Her eyes remain focused ahead, but the tension in her mouth has faltered. The armor she's worn since the day we met has cracked, and through it, I see something raw and unguarded.

The girl who never weeps is unraveling, and so am I.

The High Priestess lowers her blood-slicked hand with an eerie calm. The shimmering liquid glints down her fingers as she wipes it on her robes.

She doesn't look shaken. Instead, she looks . . . insulted.

She turns to face the rest of us, but her gaze slides past the trembling line of women from the eastern lands and lands squarely on those already broken from the Nithrin side. The ones who survived the orb but now are broken shells of their former selves.

They aren't even standing anymore. Some sit hunched and vacant-eyed, swaying in place. Others rock silently, their lips moving in fractured prayers to gods who clearly aren't listening.

I know what she's about to do . . . I feel the charged magic in the air before it happens.

"I warned you," the High Priestess murmurs, her voice soft now, almost gentle. "You were offered a chance to ascend and you squandered it."

Her next words fall like lead.

"You are not fit to return. You will not carry children. You will not pass your weakness into the bloodline."

Her hands rise and the grove responds instantly. A pulse of silver-violet magic explodes outward from her body, racing across the moss. It finds the broken women. It finds their hollow eyes, their trembling limbs, their whispered madness.

It silences them all at once.

There are no screams, only an eerie stillness.

Seventeen bodies collapse, hitting the earth with a sickening wave of finality. The glow in their eyes flickers out.

Just like that . . . they're gone.

The silence that follows is heavier than any sound.

I can't breathe. I can't think. My mind is trying to make sense of what just happened, but there's no world in which I can understand this senseless brutality.

Beside me, Thalia covers her mouth with her hands, a soft gasp catching in her throat.

Lisbeth is silent and rigid.

My body trembles beneath the weight of everything I've just witnessed, and the air I draw into my lungs feels thin and brittle.

This can't be real.

Unlike the nightmares that have haunted my sleep, there is no escape waiting for me in the slow return of the morning light. No dream-elf stepping from the shadows to pull me back from the brink, no whispered words of comfort or protective silence wrapping around me like armor.

There is no one coming to save us. No hands to steady me. No soft voice to anchor my shattering mind.

Only blood.

Only stillness.

Only the slow, methodical sweep of the High Priestess's gaze as it moves across the remains of her own destruction.

Quiet sobs rise from Thalia and strained breaths puff from Lisbeth's nose like she's counting them to avoid losing control.

Somewhere deep inside, something starts to shift. It's a heat, small and trembling, but alive.

It's the kindling of helplessness morphing into fury. It coils low and tight beneath my sternum, rising like smoke within me.

Tears still slip down my cheeks, slow and unrelenting. I let them fall for Virelle—for the woman who tried to protect us all when no one else did, who lifted her chin and met death with fire in her eyes. I let them fall for the women whose names I never learned, whose voices were swallowed by the orb and who now lie silent, broken, forgotten.

When the High Priestess begins to move again, her robes whispering against the mossy floor, her steps are slow and deliberate as she turns her attention to the remaining line of women.

She comes to a stop in front of the red-haired girl. The one whose green eyes are always too still, too knowing. The girl who never flinched at the screams and never broke rank. Who never spoke unless spoken to.

She stands tall now, her spine like a rod of iron. The High Priestess studies her for a long moment, her dark, iridescent blood still drying in a delicate line across her throat.

The Priestess doesn't speak again, merely lifts the orb. It drifts upward from her hand like smoke turned to glass, its black and white swirls intensifying with each breath. The red-haired girl watches it for a moment before laying her hands on it.

The orb hovers, pulsing brighter, drawing toward the girl until it settles just before her chest.

A moment passes and then it begins to glow. It starts as a shimmer of light, then darkens, swirling faster as the black expands outward until it swallows the white completely.

The girl's eyes remain fixed ahead, but her lips tremble now.

The High Priestess doesn't move while the orb swirls, its black glow washing over the redhead's still features. Then, at last, she speaks.

"A murderer who thinks themself above the rest." The word slices through the grove like ice. "You thought your actions would go unseen."

There are gasps of shock, but not from me.

The orb dims slightly, returning to its soft swirl of light and shadow before floating back to the High Priestess's hands.

"What you've done is prove you could never be a queen," the Priestess says, her voice sharp. "You put yourself first before all else."

The woman finally moves, lifting her chin a fraction, but there is no defense. No protest. Only a final, long exhale.

The High Priestess doesn't offer mercy, just a glance before she lifts her hand, slow and deliberate, her fingers glowing faintly. The woman doesn't beg or cry, she simply closes her eyes tightly, as if bracing for impact.

Magic unfurls in a tight, controlled pulse from the High Priestess, piercing the space between them in a single jolt of energy. The girl's body stiffens and then crumples. Her knees hit the moss first, then her side, folding in on herself. Her face turns toward the rest of us, eyes glassy and vacant.

The Priestess exhales, the faintest sound of exertion in her breath. She lowers her arm slowly and turns back toward our line.

For the first time in this nightmare I feel nothing at the death that's just occurred. For once, it was justice.

The silence stretches and my heart hardens.

Now that she's gone, there's no one left to fear among our own, only those who need protecting.

My eyes scan the line slowly, and the ache rises higher with each face I take in.

There are nine of us left.

Nine women still standing, though many of us are barely upright. One girl is trembling so hard I fear she's going to pass out. Another has sunk to her knees, her arms wrapped around her chest like she's trying to hold herself in one piece. One stares ahead with such numbness that I'm not sure she even knows where she is anymore.

Then I find Thalia, who has pushed to her feet again. She's pale, her eyes red and swollen, but her lips are pressed together, as if sealing in her own scream. Her hands shake and her breath shudders, but she's still here and staring fate in the face.

Lisbeth stands on my other side stiff as stone, her chin high despite the streaks on her cheeks, her jaw clenched like she's daring the world to push her one inch farther before she snaps. She meets my gaze, and something flickers there, fear, yes, but also trust. That quiet, unspoken trust we've forged in the fire of this journey.

I feel it again, an emotion I haven't felt since leaving my village. That tether inside my chest, stretching out and wrapping around them both.

Love.

Not the fragile, whispered kind between lovers. The fierce kind that roots itself in your bones and refuses to break.

I hear my own words again, spoken to the Elder of Edritch what feels like a lifetime ago, trembling but unflinching: *I'd rather risk everything than abandon those I love.*

I meant it then and I mean it now.

Take the step.

My body moves before I can second-guess it. My foot shifts forward and then the other. The moss beneath me gives slightly under each step as I break from the line.

Gasps echo softly behind me.

The Priestess watches with a stillness so absolute it feels sculpted from stone. Her eyes narrow, and for a breath, she says nothing. Then she tilts her head.

"You step forward willingly to be tested next?" she asks, voice quiet but sharp.

I nod once. "I want to be tested."

The silence thickens around us like the mist and shadows of my nightmares.

She studies me for several long seconds, before scoffing. "I don't know if you're brave or stupid," she admits.

"Maybe both," I answer, because it's the truth, but in my heart, I know exactly why I'm doing this.

Because if I'm found worthy, this madness ends with me and then maybe the rest of them won't have to suffer.

Maybe they can go home. Maybe they can survive.

If not . . . then at least I'll fall before they do.

CHAPTER SEVENTEEN

ELYSIA

The High Priestess steps toward me and releases the orb from her clutches.

It hovers just far enough away for me to not be able to touch it, its swirl of black and white spiraling faster the closer it gets.

Silence descends as the grove watches my fate approach.

My palms hover just above the orb's surface as it reaches me, and for a moment, I allow myself to think of my family before I shut off that side of my heart and mind.

One of my hands snakes up to touch the ribbon from Penelope in my braid.

"So you don't forget us on your journey. So you don't forget me."

My dad's voice whispers, *"My brave girl."*

Warm hands that cupped my face as my mother said with all the confidence in her heart, *"You will be fine."*

I swallow the lump rising in my throat as I bury them in the deepest recess of my heart and open my mind to him . . . to the protector of my mind when I sleep.

"When you're tested, think of me. Only me."

I may not know why he said it, but at this moment, it doesn't matter. My gut is telling me to trust him and this demand.

My hands lower.

The moment my skin touches the orb, the world disappears and I'm not in the grove anymore. There is no moss under my feet or vibrant trees that seem to breathe alongside us.

Only endless light.

It explodes inward through me. A burning surge that floods my body, probing and crackling through every corner of my being. It tears

into my chest and floods my bloodstream, spirals through my thoughts, through my memories, through the cracks in my heart.

It's like my soul is being dissected, examined, peeled open strand by strand to see what I'm made of.

I understand now what Maggie meant. The orb wants to see everything . . . who I've been, who I might become, what I'll break for, and what I'll die protecting. It's not searching for strength. It's hunting for malleability.

It wants to know if I bend. If I'll bleed without snapping. If it can shape me into something useful.

"When you're tested, think of me. Only me."

The memory of him rises, crashing through the relentless search of my soul.

His arms around me. The smell of rain just before it breaks. The press of his hand against my back as I wept into silence.

He has no name. No promises. No face I can remember.

Just the Dromin elf that feels like safety.

The orb surges again, harder, deeper. I cry out this time, the scream ripping from my throat as I drop to my knees. Every nerve burns, every thought splinters, every shred of composure I've held up until now shatters in the pressure of this unrelenting light.

I hold on to the memory of his presence. To the weight of his hand at the center of my spine as he soothed me. To the inexplicable, unwavering trust that he will catch me if I fall.

The light changes and everything slows. Then . . . silence.

In that hush, a voice slides through my mind, smooth as silk soaked in shadow.

Do you trust the Dromin elves?

It isn't spoken aloud, but I feel it.

The voice is everywhere and nowhere. It is the orb.

Do you believe in them?

My thoughts aren't clear anymore, but one rises to the surface.

I trust him.

I don't say it aloud . . . I simply think it.

I trust him.

The light fractures suddenly and the pain stops.

Suddenly I feel like I'm falling, and I slam back into my body like I've been thrown from the tallest peak of the Sacrum mountain range.

The wind is knocked from my chest and I gasp.

The grove rushes back into focus, the trees, the air, and the shimmering boundary. I'm on my knees and my vision blurs as my head moves, trying to take in my surroundings.

Then the sound comes.

Screaming, and not my own.

Lisbeth's.

I turn, dazed and aching to the depths of my chest.

She's on the ground, cradling Thalia's small body in her arms, gripping her protectively to her chest. Auburn curls drape against Lisbeth's arm, while open blue eyes stare at the barrier above us, the same as Virelle's did.

Her chest doesn't rise.

No.

My body tries to move, but it feels like I'm weighed down by stones.

Lisbeth's scream finally jolts me from my stupor, the sound raw and broken.

"You *killed* her!" she roars at the High Priestess. "You took her! She wasn't even being tested!"

The Priestess doesn't flinch. She just stands there, watching me, like she sees something now that wasn't there before.

I glance between her and Thalia as a fresh wave of agony rips through me and I splinter.

I'm moving before I even know what I'm doing. My knees scrape across the moss as I lurch toward them, my body trembling as I crawl. A wail rises in my throat that refuses to stay buried.

"No!" I scream. "No, no. Thalia!"

Lisbeth barely looks up as I reach them. Her face is pale, her cheeks soaked with tears, her hands still clutching Thalia like if she lets go, she'll lose her forever, but she relents to me.

I drag Thalia's body into my arms, fingers curling beneath her shoulders as I lift her, press her against me. I rock her like I used to rock my baby sister when she cried in the dark.

But Thalia isn't crying. She's cold and too still.

"What happened?" I scream, turning to Lisbeth with a voice that shreds itself on the way out. "*What happened to her?*"

Lisbeth's mouth opens and closes like the shock is keeping her from forming words. Her voice, when it comes, is hoarse and broken.

"When you screamed . . . when you fell, she . . . she moved toward you." Her eyes flood with fresh tears. "She reached for your hand. To steady you. To give you her strength."

I blink, shaking my head, unable to process.

"And the orb," Lisbeth chokes. "It lashed out. One strike. Right to her chest. She dropped before I could catch her."

My heart shatters.

She died trying to give me strength.

I bow my head over Thalia's shoulder and sob like never before. Not when I left home. Not when the dagger bloodied my hand. Not when I saw Virelle fall.

This is different, more raw than anything I've felt in my life.

This is the kind of grief that doesn't come with numbness. It comes with guilt that roots itself in the marrow of your bones and never lets go.

My scream rips through the grove, echoing off the trees, louder than anything that's come before.

Still, the Priestess says nothing.

When I finally lift my face, blotched and soaked and feral with rage, she's watching me and smiling.

Smiling.

"You killed her," I spit, my voice shaking.

The High Priestess lifts her chin, composed and untouchable. "She shouldn't have interfered with the process."

My stomach twists, bile rising behind my teeth.

She's not sorry, she's triumphant—because in her mind, this is all justified.

Her gaze lingers on me now, not with cruelty like before, but with certainty.

She doesn't care that I'm still cradling Thalia. She doesn't flinch at Lisbeth's wild, tear-soaked fury. Doesn't even look down at the body her magic destroyed.

She only steps forward, voice ringing across the grove with calm finality.

"We have our queen."

I freeze while the other women shift behind us. Some gasp and some go completely still.

The Priestess raises her arms like the announcement is sacred, as if anyone here even cares after everything we've witnessed.

"Elysia Virellan of Edritch," she proclaims. "You have withstood the full force of judgment. You did not break. You were chosen. The selection is complete."

My chest is still heaving from sobs and Thalia's weight is still pressed against me. The taste of grief hasn't left my tongue, but something cold and clear cuts through the haze of it all.

Power.

Not because I want it and not because I asked for it, but because if she just handed me a crown, then I will wield it as a weapon.

My mind is unsteady and my heart is wrecked, but my voice comes strong.

"Then if I am your queen," I say, voice rough but rising, "I give my first order."

The High Priestess stills.

"Lift the barrier," I continue. "Let every single one of these remaining women go. Alive. Right now."

A murmur ripples through the line as the Priestess's eyes narrow, her expression unreadable now.

The air tenses like the universe itself is waiting to see what happens next.

I hold her gaze, daring her to deny me.

I am Elysia Virellan of Edritch and I am done watching them fall.

The High Priestess studies me in silence for a moment longer, then she smirks, not out of amusement but condescension. It drips from her like invisible sweat.

"You'll learn soon enough," she murmurs, voice dipped in silk and something far more cruel. "What that title truly means."

With a flick of her wrist, she turns away, stepping back toward her altar.

The air shifts and the veil that enclosed the grove shudders once, then splits like mist parting. The magic bleeds out of the trees, the glow in the moss vanishing in a blink. Light and color fade until what's left is only a sparse, plain, snow-covered forest.

The barrier is gone.

Behind me, footsteps erupt. The remaining offerings waste no time . . . they flee.

They vanish back toward the town, tasting freedom with blood on their boots and scars in their minds.

"You have ten minutes before we ascend."

The Priestess's words are sharp and final, yet I can't process them as I stare down at Thalia's lifeless face.

A memory hits me hard, causing a broken cry to catch in my throat.

Us standing in the inn where we met, stopped at the door of her room as she glanced back at me. *"We'll be okay, right?"*

"Of course we will," is what I told her.

I bite down on my lip hard as fresh tears pour from my eyes and I curl myself around her, holding her to me as if I could will my own life into her.

"I'm so sorry," I mutter over and over again through my sobs.

Eventually my sobs fade to shudders.

Lisbeth leans forward and brushes a strand of hair from Thalia's face as I pull back.

Then she swings her gaze to meet mine. Her eyes are red-rimmed and hollow, but there's steel beneath.

"You have to do it," she says hoarsely. "You have to be Queen."

I blink at her, throat thick, lips parting to protest, but she holds up a trembling hand to stop me.

"You don't have a choice anymore," she whispers. "Not after this. Not after *them.*"

She glances down at Thalia, then toward the many fallen bodies around us, and her voice shakes, but she forces the words out anyway. "You need to take the throne, and when you do, you change this. All of it. For Virelle. For Thalia. For every girl who died on the road here and in this grove."

I stare at her, the words sinking inside of me like stones in deep water.

Lisbeth wipes her cheek, breath hitching.

"You remember this moment," she says, "and you burn it into everything you become."

I nod slowly, unable to speak.

I will not wear this crown for power. I will wear it for the women who were never given the chance to take another breath.

CHAPTER EIGHTEEN

ELYSIA

The weight of the High Priestess's gaze burns between my shoulder blades.

Cold seeps through my fingers, numbing my bones as I lower Thalia's body to the ground and take in her gentle face for the last time. Her curls are tangled against her cheek, her lips slightly parted, as if she might still exhale. Tears fall from my face, dropping onto her cloak as I take her hand in mine, wishing I could go back to her holding my hand last night one more time.

Lisbeth kneels across from me, brushing dirt from Thalia's cloak. Her movements are slow and deliberate, like she has to stay in motion to keep from unraveling any further.

I know the sentiment well. All I can do at this moment is to keep moving, to find justice somewhere in the wisps of clouds above. If I don't, I'll wallow here forever, and I'm beginning to learn that all of us living beneath the clouds need a voice.

A protector.

My throat aches as I finally look up. "Take Thayus," I tell her, voice raw from my cries. "Who knows what those guards will do to him if he's left alone."

Lisbeth nods once, her eyes still red-rimmed, but focused. "I will get everyone home." Her voice is steady as she vows, "Every girl who died here—Virelle, Thalia, the ones we didn't even know—I'll make sure they're returned to their villages. To the people who loved them."

With her words of certainty, a knot loosens in my chest. I know she will see them to a peaceful rest for eternity, just how I would. Nothing will get in her way.

My heart squeezes. "Thank you."

I rise on trembling legs, forcing myself away from Thalia. It feels like her small hand is wrapped around my heart and tugging me back the farther away I get. I want to compartmentalize. To shut off the emotions raging like storm clouds inside my chest, but I never learned how to do that . . . I was never built to endure without feeling every emotion deeply.

So I carry it at the forefront of my mind and heart: the grief, the guilt, the fear.

I glance toward the High Priestess, waiting for me at the altar. My stomach turns, threatening to empty itself, but my spine straightens.

I have to go.

"She'll be punished," I whisper softly to the wind, hoping the souls of the fallen can hear me wherever they are now. "I'll find a way."

Even if the crown is the only weapon I'm allowed in this new world, then I'll learn how to wield it with blood in my teeth and their names in my heart.

I take one last look at the fallen around me, eyes lingering on Virelle as I try to breathe in the fire that filled her soul like a warrior going to battle.

Take the step, Elysia.

The words echo in my chest as I walk, boots sinking into the damp snow-covered ground now stripped of the magic of the grove.

I get only a few paces before Lisbeth's voice calls out from behind me.

"Elysia!"

I stop and turn, finding her figure rushing to me. Without a word, she crashes into me roughly, pulling me into a hug.

Lisbeth. Hugging me.

For a heartbeat, I just stand there, startled. Then her grip tightens and my body responds, arms sliding around her, holding her just as fiercely. Her breath hitches, her muscles trembling faintly as we cling to each other. We say nothing, because there is nothing to say. This embrace is grief, pain, and promise, all wrapped into one.

When we pull apart, she gives me that no-nonsense, confident gaze that I've somehow grown to love.

"Don't forget why you're going," she breathes out, "and don't let them turn you into something you're not, Elysia."

I nod, unable to speak past the emotion burning in my throat.

We don't say goodbye, because no matter what happens next, we'll carry the weight of surviving this together, and always.

I move toward the altar where the High Priestess waits, her robes swaying in the thin mountain wind.

The grove has vanished alongside the barrier, the magic stripped from the trees, leaving behind nothing but a patch of bare earth and brittle grass poking out of clumps of dirt. The altar still remains, the anchor of something eternal and ancient.

Its curved surface is now etched with a glowing sigil, bright and pulsing with a violet energy.

The High Priestess raises her arm, palm outstretched. "It is time," she says.

I hesitate. That hand stained with death is the last thing I want to touch.

"We don't have time for this," she snaps, shoving her hand at me again. "You cannot travel without taking it."

I let out a breath and reach forward. The moment our fingers connect, magic lurches through me, not soft or gradual, but like being yanked by a tether attached to my spine.

The world splits apart beneath my feet and light floods my vision. For a breathless moment, there is nothing but wind and color and sound curling around me.

Until suddenly everything slows and clouds swirl below my boots. They're supportive beneath me as I gingerly pick up my foot and place it back down. It's like stepping onto spun silk that's somehow infused with the strength of stone, that refuses to give way. It ripples gently beneath each footfall, but doesn't break.

My heart beats wildly in my chest at the thought of falling through in the off-chance it suddenly chooses to evaporate beneath me. It's going to take a while to trust it.

We stand still at the convergence of the two elven courts, and as I glance up from the questionable ground, my jaw drops. It's the only spot without clouds floating through the air. The sky stretches wide and endless above us, painted in hues of lavender shifting into dusky blue. The air is thinner, and I expect it to be colder, yet the way the sun shines down on me, unobstructed for the first time in my life, is a moment I'll never forget.

I want to close my eyes, to bask in the warm rays chasing away the cold in my body, alongside the shadows of fear, but I can't. Not when this beautiful land is full of unknown dangers, be they magical or elven.

To my right, the Nithrin lands gleam. Sprawling towers of blackened glass and shimmering obsidian twist into the sky, each one adorned with curling silver spires that pierce the wisps of gray clouds that keep most of the land obscured from my eyes. Dark clouds beneath it churn with violent lightning, casting flickers of light across the reflective buildings.

Swinging my gaze to the left, the Dromin Court dazzles in contrast. I'm instantly awe-struck and drawn toward it.

Pale ivory towers spiral high and elegant, glowing faintly with the sun's reflection. The air around the city glints, catching and refracting the morning light. Golden bridges connect sections of the city through puffs of thin white clouds.

"Let's go," the High Priestess snaps from my side.

My head jerks forward as she begins to move and I hurry after her.

Everything in me screams that I'm not meant to be here. That I'm helpless to a world full of magic.

The clouds beneath my feet ripple with each step, parting in thin veils that begin to reveal a pathway of interwoven stone buildings, allowing me to breathe a small sigh of relief at a solid ground. The High Priestess walks ahead of me, silent, regal, unbothered by the death and trauma she'd left below. I follow because there is no other choice, but each step that keeps me near her ensures I stay on alert.

I know exactly the danger she presents now, yet I have no clue if she's an anomaly amongst the elves or the precedent.

We cross into the shadow of a towering structure that rises from the center of this world like a carved mountain. The building is carved entirely of smooth, slate-gray stone, inlaid with veins of silver that shimmer as we approach, reminding me of *him*.

I can't help but wonder if he knows I'm here . . . if he can sense it.

Arched columns hold the weight of a massive domed roof, and carved patterns run across every surface—vines, flowers, and a flowing script I can't read. It's stunning, but what makes my breath catch in my throat is the statue above the entrance.

A single figure is carved into the upper arch, so large it stretches from base to peak.

It's otherworldly.

Three eyes are carved into a serene, angular face, the third centered in her brow, closed in eternal slumber. Her hair flows around her like wisps of water, long, wild and endless. Sharp, elegant ears crown either side of her head, and her hands are outstretched. One is open in offering while the other is curled into a fist.

A chill rolls down my spine.

"She sees all," the High Priestess says, finally breaking the silence. "Even now. Especially now."

Their goddess.

We step under one of the archways, into the temple's grounds, and instantly I'm filled with a hum beneath my skin.

The interior is dim and echoing, filled with soft light that bleeds down from circular openings in the ceiling above. Each breath I take feels louder here, like the space itself is listening.

I don't know where I thought I'd be taken, but it wasn't this.

The High Priestess doesn't slow as we climb a wide stone stairwell. At the top, she stops and turns, her face as unreadable as ever.

"There will be no preparation," she says dryly with a tight set to her jaw. "The crowning ceremony is about to begin."

I stop in my tracks. "What?"

She lifts a single brow, as if my panic is inconvenient. "You are chosen. The moment demands acknowledgment in front of our goddess now."

I swallow harshly and blink repeatedly, trying to catch up to the moment I find myself thrust into. "Now? Just like that?"

"Is there a reason to delay?" she asks, already turning again, as if I couldn't come up with a singular one that would matter.

I scramble to follow, my breath uneven. "Wait, you said ceremony. That means . . . a king, doesn't it?"

Her silence is answer enough.

I'm not just being crowned . . . I'm about to meet the elf I'm expected to rule beside.

How is it that the simplest train of logic eluded me until now? Of course there is a king with a queen here. They wouldn't allow a human queen to rule over them alone.

My palms sweat and my mouth dries out.

What if he's cruel? What if he's like her?

My thoughts lurch sideways as my nightly visitor comes to mind.

What if I never have a chance to meet him now?

My heart stutters as the doors groan open with her touch. I follow, ready to learn the answers to my questions.

I expected this to be a grand spectacle, to be leered at and judged by hundreds of elves, but inside it is completely quiet and mostly empty.

At the far side of the grand hall stands a single, enormous tree, its roots and branches curling up into the vaulted ceiling. Its bark is swirled black and white, twisting through every branch and leaf. The tree is alive with quiet magic, glowing softly from within its veins. I stare too long and it feels like it stares back somehow.

Before it, on a raised platform, stand three figures.

Three elves, discernible by the long, pointed ears on each.

One stands centered with his back to us, only his short, silver hair on display, flanked by the others.

The one on the left has pale silver eyes and lips pressed into a thin, grim line. His skin is a muted violet-gray, his features sharp and unreadable—cold and distant.

The one on the right watches us with a warm expression, his golden eyes bright, almost glowing, as if lit from within. His skin has a dusky blue hue, and his smile feels like sunlight glinting off snow.

They each wear crowns that instantly remind me of each opposing court, black and silver twisted metal on a head of black hair neatly braided, and white and gold for the head of long, wavy white hair.

"My Kings," the High Priestess greets them, much more respectful and soft than I've ever heard her.

The sound of it has my lip beginning to curl in disgust at her change of tone, but I stop it from appearing fully on my face.

These are the two courts' kings, but who was I to stand next to as the Queen? Surely the Dromin, if I'm from beneath his lands?

My jaw clenches as I think of Virelle and the other offerings from beneath the Nithrin. Are there supposed to be two queens, one for each side? If so, where is the Nithrin Queen, if only ours recently passed?

My brow furrows as I glance at the wide back of the figure between them.

He's not dressed in fine garments that gleam with filigree like the two kings, with no crown on his head, but the way he stands tall and composed tells me he's still of importance. His shoulders are broad, arms folded behind his back, his dark tunic giving nothing away of his court status.

Something tugs at my chest as we come to a stop before them. A familiar scent.

My thoughts snag as the High Priestess lifts her voice, echoing through the vaulted chamber.

"I present to you, Elysia Virellan of Edritch. Crowned by the will of our goddess. Your queen."

Suddenly I feel very, very small beneath these towering elves staring down at me. Even if I were to stand next to them on the platform, I'd merely come to their mid-chest.

Still the one in the middle doesn't move . . . not at first.

Then, a breeze stirs through the great hall, soft and unnatural, carrying a scent I know better than my own breath.

Storm-charged air just before the first drops of water are unleashed.

My breath catches and he turns.

Slowly, deliberately, the figure in the center lifts his head and pivots toward me.

I know it at that moment . . . it's him.

"Think of me. Only me."

The Dromin elf from my dreams.

I once thought his skin to be of a purple hue, but between the two kings, it's like he's the perfect blend of a dusky sapphire and violet laid over a smooth gray river stone. A stunning mix of the two. The same faint silver veins cover the tops of his hands and run up the sides of his neck, leading to the most striking face I've ever seen.

Yet I can't even take in every feature, finding my eyes inexplicably pulled in toward his gleaming violet eyes.

They meet mine and, for a heartbeat, I want to smile because somehow, he's real. He's here with me. For the first time in what feels like days, a sense of safety finds me in this foreign sky.

Then I watch as his neutral stance and energy shifts.

It's not soft . . . not safe.

His eyes rage.

They crash into me like a strike of lightning to my chest. They don't hold warmth or welcome, but indifference.

I don't know what I expected if I found him, but it wasn't this. Not the coldness. Not the silence. Not him looking at me like I'm the one who doesn't belong.

I thought finding him would bring me relief. Instead, I'm more lost than ever.

CHAPTER NINETEEN

ELYSIA

The High Priestess's fingers close around my wrist before I can brace myself.

Her grip is cold, firm, and merciless as she pulls me up the stone platform without so much as a glance back. I stumble up the first step, my boots slipping slightly against the polished floor before I catch myself.

I notice my dream-elf's hands twitch at his sides, like he is ready to catch me, but maybe it's a figment of my imagination. My heart aches to see any semblance of the elf who held me as I broke apart in his arms.

I'm close enough now to see the crown clearly. It's smaller than I imagined. Not ornate or sparkling with jewels. Just metal that's interwoven bright silver and shadowy steel, shaped into thorny curves and delicate arcs.

My fingers twitch at my sides as she reaches for it and turns toward me. I want to back away and say I'm not ready, but where would I run to that I wouldn't be found and dragged right back to this temple?

This is happening now, whether I want it or not.

Before I stepped foot into this room, I would have daydreamed about running to find the elf from my sleeping world, thinking up a scenario where he swept me into his familiar arms and hid me from my fate.

That's neither here nor there any longer. That elf is just a figment of dreams that will never come true now. Add it to the list of beautiful things that this twisted world has destroyed.

"Bow your head," she instructs, taking me from my thoughts.

I hesitate just for a breath and then I lower my chin.

"The Goddess has chosen."

Cool metal touches my forehead, and I brace for something more. A jolt, a burn, a rush of magic, but all I feel is the weight of the crown settling against me.

"Welcome to our world, Queen Elysia," the High Priestess says before taking a step back from me. "Your formal joining ceremony will take place once your choice has been made, tying you to our people and the Goddess forever."

I have so many questions swirling, but one comes to the tip of my tongue as I raise my head up. "What choice do I have to make?"

The thought of being free to choose anything in this world feels as foreign as the magic pulsating through the tree like a system of veins.

Movement catches my eye to the right and I turn to find him stepping forward. The elf from my dreams, the stranger with beautiful lavender eyes and a name I still don't know. He folds his arms behind his back, expression unreadable as he faces me directly.

Unlike the two kings with their long hair, his silver hair is cut short all around, but with a bit more length on the top.

"You must choose between the kings," he says, voice flat, like he's reciting from a scroll. "You will choose which court your soul belongs to and that court will rise in power throughout your reign, alongside your village. Your choice binds our fates together, providing a balance in the power we hold over humans, as is the will of our goddess."

He might as well have said I control the moon. It makes no sense.

"But . . . I don't know enough about either court to make a choice," I argue, clenching my hands lightly at my side.

"It is law. Divine law. The one thing that has kept peace since the Blood War's end."

A flicker of pain passes across his face, like he's been wounded.

He lifts his chin, a flare of anger in his voice. "You'll be given time with King Sorryn of the Dromin and King Zayvin of the Nithrin."

I don't understand what I've done wrong and why he sounds so far away, when just days ago he held me together.

The Dromin King steps forward, white hair and golden eyes gleaming. His smile is easy and open. He bows at the waist, fluid and elegant.

"Forgive Rhune," he says gently, and just like that, I have a name.

Rhune.

"He forgets how overwhelming this must be for you."

Sorryn's presence is a minor balm to my frazzled nerves. His eyes gleam with warmth and the way he speaks is slow, thoughtful, like he actually cares how his words will be taken by me. "You'll come to the Dromin side first since you are from beneath our lands. We'll give you time to adjust and to understand who we are and our history."

I nod, forcing myself to swallow despite my throat feeling dry as sand.

My gaze shifts to Zayvin. He doesn't step forward and he doesn't speak. His eyes stay fixed on me, sharp and unreadable. Not cruel . . . just guarded, a look he shares with Rhune.

"Is it always this way?" I ask, looking between the four elves here. "Is there always one queen and two kings to choose between?"

I know there is likely a reason for the elves to keep so much of their world a secret from us, but why this?

The High Priestess steps in, voice smooth and full of pre-planned explanations.

"Traditionally, the kings are twins," she answers, "born of a human queen. The Goddess splits them, one for the Dromin and one for the Nithrin."

She pauses, eyes flicking to Rhune. A trickle of unease runs down my spine.

Why *is* he here if he isn't a king?

"This time . . . there were three born."

The breath leaves my lungs and my eyes flick to him as the High Priestess continues. "Rhune bears both courts' powers within him. They're weak, but there."

Suddenly, everything slots into place. His blend of features between Sorryn and Zayvin. His question to me when he'd saved me from the valgys: "*How do you know I'm Dromin?*"

I turn fully now, staring at him with hope in my heart. "Then you are a king as well?"

His eyes drift to the ground, unable to hold my gaze.

"In order to honor our goddess's will, yes, you must spend time with each king," the High Priestess interjects, and I drag my focus back to her. "However, because Rhune is both Nithrin and Dromin, he has no court to rule over or for you to visit. He will serve as your guard in both courts, ensuring we've honored the sacred laws for him to spend time with you."

Her words ring out clearly, but I only hear the silence that follows. The one growing in Rhune's eyes as he looks back up at me. The stillness of an elf who's been told he's lesser than his entire life.

He has no court, no claim, and now, he has to watch me be courted by his brothers.

It hits me like a punch to the ribs . . . maybe that's why he's pulling away. Why the man who once felt like the calm amongst the storm of my life now looks at me like I'm a danger to him.

A question rises in my throat, trembling on my tongue before I force it out.

I look at the High Priestess and lift my chin. "Is Rhune one of my options, seeing as he *is* a king despite having no court? He was born alongside the others and from the chosen queen."

Rhune's and Zayvin's heads jerk toward me, a shared look of bewilderment on their faces, but it's the first I zone in on.

For a moment the guarded anger isn't lining his rigid body and causing storms to brew in his eyes as he stares at me. For a moment, he looks at me like maybe I do control the moon.

Like no one has ever stood up for his claim.

Zayvin shifts beside Rhune, arms folding across his chest as he casts a sidelong glance at the High Priestess. His voice is low and steady when he finally speaks, surprising me with its smoothness. "Perhaps Rhune should be treated as a choice."

His words fall into the room like a stone dropped into still water, rippling tension outward from their source.

The High Priestess straightens, flipping a strand of hair over her shoulder. "His powers are too weak to be a choice. Sorryn and Zayvin are masters of their individual powers and that is what matters. This has already been determined by the Elven Council."

The finality in her tone cuts off any room for debate. Zayvin doesn't argue, but his gaze lingers on his brother, unreadable.

Beside him, Sorryn lets out a breath and steps forward with easy confidence. He claps a hand onto Rhune's shoulder, the motion too casual for the weight of the moment.

Rhune recoils back from the touch. It's subtle . . . a tension that lines his sharp jaw, a flicker of disgust in his narrowed eyes. He shrugs off the touch with a barely concealed sneer and steps away.

There is clearly no love lost there.

By the time Rhune turns back to me, the mask is back in place. Cold. Impenetrable. The warmth I'd felt from him in dreams is nowhere to be found, still.

He folds his arms behind his back again, spine perfectly straight. "The High Priestess is right," he says, and his voice is steady now, stripped of the hurt I thought I'd seen a moment ago. "You must choose between Sorryn and Zayvin. That's how it's always been. That's what maintains the delicate balance."

I want to interrupt him. I want to ask why that balance doesn't include him, but something about the way he says it makes me pause. It's like he barely believes in his own words but is forcing them out.

"You don't understand what your choice means," he continues through gritted teeth now, his voice growing quieter but no less intense. "It's not just ceremonial. It isn't symbolic."

His gaze locks with mine, unwavering and hollow. "The court you choose gains power from our goddess. The blessing doesn't just happen for your village, but here in our world as well. Her blessing enhances the elves' magic and extends their lifespans. Your choice shapes the tides of our people's future."

A lump lodges in my throat.

"You think that means you shouldn't be an option?" I ask softly, needing clarity.

His face twists just for a second and then it's gone. "I think," he says, voice barely above a whisper, "that you shouldn't waste that blessing on the King of Nothing."

A silence falls between us all in the aftermath of his words. It settles over the room like dust, clinging to every breath I take.

I want to speak and to tell him he's wrong, that he matters to me, but I can't seem to find the words . . . not when he won't meet my eyes anymore.

He turns slightly, just enough to place distance between us again, shoulders squared like a wall has been built where the chance of a different fate used to live between us.

Still I look at him. At the way the light from the tree glints along the edge of his jaw and the way his hands remain clenched behind his back, like he's holding in all the pieces that could shatter.

I think back to the moment in the dream where I told him I was going to the selection.

The shift in tension between us then, the silence that descended. I was worried then that he thought of being punished if he visited me again.

I didn't understand it then, but I do now.

He wanted me to survive. He wanted to protect me and guide me. Even if it meant watching from the shadows while someone else stood at my side, if I made it to the other side of the selection.

Even now, with everything stripped away, he's doing what he believes is best for the courts. He's willing to give up whatever . . . this possibly could be between us, to make sure the elves are given the future they deserve.

I see the goodness of his heart in his words and actions, but it hurts more than I want to admit.

I will never be able to choose him. Not because I don't want to . . . but because he won't let me.

Our eyes meet, finally, in the stillness and silence of the room.

In that moment, I swear I feel everything we'll never be. The quiet ache of could-have-been threads itself through my ribs like a secret only meant for us.

I want to take a step toward him and ask him to fight for us, for *me*, but the look in his eyes says he already made peace with letting me go, and it breaks a piece of me I didn't know was still whole.

CHAPTER TWENTY

ELYSIA

Rhune doesn't look at me even once after that.

Even when the High Priestess calls the three brothers forward. Even when his name is spoken in the sacred hush of this glowing temple, he remains locked behind that invisible wall—shoulders rigid, mouth tight, eyes focused on some point beyond me.

I don't know what's worse: his distance . . . or how familiar it's beginning to feel.

We stand beneath the massive tree that pulses with quiet magic, its swirled black-and-white trunk looming over us like a deity carved from wood and light. Its roots twist across the floor like veins, and its upper branches stretch toward the domed ceiling, where pale light spills in from a skylight above.

The High Priestess steps forward with a small obsidian dagger, its handle etched with a script I can't make out. "As it has been since the first queen rose," she says, voice echoing through the space, "so it shall be now."

She presents the blade to Zayvin first. He takes it wordlessly and draws it across his palm without hesitation, the silver sheen of his glimmering dark blood gleaming as he presses his hand to the trunk of the tree.

For a second I'm reminded of Virelle drawing the same-colored blood from the High Priestess. My eyes narrow as I glance back and forth between them, wondering if the High Priestess is a Nithrin? It would line up with my fears of the nightmare court—her callous and deadly actions.

The bark absorbs his blood instantly at the first moment of contact. Black veins flicker throughout the tree, as though drinking it in.

Sorryn is next. He doesn't flinch, slicing open his own palm before placing it on the wood with a reverent dip of his head. His blood is lighter, more luminous, like a swirling silver. The tree's lighter veins flare this time, expanding upward, glowing like stars lit beneath the dark parts of the bark.

Then it's Rhune's turn.

The blade whispers across his skin and his hand meets the tree, his blood a deep violet-silver that pulses like storm light.

The tree responds differently this time.

It shudders just slightly, but I see it. The leaves above tremble and the trunk glows brighter where his hand touches, and for the briefest second, I swear it leans toward him.

He pulls away immediately, jaw tightening as he wipes his hand on the hem of his tunic, like he wants to forget the touch before moving back into line.

The High Priestess lifts her arms as the last glow recedes into the tree. "You are now bound in vow. Witnessed by the Goddess. A new queen has risen, and her courting begins now."

She lowers her arms slowly, turning to face the brothers fully.

"As you know, there are rules you must abide by," she says, sweeping her gaze across them. "You are not to speak ill of each other. The Queen's choice must be her own, untainted by slander."

None of them react.

"You are not to extend your courtship. Each of you will have three weeks. No more."

Silence reigns and I begin to shift uncomfortably under the weight of it.

"You are forbidden to speak of the queens who came before her. The past is not to shape the present."

A chill settles along my spine at that one.

The High Priestess's voice slices through the silence, calm and absolute. "With the vows made, the first courtship begins now."

I blink at her words.

That's it . . . just like that, I'm to allow myself to be courted by a king.

Sorryn steps forward with a smoothness that feels rehearsed. He smiles, wide and gleaming, the kind of smile meant to disarm and dazzle. "My Queen," he says with a faint bow, offering me his hand, "allow

me the honor of escorting you to the realm that now waits to welcome you home."

There's something undeniably charming about him. His voice is warm, like the low thrum of firelight, and I can feel it trying to soften my panic. To coax me gently into this next chapter.

I hesitate before taking his hand. As I do, Rhune's expression tightens. His jaw locks, eyes flashing with something sharp, something that looks too close to fury. Not rage at me . . . but at this.

There's a glint of satisfaction in the High Priestess's eyes as Sorryn's hand squeezes mine.

His grip is warm and sure, his skin smooth despite the faint calluses. It should feel like comfort, but all it does is make my skin crawl.

He's not the elf I want to touch.

"Tonight," he says as he begins to lead me off the platform, "we'll host a ball in your honor. Music, dancing, food from the finest Dromin chefs. The court will gather to meet you, to celebrate you."

He glances down at me with that golden smile. "It's time you felt joy in this new life, my Queen. Tonight, you'll see that we're not just courts and politics—we're people, too—and we'd be lucky to have you as our queen."

I nod stiffly, trying to mirror the poise I don't feel.

A ball.

After everything.

The image of Virelle falling with fire in her eyes flashes behind my lids. Then Thalia. Then the empty faces of the other women whose names I may never know.

A hollow echoes in my chest, but I offer a nod, because I don't know what else to do.

"I'll see you in three weeks," Zayvin's voice cuts in, sharp and grounding.

I turn to face him as he stays atop the platform. His posture is impeccable, his face carved from restraint, but there's something in the way his eyes flick to Rhune, like they're sharing a language I don't speak.

Then Zayvin pulls a small stone from inside his pocket.

It glows the same soft violet as the symbol etched into the altar we used to travel here. He gives one final nod and vanishes in a shimmer of wind and light.

Sorryn wastes no time in guiding me toward the exit and I resist the urge to glance back and see if Rhune is following us. The temple doors creak open as we step into the light.

The shift from stone to sky is jarring, as if I've been held inside some breathless, sacred box, and only now the world is exhaling again. Waiting at the path that connected the two courts, bathed in that soft golden light, is the most stunning carriage I've ever seen.

It's crafted from pale wood and inlaid with delicate gold filigree that curls around the edges like vines. The doors shimmer faintly, as if kissed by enchantment, and two creatures stand harnessed at the front.

They aren't horses. At least, not in the way I know them.

Their bodies are long and sleek like stags, but covered in a soft, pearlescent fur that gleams with every breath. Translucent feathered wings rise from their shoulders, half-folded at rest against their backs. Their eyes are pure silver with no pupil, but when one turns its head toward me, something powerful stirs behind its gaze.

I don't realize I've moved until my palm is pressed gently to its neck. Its breath huffs warm against my cheek, and I lean forward, forehead resting against the velvet-soft fur as I exhale.

The creature leans in, just slightly.

A quiet thrum rises beneath my skin at the connection. It hums low and gentle, touching a place deep within my bones.

"They're called aerwynth," Sorryn says softly behind me. "They exist only in our court. I'm glad you can see their beauty."

I glance back at him, then over his shoulder.

Rhune stands just beyond the stairs. Still and silent, his gaze going over my shoulder like he refuses to look at me.

"I'll meet you at the castle," he says, voice clipped and distant.

I glance at the carriage and the two plush seats waiting inside.

Of course there's only room for two.

He doesn't wait for a response, simply pulling out a stone the same as Zayvin did, and disappears like mist.

Sorryn offers his hand again. "Come. The city awaits."

I climb in, letting Sorryn guide me into the seat beside him as the door closes with a soft click. The aerwynth shift, their wings lifting and extending before the carriage begins to move.

Upward into the clouds and toward the Court of Dreams.

The carriage glides higher and the clouds thin as we rise above them. A breeze curls around me, soft and cool, scented faintly with some floral sweetness I can't name.

My hand rests in my lap, fingers curled tightly in my skirt as the city begins to reveal itself ahead.

The same massive ivory towers I saw glimpses of earlier stretch into the sky like needles, the tops lost in drifting clouds. Bridges of gold are littered across the expanse, winding over cloudbanks and curling between structures that shimmer with magic.

It's beautiful and completely, utterly unreal.

I should be in awe, but all I feel is hollow.

Sorryn watches me from the corner of his eye, his smile still warm, still present—but he says nothing. He doesn't press me to speak or smile, and for that I'm grateful.

While this realm is far more than I could have ever imagined, I can't stop thinking of the blood that got me here.

Thalia's still body. Virelle's final strike. The broken women in the grove.

Even riding in this carriage, with its glowing trim and soft seats, feels like a betrayal to them. The guilt of being alive when they no longer are.

I shift slightly, staring down at my hands.

The ache within my chest isn't just grief, it's also the rising awareness that I am alone now in a way I wasn't before.

A thought creeps in like cold air: *Rhune should be here.*

Not just because I want to see glimpses of the elf I was growing to know from my sleeping thoughts. Not because I dream of soft looks or secret touches, but because when he stood beside me—even silent and unreadable—I felt like there was one person in this strange world who *saw* me. Who would step forward if danger struck, or simply to stand in support while I learn how to navigate this world and my new role.

"I don't know how to be queen," I murmur, my voice barely a whisper. "Whatever you expect of me . . . I don't know how to do it."

Sorryn shifts beside me but doesn't interrupt. I continue as I glance up at him.

Will he be spiteful and angry if I don't carry myself like I'm anyone other than Elysia Virellan of Edritch, the woman who braids her sister's hair before bed and daydreams atop a hill?

I may wear a crown now, but it doesn't suddenly give me the confidence and clarity that I imagine a queen should have.

The Dromin King leans back, his posture easy and relaxed. "You don't need to pretend to be anyone other than yourself. You were chosen by the Goddess to be our queen. You are enough as you are."

His words settle over me like a comforting blanket I didn't know I needed.

I give him a nod of appreciation before I glance out at the sky again. The carriage crests a gentle curve in the clouded path, and suddenly the city comes into view.

In the distance, the clouds still conceal parts of the city, but I get a glimpse of a vast forest painted in unnatural hues—pinks, blues, and shimmering silver. Birds—no, not birds—but creatures winged and unknown soar among the treetops.

Even with all the beauty spread out before me, I don't feel safe, because I know what beauty can hide.

This isn't home. This isn't salvation. It's the place I'll be courted like a prize and watched like a threat. The decisions I make here will change the lives of everyone I've ever known and possibly those not even born yet.

I can't afford to be dazzled by this world.

Still, I study everything. The layout, the symbols etched into the arching bridges, the way the buildings glow faintly even without sunlight. If I'm going to change anything, if I'm going to uncover the truths buried beneath centuries of selection ceremonies and power games, I need to understand this world in its entirety.

The carriage descends and we pass beneath a sculpted arch and into the heart of the court. This is where it begins . . . my first test of what kind of queen I might become.

Already I feel the weight of every step I take here. For my family. For Thalia. For Lisbeth. For Virelle. For all of the fallen chosen and the selections yet to happen in the future.

I won't let beauty lull me into forgetting what's been lost.

Not ever.

CHAPTER TWENTY-ONE

ELYSIA

The moment the carriage slows and touches down, the air shifts.

Elves are everywhere. Men and women alike step forward with graceful purpose, dressed in elegant garb that glimmers with woven threads of gold and white. They bow slightly as the carriage pulls in, and the sheer number of eyes trained on me makes my chest tighten.

Sorryn stands as the door is opened. He doesn't seem surprised by the crowd. Instead, he leans toward me and murmurs, "Don't worry. I assume you'd prefer a moment to breathe before the ball tonight. You're not expected to meet anyone right now."

Relief rushes through me. "Thank you," I manage, keeping my voice low.

Maybe he is a decent elf. He isn't Rhune, but so far he's shown compassion and kindness.

He offers a smile and steps out of the carriage first, greeting the gathering crowd with practiced ease. I hesitate before stepping down, careful not to trip on the delicate steps. As soon as my feet touch the ground, a new figure steps forward.

She's striking in a colder way than the others, tall as are all the elves compared to me, sharp-featured, with raven-black hair braided into a crown atop her head. Her robes are pure white, trimmed in deep navy and gold, and her eyes are a shade of pale blue that borders on frost. Her presence is less welcoming and more clinical as she gazes at me.

"This is Maerel," Sorryn introduces, gesturing toward her. "She's my most trusted advisor. For the duration of your stay she will be your point of contact if you need anything."

Maerel doesn't bow like the others, only inclining her head slightly. "It's my task to ensure you don't get lost. Or, more likely, cause a political incident."

Her tone is cool, almost amused in a detached way, but it rubs at the raw edge of my nerves. "I'll try not to ruin anything," I reply, my voice flat.

She blinks slowly. "Good. Come with me."

The castle swallows us quickly with its vast, glowing halls lined with high, arched windows and drifting candles that hover midair. The walls hum faintly with magic, and at least twice I pass some kind of enchanted mirror that seems to flicker with movement just out of sight.

Maerel moves quickly, sparing no time to explain what we pass, and I don't ask. The silence suits me fine.

She leads me to a corridor of white stone, lit by more floating candles and flanked with tall windows that overlook a bed of clouds.

A figure beside the door at the end of the hall turns toward us.

Rhune.

He's leaning against the wall, arms folded. His expression is unreadable, jaw set tight. His eyes flick over me once like he's inspecting me for any wounds, but he says nothing.

I freeze for a breath too long, then glance at Maerel as we come to a stop. "You will not go anywhere without me or your guard."

"Of course," I mutter, hoping my voice doesn't betray the twist in my chest as I fight the urge to glance at him.

I offer a nod, and Maerel opens the door to my chamber. "I'll return in two hours," she says. "Be ready."

Then she's gone, leaving me alone with the elf who once held me as I shattered and is now guarding me like I'm a stranger to be protected.

He's still leaning against the wall just beside the door, arms folded, posture lazy but eyes sharp. He doesn't look at me right away. Just stares straight ahead like I'm not here, like I'm not the woman who once cried into his shoulder in a dream and whispered things I can't seem to forget.

I hesitate, fingers curling against my palm. "I didn't truly think you'd be with me at all times as my guard."

He doesn't move. "It is my duty."

The response is clipped. I should thank him for his protection and step inside and pretend none of this matters, but I don't. I can't.

His eyes flick toward me briefly as I continue to stare at him and I wish they hadn't. Because what I see there isn't the warmth from my dreams. It's something colder. Weighed down. Like every word he wants to say is being shackled inside him.

"Do you know what happened this morning?" I ask after a beat. "The grove. The testing. All of it."

He shifts just slightly.

"My brothers and I know what happened," he answers. His voice is low now, rough around the edges. "I'm sorry. For all of it."

My throat tightens as the images return too easily. Thalia's lifeless body in my arms. Virelle's defiant final breath. The screams. The silence.

"It's horrendous," I whisper.

Rhune exhales slowly, and this time when he looks at me, there's something breaking through. A crack in the ice.

"You'll carry it with you," he says. "Every day. That's the cost of surviving something like that, but I won't apologize for being glad you made it out."

There's a weight behind those words that surprises me after the cold exterior he's presented until now.

"I'm not supposed to say this," he mutters, almost to himself. "Not now. Not anymore."

He steps forward, just once, and the air between us tightens.

"I wanted you to make it. Even if it meant you'd never look at me the same again. Even if it meant you'd end up somewhere I couldn't follow."

"Why?" The word leaves my mouth before I can stop it. "Why would that matter if you knew we could never . . ."

His expression hardens and I clamp my mouth shut. "Because your soul is the most pure I've ever witnessed and this world needs more of it, not less."

My mouth pops open at the soft sentiment and my shoulders sag as I begin to feel comfort between us once more. Like this is a place where I don't need to pretend I'm okay.

"Don't do that," he adds, voice quieter now. "Don't look at me like that anymore."

My brows pinch together. "Like what?"

His jaw clenches and he lifts his eyes to mine, and this time, he lets me see the weight behind them.

"Like I'm worth fighting for," he says, each word deliberate. "We both have a duty now and none of it ends with you choosing the one who doesn't have a court. The one who doesn't belong."

My mouth parts quickly to rebut. "You're more than—"

"No, I can't be anything more to you," he cuts in. "Not here. Not anymore."

The silence stretches between us again. Even though his words feel like the bite of cold from the winter cycle settling into my bones, I can't stop the memories from rolling through my mind. The way he once touched my cheek, the way he anchored me with nothing but his presence, the way he worried when I didn't dream and he couldn't find me.

My eyes flutter shut as I let out a heavy breath. That elf doesn't exist here.

He turns, steps back into place beside the door, eyes forward again like the conversation never happened, and I know what he's doing. He's building walls between us before either of us gets the chance to try to knock them down.

I walk into my new room and the door clicks shut behind me with a softness that still manages to feel final.

Silence settles over the room, broken only by the faint hum that seems to linger in the castle walls. I take a step forward, hesitant, eyes sweeping across the space.

It's beautiful, but of course it is.

The chamber is carved from smooth ivory stone, accented with flowing gold trim and tall windows veiled with sheer curtains that flutter with the breeze. The bed is massive, draped in pale linens that shimmer faintly like starlight, and a gilded vanity sits near the far wall, its surface littered with delicate glass jars and brushes.

It hits me then, the emotional toll of this day, and it's not even over yet.

This morning I saw women senselessly killed, and tonight I'm expected to dance and chat with new people, like none of it ever happened.

I sink onto the edge of the bed, fingers curling into the fabric, grounding myself in something real. Something solid. Because my chest is caving in and my throat is tight and I'm not sure how to exist here without falling apart completely.

This place is more than what I dreamed about, back when Pat and I used to climb the hill behind the house, watching the clouds drift above the mountains.

I thought if I ever made it outside of my village, I'd feel like I had accomplished something. That I'd follow that sense of feeling like I was meant for more than our lands and feel at peace when I found it.

All I feel now is hollow.

I blink rapidly and stand, pacing toward the window. The city gleams in the distance, breathtaking in a way that doesn't feel real.

I press my hand against the cool glass and exhale. My breath fogs the pane for a moment before fading like everything else that once felt close.

It's funny how now all I wish is for a glimpse of the place I dreamt of leaving behind.

Is my mother tending the hearth and fussing over Penelope's braid right now? Is my father still watching the road when the sun sets, wondering if his bravest girl will ever come home?

Is Pat finally at peace now that he's been allowed to choose love freely?

I hope so.

I hope he's wrapped in warmth and laughter. I hope Persephone said yes and that they're planning an intimate and beautiful wedding.

My fingers reach for my braid, quickly brushing over the fabric Penelope pressed into my palm that final morning. It's slightly frayed now, a little dusty from the road and everything since, but it's still there. Still tethering me to them.

I press it to my lips, then to my heart.

"I miss you," I whisper into the stillness.

The ache swells in my chest.

I wish I could crawl into my mother's lap like I did when I was small and bury my face in her shoulder. I wish I could feel my father's hand steadying mine, telling me everything will be alright, even when I knew it wouldn't be.

I wish for a hundred things that will never be again.

My knees buckle slightly and I sit down on the edge of the bed once more, hands gripping the ribbon like a lifeline as the tears fall in silence. Not in gasping sobs or shattered cries, just soft, quiet heartbreak leaking from a girl trying not to fall apart.

Because I can't.

I have to hold on to the promise that this pain will mean something. That my village will be blessed. That all of this—every death, every scream, every choice—will amount to more than just survival.

It has to. It's the only thing keeping me together.

The next thing I know, I'm waking to the sound of gentle knocking and the soft creak of my door opening.

A woman steps inside. She has faint blue tattoos along the sides of her arms. Her dark hair is braided in a thick rope down her back, and her expression is unreadable as her warm-brown eyes flick over me.

She gives a short bow. "I've been sent to prepare you for the ball, Your Majesty."

The title still makes my stomach turn.

I push upright in bed, heart thudding from being yanked from sleep. There were no dreams. No nightmares. Just a void that should've been restful but instead left me groggy and confused at the silence.

"I . . . right. Of course." My voice comes out rough, my throat dry.

She gestures toward the adjoining room where a steaming bath waits.

I rise, still sluggish, and move to the room, quickly taking out the ribbon from my hair as I run my fingers through the braid. Setting it on the smooth stone counter, I call out, "Please don't move this ribbon. It's important to me."

A soft response of understanding carries through the space.

The moment I step into the water, the tension in my shoulders finally begins to unravel.

For the first time in days, I can cleanse myself.

A fruity, floral scent clings to my skin as I quickly wash. I close my eyes as I sink lower into the warmth and scrub away the evidence of the journey here, but the memories are harder to wash away.

I think back to the moment I saw Rhune for the first time, still cloaked in dirt and stench, my braided hair a wild mess. Here I thought the worst part of that moment was how he looked at me like I was nothing. Now I realize I probably *smelled* like I'd been fighting wolves in the mud for three days straight.

Not my finest moment.

The Dromin attendant doesn't speak much as I emerge from the bath. She dries my hair with a gentle wave of her hand, the strands

lifting and twisting as warm air surrounds me. I'm startled by the magic, but quickly compose myself so I don't offend her.

I try to offer a soft smile and ask what her name is, hoping to establish an acquaintance, but she simply says, "Call me Enari," and moves on.

Perhaps the previous queens preferred quiet relationships. I try to not dwell on the abrupt answer and continue on.

The dress she helps me into is unlike anything I've ever worn. Light blue silk that ripples like running water every time I shift. When I turn slightly in the mirror, it catches the light and shimmers, almost glowing. My wavy hair is pinned half-up, the rest cascading down my back in soft curls.

Then comes the crown.

Enari lifts it with reverence, as if it's not just metal, but something sacred.

The moment she sets it back on my head, I feel the weight of what comes with it. A reminder I don't need.

I glance at her reflection in the mirror and try again for a connection. "Do you like it here? In the Dromin Court?"

Enari's hands pause for only a heartbeat before she smooths down a fold in my gown. "I serve," she says simply. "That is what matters."

I nod, unsure what to say to that. Her tone isn't unkind, but it is distant and clear she doesn't wish to lower her walls.

I hope not everyone treats me this way, or else the depths of my loneliness will truly know no bounds.

I press my hands to the fabric of the dress and take a breath.

A ball awaits. A court awaits.

I can do this.

A soft knock echoes against the chamber door and Enari turns without a word and opens it. Her head dips slightly in a bow for whoever waits beyond the threshold.

"Your escort is here."

I barely have time to register her words before she glides from the room.

Then Rhune steps in.

His boots are silent against the stone floor, his posture sharp and guarded, but the second his gaze finds me, everything about him changes.

He stops mid-step, as if the sight of me has knocked the breath from his lungs.

The silence stretches as his eyes drag down from the crown nestled in my hair, over the shimmering folds of blue silk clinging to my frame, then back up to meet mine. There's something unspoken in his stare. Something dangerous and spellbound and entirely unguarded.

My skin prickles with his attention as my heart skips far too many beats.

He doesn't say anything and he doesn't have to, because I see it—the awe, the hunger, and the confusion.

I shift slightly and his throat bobs as he swallows. His hands stay clenched at his sides, as if he's fighting himself not to reach.

Heat rushes to my cheeks. I feel bare beneath his stare, exposed, as if I weren't wearing a dress. My fingers twitch at my sides, suddenly unsure of where to put them. My entire body buzzes with the weight of his attention.

Then he blinks, his expression shuttering again, and I remember where I am . . . who I am now.

I'm not a girl in a dream anymore. I'm a queen about to walk into a room full of strangers who expect something from me that I'm not sure I know how to give.

My hands shake as I smooth them down the silk at my sides.

I cannot reach for him and I cannot fall apart.

So I step toward the threshold and brace myself for the weight of every eye waiting for me.

CHAPTER TWENTY-TWO

RHUNE

I navigate us through the castle, quiet and careful to keep my gaze ahead of me and not on the woman unraveling my carefully constructed restraint.

The stone beneath my boots feels unsteady tonight, though I know it isn't. It's the weight of too many lies pressing down at once.

I've spent years breaking laws in silence. Visiting her night after night when I had no magical need to feed, unlike the others. Falsifying each entry in the dream logs with practiced ease.

While she was getting ready for the ball, Myren—the Dromin responsible for tracking dream connections—sought me out.

He's begun asking too many questions now that I've suddenly stopped showing up for feeds. I diverted him with a half-truth about shifting to nightmare-feeding, a carefully timed misdirection, but I can tell he's growing uneasy.

If he ever uncovers the truth, I'll be dragged before the Council—title or not. My involvement in Elysia's dreams and nightmares would be seen as a violation of the highest order. They'd claim I influenced her and manipulated her path to being queen.

My upper lip curls at the absurdity of it.

Sorryn would love the chance to remove me from the equation entirely, and I can't allow that.

Who knew my early pining over a random woman I was assigned one fateful night would lead me here? Especially when all I was attempting to do was keep up the facade that I had to replenish my magical reserves.

We arrive at the ballroom doors and I give the guards lining the walls a strict nod that they may open them. I keep my spine straight,

hands folded behind my back, and my jaw clenched as she moves to stand at my side.

Allowing myself to glance at her out of the corner of my eye, I watch her tug her bottom lip between her teeth and bite down as she gazes at the heavy double doors.

She's nervous.

I can hear the quiet rustle of the crowd inside, the soft notes of stringed instruments playing beyond the doors.

Her head swings toward me, lips parting to say something, but I quickly avert my gaze. My heart pounds within my chest, waiting for the beautiful sound of her voice that I've committed to memory.

It haunts me now, the two worlds clashing in reality.

I told myself after the first week of feeding off of her dreams that I needed to let go. That I couldn't continue to break our laws for a human I didn't even dare to reveal myself to. The weeks bled into months and eventually into years.

The doors swing open, saving me from whatever she wanted to say.

The herald announces her name in a booming voice that echoes through the gilded hall: *"Our new queen, chosen by the Goddess's will. Queen Elysia from Edritch."*

She's hesitant at first and I let myself watch as she steps forward. Her shoulders dip slightly, and her steps are small, like she's trying to put off fully stepping into the room for as long as she can, but then I watch it happen . . . that quiet shift I've seen only in her sleep.

She lifts her chin as her shoulders draw back and she walks forward. As if she is daring the universe to give her its worst.

She walks like the light of the sun trying to pierce through a storm, soft yet unyielding.

The silk of her gown whispers across the floor, and the crown atop her head catches the light with every measured step. But it's not the dress or the glow of the room that steals the air from my lungs.

It's the strength it takes to walk into that room, after everything she's been through. What I had to watch her endure from the temple as the High Priestess laid waste to the humans who trusted us with their greatest offerings.

I'd struggled to watch, yet Zayvin had forced me to with a silent, steadying hand to my shoulder.

Now, here she is, walking into a room full of elves in a world she doesn't recognize, who will smile and lie. To try to claim her as their queen, as if the Court of Nightmares has no chance.

My hands curl into fists behind my back. They don't deserve her. No one does.

Least of all me . . . but still, I can't look away.

I move to the shadows inside the ballroom doors as she continues forward. I stand with my shoulders squared and arms crossed in an attempt to appear unbothered. Just another guard. Just another figure in the corner, forgettable in a sea of glittering gowns and robes.

She hesitates at the threshold, eyes scanning the vast, gold-drenched room like she's looking for enemies already. Quiet strength and defiance pour from her.

It undoes me in ways nothing else ever has. Nothing prepares me for the quiet ache that builds when I look at her, knowing I can't reach for her like I did in the privacy of her dreams and nightmares.

Not ever again.

She's not the woman from the dreams I watched anymore—she's the Queen—and I'm just the glorified guard cursed with knowing the way her soul tastes in the veil of sleep. The only elf reckless enough to shield her mind from others when she dreamed, even when it meant skirting the edge of treason. I blocked them from reaching her . . . every single Dromin who tried to pull power from her while she slept.

I was drawn to her long before I understood why. I never planned to reveal myself. Never believed she'd be chosen for the selection, let alone stand in this room in my world.

She crosses the floor toward Sorryn, and I feel the tension coil through me, squeezing my heart. He's already smiling, flawless and rehearsed. He reaches for her hand with all the charm of someone who's never had to fight for anything in his life.

I want to rip it away before she can touch him, but she takes it quickly. I notice her initial wariness of him seems to be fading and my jaw grinds at the idea.

I'm supposed to be her safety. The one she trusts.

He guides her up the dais like he's presenting a rare jewel, and the court erupts in applause. From my post, I see the pride on his face, but beneath it there is a flicker of triumph. His gaze cuts toward mine, and for a heartbeat, I see what he's really thinking.

This is his victory . . . that he won again.

The vow binds my tongue from slandering my brothers, but no vow forbids me from breaking his bones. From spilling his blood and breaking him down if he so much as bruises her spirit.

I force myself to look away at the rest of the room. To breathe. To remember that I am not a king courting her.

I am not hers.

The applause fades as the music swells. I watch her get passed from one noble to the next, each offering a dance, each drinking in her presence like it's their right.

My jaw clenches with every turn of her body, every strained smile, every moment her shoulders sag more beneath the weight of their attention.

Sorryn doesn't even look for her, too busy laughing with nobles and Council members while she's left to endure the court alone.

I tell myself not to interfere. To let the dances end, to let her endure this with her head held high like she always does. She doesn't need me.

Yet every time she's passed from one pair of hands to another, my restraint slips further.

I watch her smile. It's small and tight, the kind that doesn't reach her eyes. I watch her try to keep her shoulders back and her head up as if she's not retreating mentally. The nobles swarm around her like moths, all charm and pretense, trying to bask in her light as if they've earned the right.

They haven't.

Her gown ripples like water with every turn. Her crown catches the light, making her seem untouchable, otherworldly. Yet . . . she looks like she's about to shatter.

Sorryn doesn't notice. Or maybe he does, and he simply doesn't care.

My hands are so tightly curled, I feel my bones will shatter. My jaw aches from the tension lining my entire body.

It's been too long. She's danced with seven different elves now, each one taking just a little more from her light. My legs move before I realize I've made the decision.

I cut across the ballroom floor in a straight line, dodging dancers without apology, my gaze fixed on the one place it's always anchored—*her*.

She's with a new partner now that I don't recognize, with his hands just a little too low on her waist. Her smile is gone but as she sees me approaching, her eyes widen slightly. Relief flickers there.

The male turns as I reach them, a question forming on his lips.

I don't let him speak.

"Get out of the way," I say, voice low but firm, and I don't give him the chance to argue. I take her hand in mine and step in, leading her away before anyone can protest.

She doesn't resist and we move into the rhythm of the dance, but I don't care for the steps. My only goal is to put space between her and everyone else.

Her chest rises and falls with shallow breaths, and she doesn't look up at first, keeping her eyes on my chest. I feel the shift in her, just slightly. It satisfies in a way it shouldn't, feeling her body relax into me.

A beat passes between us.

"I didn't think you'd step in," she says quietly.

I shouldn't have. Every instinct told me to stay back. To let her learn, let her choose, let her forget.

However, the moment her body slumped beneath another stranger's hands, I knew.

There are things I will never be allowed to say aloud, but this is part of my duty. Her safety. This I can do.

"I am just doing my job," I murmur, drawing her in as we turn beneath the gilded arches of the ballroom. "His hands were far too low."

She doesn't answer and I don't press her to.

The music swells around us, light, delicate, and orchestrated to keep the mood festive, but none of it reaches me as she finally looks up at me. The entire room fades away until it's only her.

Only the feel of her hand in mine, the way her fingertips tremble just slightly, the way her gaze lingers.

We move together in silence. It's not practiced or polished, but it's easy and comfortable. The silence stretches long, but it doesn't strain. It wraps around us like something meant just for us. A world all our own carved out from the chaos of the court. Her eyes hold mine, questioning and steady, like she wants to speak but doesn't trust what might spill free.

For a fleeting moment, everything disappears.

There's no crown, simmering war between courts, or duty biting at my heels.

There's only her.

Only her devastating beauty and the terrifying calm that settles inside me as we hold each other's gaze.

My hand tightens just slightly at her waist and her breath hitches. I feel it . . . that pull that's been there since the first time I found her soul in a dream—wild, aching, and brilliant. It coils low in my chest, a feeling that has terrified me yet held me in its rapture for years.

She opens her mouth and a breath escapes.

"Your Highness," Sorryn says smoothly, clearing his throat from the edge of the dance floor.

The spell snaps like brittle glass around us.

Elysia flinches, breath catching as if waking from a place where she never meant to linger. Her hand slips from mine quickly, almost guiltily, before she turns from me without a word.

Maybe this was a mistake.

Sorryn's smile sharpens as she nears, his gaze locked on mine over her shoulder. Triumphant and possessive.

He thinks he's already won her hand, providing this extravagant ball for his hand-picked guests to fawn all over her. Like the previous queen he wooed into his web of lies.

I stay where I am, jaw clenched, spine straight, letting the weight of my stare settle heavily between us. As soon as her hand slips into his, they turn and head back toward the dais, where two thrones await.

The second she settles into the golden monstrosity, when she lifts her gaze across the ballroom, through the glittering crowd and dancing nobles, she finds me.

The hope in her eyes is gone and so is the brief glimpse of her desire.

What's left is blank and distant. A careful emptiness that feels like the mirror of everything I've shown her since she arrived.

She's doing exactly what I told her to do . . . forget me and let go.

So why does it feel like something is being torn from my chest as I watch her slide her hand into Sorryn's without him offering this time.

The music swells and the crowd spins around me. I remain frozen beneath the chandeliers, nothing but a guard at the edge of her court.

Such a pretty little dove, in such an ugly, gilded cage.

CHAPTER TWENTY-THREE

ELYSIA

Sorryn insists on walking me back to my chambers, and I finally relent, if only because my body is too exhausted to argue and my mind too full to think.

The corridor stretches long and gleaming before us, its floors inlaid with silver-veined marble.

Rhune follows a few paces behind, a silent shadow trailing us both. I can feel him there, just at the edge of my senses, the pressure of his presence folding around me like the remnants of a storm.

I take a deep breath and push the sensation away. He's just a bodyguard ensuring my safety.

When I walked away from him after our dance, I told myself that it would be the last time I allowed my mind to be distracted and confused with the ache I feel for him. I made a promise to Lisbeth and all those we'd lost. Matters of the heart have no place in my life now. Not when there is so much on the line.

"You don't need to follow," Sorryn says over his shoulder, not bothering to slow his long strides despite my struggle to keep up. "She's with me."

"I wasn't asking," Rhune replies, his voice low and sharp.

The tension hums louder than our footsteps.

Sorryn says nothing more, but I catch the narrowing of his eyes, the tightening of his jaw. I knew I hadn't imagined the bubbling animosity between the two brothers at the temple, yet I still don't have a grasp of where it stems from.

Rhune stays just steps behind me. Unshaken. Unbothered.

Eventually we come to a stop before my chamber door. I reach for the handle, ready to slip inside and vanish from everyone and

everything. This has been the most agonizing day of my life and all I want is to close my eyes and let reality slip away for a few blissful hours.

Sorryn steps into my space, preventing me from moving forward.

"Today was difficult," he says softly, bringing his large hand up to cup my cheek. "But you carried it with grace. I hope tomorrow is gentler."

He leans in, eyes on mine, and I know what's coming. My stomach tightens and I don't move until the very last second. Then, I turn, offering my cheek.

It should feel flattering. He's a king. Powerful, graceful, and impossibly revered from what I glimpsed at the ball.

I should feel chosen, but as his mouth touches my cheek, my eyes find Rhune.

He's watching.

There's fire there flashing through his expression before he turns away—jaw locked, shoulders coiled. It's gone too quickly to comment on, but not quickly enough to forget.

Why does he insist on saying one thing to me, while lacking the ability to display matching emotions on his face? Everything about him has been a contradiction.

He's told me himself that he isn't an option. He's sworn it with his distance, with his silence, with the way he pulled away when I needed him most.

Yet it's not Sorryn's lips I imagine on my skin. The thought has my lips thinning just as Sorryn pulls back to look down at me.

"Rest well, my Queen," he says.

I nod and let out a breath. "Good night."

He leaves without another word and my shoulders instantly sag. There's an overwhelming pressure to present myself as well as I can around everyone besides the shadow that moves into place next to my door, silent as ever.

I continue to pause in the doorway, hand still on the handle.

After a breath, I lift my eyes to the sharp and beautiful lines of his face, hating the way his beauty continues to steal my breath.

Maybe in time I will stop thinking of him as the protective, nurturing elf from my dreams. The one who broke laws to see me. The one who admitted his fear for me when he couldn't find me at night. The

one who cradled me as my soul cracked open to reveal a new version of myself.

My jaw clenches as I shove that tender moment into the depths of my mind. That isn't the elf in front of me now. Maybe if I finally agree to his demands of not being an option, he will stop making this so confusing.

"You already denied my attempts to make you an option," I say quietly as he blinks. "I'll respect that, but I expect you to respect my decisions moving forward—especially the ones that don't involve you. If you have anything left to say, say it now."

Silence stretches and still he won't even meet my eyes.

I wait, despite knowing I should walk through my door without looking back. I watch for a flicker of emotion. For a falter. For anything.

Maybe I imagine it, but just before I turn the handle, I think I see something slip through the mask—regret, sharp and fleeting.

No. I don't let myself believe in what-ifs or looks that may or may not linger. Not anymore.

I step inside and close the door behind me, instantly sinking against the solid wood for support.

My chambers are still, touched only by moonlight through the windows. I don't bother lighting the lamps, loving the quiet and ethereal moment. It brings a sense of quiet to my mind as I strip the gown from my shoulders and let it fall into a pool of silk at my feet. I remove the crown with steady hands, staring at it in disbelief for a moment as the light gleams off the metal.

This morning I had greeted the day with Thalia's small hand in mine and the desire for us all to survive the day with our minds intact.

I don't stop the tears that fall freely down my cheeks as I lay it on the small pillow atop my vanity and begin to work on removing every pin from my hair.

The silence in the room tightens around me.

I toss the last pin aside and drag my fingers through my hair until it falls loose around my shoulders, wild and tangled. My breath trembles as I stand there, surrounded by an opulence that would take the combined wealth of the eastern lands where I'm from to emulate.

The bedding is silk and the floors gleam to perfection. The windows open to glistening stars and I hate it. I hate every inch of it.

Because Thalia is dead and I'm standing in a palace atop clouds.

Because Lisbeth had to watch me walk away and handle the fallout alone.

Because no matter how refined this room is, no matter how lovely the furnishings or how soft the sheets, nothing can hide the truth that I was handed a crown shaped from suffering and told to smile like it was a blessing.

My throat burns as I force a silky nightgown over my body, hating the way it clings to my skin, ever-present like the duties I can't escape.

The tears don't stop this time, but they're different now. They scald my skin as they fall, and I welcome the heat, the ache, the fury that churns beneath every soft part of me that I've tried to protect.

I turn, pacing the room like a caged animal. My bare feet slap against the stone and fists curl at my sides until my nails dig into the tender flesh of my palms.

They made me watch her die.

They made me kneel in front of corpses and call it destiny.

This unrelenting fury is proof of the stranger that I've become.

I'm not the girl from Edritch anymore. Not the girl who braided her sister's hair. Not someone who felt so weak despite her father calling her brave.

I'm not the woman who wears sorrow like a second skin in silence.

I want to scream and tear this room apart with my hands and make it look as torn as my soul is. To shatter every glass bottle on the vanity and throw the crown out the window.

Yet I can't let it out. It's trapped within me, simmering.

I prowl through the room, chest heaving, like it's a battlefield.

"I didn't ask for this," I whisper as my cheeks flame with heat.

The words echo against the marble. They feel too loud, reverberating back to me.

"I didn't ask to be a chosen. I didn't ask to be a queen. I didn't ask to watch my friends die so I could stand in a room fit for a goddess while the women who bled for this crown rot beneath the soil."

My voice shakes. My legs do too, but I don't stop, needing to get it out.

"I'm tired of pretending this is fine. That I'm fine. I'm tired of swallowing every ache just to be what they expect."

I reach for the edge of the vanity, gripping it so hard I think the wood might crack.

This fury . . . it's not weakness. It's not shameful. It's mine and it's about damn time I let it breathe.

"I will wear this crown," I say through my teeth. "But I will burn down everything that made it."

The last words leave my mouth in a rush, and I don't realize I'm not alone until I feel it.

That unmistakable pull.

I whirl toward the door, breath caught in my throat.

Rhune stands there, silent and unmoving, just within the threshold with the door closed behind him. His expression is unreadable, but I don't miss the way his shoulders rise with each breath or the tightness around his eyes.

"How long have you been standing there?" I ask, voice hoarse.

He doesn't answer, instead choosing silence, his favorite defense since I ascended to his world.

I've bled too much for this crown, cried too many tears into the ground thousands of miles beneath us, and I'm done being met with silence when I deserve truth.

I storm toward him, anger giving my bare feet purpose as I cross the room and stop just a breath from his chest.

"Why are you even here?" I ask with a cold bite to my words. "Standing there like you care about anything I just said. If you're only going to watch me break and say nothing, then get out."

He flinches.

I press forward, shoving my finger into his chest. "You don't get to glare when Sorryn touches me and then pretend you're a statue again the second I try and fight for you. You don't get to do both."

Still, he says nothing and it makes my blood boil.

I hit both of my palms against his chest. Not hard. Just enough to make contact. To feel something solid under my hands instead of the crumbling edge of my restraint.

He grabs my wrists firmly and holds them between us. Our breath comes fast and uneven as we stare at each other, close enough now that I can feel the heat of his body and the trembling of my own hands.

His voice is ragged when he finally speaks.

"You think this is easy for me?" he says. "You think I haven't spent every second of this damn journey fighting the instinct to reach for you?"

His fingers flex around mine, and his gaze drops to the space between us, as if the weight of his own words is too much.

"I don't want to be the King of Nothing, Elysia," he says quietly. "I was born outside both courts. I've never belonged—not to the Dromin, not to the Nithrin, not to anyone."

His voice cracks just barely. "I hate that I've spent my life trying to be enough for people who look at me and only see failure, and now . . . now I'm forcing myself to walk away from the one person who's ever looked at me like maybe I'm worth something."

My heart stutters, but the heat in my veins doesn't die down. It changes, shifting into something far more dangerous.

"I don't want to do this without you," I say, voice breaking. It feels like my soul tears with every word. "You're the only soul atop these clouds I don't fear."

He lifts his eyes to mine, and the longing in them steals the air from my lungs.

"That's interesting," he whispers, "because yours is the only soul I do fear."

I blink.

"I fear the way you make me want to throw my role and responsibilities into the sky. I fear the way I need more of you each time you leave my sight. I fear the way I've not been able to get you out of my mind for years . . ."

His voice lowers further, raw and trembling.

"Well before we ever exchanged words in your first nightmare."

I inhale sharply, but the room feels too small now.

Years?

I thought his visits began just before I left for the selection. I thought he found me then. Not years before. Not when I was still just a girl in the village, plucking berries from bushes and sitting atop a hill longing for something more.

"You've been in my dreams that long?"

He doesn't answer, but he doesn't have to.

His hands lift slowly, gently, to cradle my cheeks. His touch is reverent, like he's afraid I'll vanish if he blinks.

We lean in until our breath mingles. I can feel the promise of it on his lips, feel the war raging in his hands as they tremble against my skin.

We pause and the world holds still.

"We can't," I whisper, voice already breaking as my hands come up to rest atop his. "Can we?"

He doesn't answer. Just stares at me like the question itself is agony.

Then, softly, he says, "I watched you step forward before all those women from your lands. I watched you stand between them and that orb, hoping to stop them from being broken the way the High Priestess meant to break them."

His thumb brushes across the back of my hand, almost absentmindedly. Like he doesn't even realize he's reaching for something he's already told himself he can't have.

"You did it," he murmurs, "because you aren't capable of putting yourself first when it means hurting others."

The words gut me. Not because they're cruel, but because they're true.

My voice is quiet when I say, "You can't put yourself first either."

His jaw clenches.

"For the sake of the courts," I continue, "and the blessings you want the Goddess to bestow. You want one of them to win, so she might bless their lands again, and to do that . . . you walk away from the one thing that makes you feel like you could belong."

He looks at me for a long moment, anguish flickering behind his eyes.

Then he lifts his hand and gently brushes a tear from my cheek.

"Yes," he breathes. "I can't rip that chance away from our people. One court desperately needs it. They've been crumbling from within for too long. The magic isn't flowing the way it should."

I search his face, my breath catching in my throat. "So where does this leave us?"

The question hangs between us, heavy and fragile.

I see his answer in the tight set of his jaw, in the way his eyes drop like he's already mourning a life that he never had the chance to live.

Somehow I want him more for it, not less. Not despite his restraint, but because of it . . . because I understand it now.

I understand what it means to carry an entire realm on your back for the sake of people who will never know the weight of that choice.

I understand what it is to want and to withhold in the same breath.

I understand why we can't.

My feet slowly return to the ground, and I take a step back. Then another. I walk to the bed, feeling like each movement unthreads something inside me.

As I slip beneath the covers and close my eyes, my heart still pounding against my ribs, I whisper into the quiet, "Good night, Rhune."

The door closes softly behind him.

CHAPTER TWENTY-FOUR

ELYSIA

When I open my eyes, the sky outside the windows is streaked with orange and pink, the soft light painting the room in a warm glow. I don't remember falling asleep. Only the pounding of my heart and the ache in my chest from last night.

Once again, I had no dreams or nightmares.

Is it because I don't live amongst humans anymore?

Maybe because I'm the Queen. Perhaps it makes me off-limits.

Enari is already in the room, quiet as always, helping me into a simple silver gown the moment I sit up. She still doesn't speak unless prompted, but when I murmur a soft "Thank you," and add, "I hope your day is kind to you," I catch the faint flicker of surprise in her expression.

Perhaps one of these days she will open up to me.

She hesitates, then nods. "And to you, my Queen."

I follow her into the hallway, the hush of the castle broken only by the distant sounds of waking life. The air is cool, and the faint scent of citrus and smoke lingers, a strange but pleasant mix.

Voices drift from ten feet away, sharp and tense. When I step into their view, I freeze.

Rhune and Maerel stand just ahead, their bodies angled toward each other like twin blades about to clash. Their voices are low, but not low enough.

"I said, leave Zayvin out of it," Maerel hisses.

"You already involved him the moment you—" Rhune cuts off the second his eyes meet mine.

Both of them straighten at once, their expressions smoothing into careful calm.

"My Queen," Maerel says with a tight smile, stepping back from Rhune as if her proximity to him had been accidental.

Does she think I'm daft?

"Good morning," I offer, my tone cool, but my curiosity sparking.

Why would Sorryn's most trusted advisor be whispering about the Nithrin King?

Rhune falls into step behind me without a word. No tension touches his face now, but I can feel it rippling beneath his calm exterior. Whatever their conversation had been about is far from over, it seems.

Maerel gestures for me to follow her down a branching corridor I haven't explored yet. "There's much to prepare you for," she says. "Before a queen receives the Goddess's blessing when she chooses her king, it is common practice to determine if she carries the seed of magic within her. Many before you have."

No pressure or anything.

I glance over my shoulder, eyes briefly catching Rhune's. He doesn't speak, but I don't miss the look he gives Maerel, sharp and measured. Is it because he can't speak of previous queens?

"Sorryn thought it best to begin familiarizing you early. The blessing can be . . ." she trails off, "*overwhelming* for those unprepared."

My brow knits at the specific choice of wording and hesitancy.

"That's kind of him," I hedge and silence descends over our small group as we make our way through the castle.

Sorryn's gestures so far have been gracious, but I still feel like a bird in a cage when I'm near him.

I keep my eyes low as we walk, uncomfortable with the number of elves who stare at us as we go, whispering amongst themselves. I'm not sure I'll ever adjust to having such a focus on me.

The training wing is unlike anything I've seen within the castle. It's spacious and warm, with slanted light pouring through clear skylights. Alcoves line the vast room, each one glowing with faint magical ambiance.

Waiting near the center of the room stands a Dromin cloaked in layered violet robes trimmed with gold threads. Her hair, long and white as frost, is braided down her back with rings of gold woven in.

She takes my breath away with her beauty, but it's her inviting hazel eyes that draw me in the most.

"This is Serenath," Maerel says. "She will assess your potential, and if any affinity presents itself, begin your training. You are in excellent hands. She has worked with more elves than any other alive."

Serenath turns to me and smiles. "Welcome, my Queen. I've been expecting you."

Her voice is soft but carries the weight of power behind it.

Maerel nods to me once, then to Serenath, before exiting the chamber without another word. It doesn't escape me that she ignores Rhune completely.

When the doors seal behind us, a calm hush falls over the room.

"You're nervous," Serenath observes gently, the fine lines around the edges of her eyes crinkling. It's the only trace of her age that I can find, and I can't help but wonder how long she's been alive—what she's seen and the stories she could tell.

"Shouldn't I be? This moment feels fairly important," I reply, surprised by the steadiness in my own voice, belying the comforting energy she exudes.

She chuckles and pats my shoulder. "A queen with caution is a good thing. Come, walk with me."

She leads me past several open archways. Each alcove pulses with distinct magical energy, but I'm at a loss for what each represents. I see mirrors rimmed in runes, trees growing from stone, and shallow pools with smoke curling over the surface instead of water.

"This is where our magical users come to train. Each affinity is unique, but all are sacred gifts from the Goddess."

She brings me to a smaller door tucked at the back of the hall and opens it without hesitation.

Inside, the chamber is circular and dim, the walls carved with the same face of the Goddess repeated over and over. Identical and unblinking.

The sheer number of them makes my skin crawl. No matter where I turn, I feel her eyes following me.

"She sees all," Serenath murmurs, stepping inside behind me. "But she does not judge. Not here."

In the center of the room stands a raised dais, and at its heart, a flame glowing purple, with threads of silver winding through it like veins of starlight.

"This is the Calling Flame. If you have an affinity, it will respond in kind."

She walks to the edge of the platform and turns to face me. "Come, my Queen. Let the flame meet you. It will not hurt you."

I hesitate. Not from fear, exactly, but from the weight of this moment.

I've had countless dreams, both while awake and asleep, as I imagined the mysterious and magical world of the elves living in the clouds above us. Never did I have an image of myself with . . . magic.

Is it possible?

The flame stirs as I approach, growing larger. I raise my hand slowly, hovering it just above the flickering energy.

The purple energy coils upward, reaching for me, and for a moment, it's like the silver threads flare brightly. It's almost like the beat of a heart and I find myself drawn to it, unable to look away as it pulsates over and over.

Finally the flame shifts beneath my palm. Shapes form inside it—a fox with many tails, a bird made of ash, a coiling serpent. One by one, they change, morphing and growing in darkness.

Then it appears.

A shadowed beast. Sleek and powerful. Its silver eyes gleam through the fire, familiar in a way that makes my breath catch.

The flame flares once more, until my entire hand is engulfed. I rip it out as a searing pain burns along my skin. As soon as I break contact, the beast is gone.

A tremble moves through me and I stagger back a step, heart pounding.

Serenath steadies me and I look at her with wide eyes, hoping she understands what just happened.

The warmth is gone from her expression, replaced by caution. I can feel it vibrating off her, the way her fingers tremble just slightly against my skin.

"You saw it?" I whisper, voice shaking as I continue. "You . . . you felt its power?"

Her hazel eyes are fixed on the flame, which has quieted again to a slow, natural flicker. "Yes," she breathes. "Goddess above . . . yes."

There's no reverence in her voice, only fear.

Before I can say another word, Serenath turns to the door. "Summon him," she commands, her voice as sharp as a blade. "Bring Rhune inside. Now."

My breath catches. "Why?"

She doesn't answer me. She's already moving, muttering to herself in a language I don't know. She glances at the Goddess's carved faces as though expecting one of them to open its mouth and speak.

The door opens behind me and Rhune steps in, his shoulders tense, his eyes locked onto mine.

"I was just about to come get you," I breathe out. "Serenath wants you here."

"What happened?" His voice is low and guarded as his eyes do a sweep over my body, seeming to assess for damage. "I felt . . . I don't even know how to explain what I just felt."

Serenath doesn't hesitate. She points to the flame, which now pulses faintly violet-blue at its base.

"It stirred within the flames," she says, voice hoarse. "It's . . . awake."

Rhune goes completely still. His eyes snap to the flame, then to me, then back to Serenath.

"That's not possible."

"It shouldn't be," she replies. "Not after what happened at the end of the Blood War. Not after it was put to sleep with her death."

Panic curls inside me like smoke, suffocating me from the inside out.

"What was it?" I ask. "What did you see?"

Neither of them answers.

"Tell me," I snap, louder now, frustrated at feeling left in the dark. "Why is this so bad?"

Rhune inhales like someone bracing for impact, his wide chest expanding until he lets out a controlled breath.

"There was a creature long ago during the Blood War," he says carefully. "Born of nightmares and blood magic. They say it was harnessed by the right hand of our greatest enemy during the Blood War. She was a Nithrin who defected and swore fealty to the Dark God, yet she wasn't twisted into Valgys like all the other elves that followed to his side."

Serenath's voice is quiet now, almost reverent again, but with no comfort behind it. "The elves called the creature *Vayrith*—the harbinger of death. It obeyed no master but the one who awakened it. It swept through the lands, killing humans and elves alike. The texts say that its fire was able to break through all magic, completely impervious to it. When its master was killed, Vayrith was never seen again."

"It just . . ." I swallow hard. "Stirred. Because of me?"

They both look at me and suddenly chills cover my body from head to toe.

"I didn't do anything," I rebut, feeling as if I have to defend this connection to Vayrith that I didn't ask for. "I just stood there and touched the flame as instructed. Can't we just forget it ever happened?"

My tone has descended to a hysterical plea. "Please. We don't even know if anything will happen."

"You're human," Rhune finally answers, his expression pinched with deep thought. "You weren't raised on these stories from our history. You don't know what this means to our people."

"I'm standing right here," I snap, the fear shifting to anger. "So tell me! What does it mean?"

Serenath's expression softens, but the urgency doesn't leave her eyes. "It means no one can know outside of the three of us."

She looks to Rhune. "If word gets out, if anyone learns that Vayrith stirred in her presence, some will want to use her to awaken it fully. Others will want her dead before it ever opens its eyes."

The floor feels like it tilts beneath me and I stagger toward the wall with a hand up, trying to find my balance.

I always knew there would be dangers when ascending to the world of elves, but never could I have prepared for *this*.

"I didn't ask for this," I say, the words barely more than a breath. The tips of my fingers scratch against the stone carvings of the Goddess.

"I know," Serenath replies soothingly. "That's why we will protect you, but you must understand, Elysia, this can never be spoken of outside this room."

Rhune nods once. "Agreed."

Serenath exhales and pulls her shoulders back and glances at Rhune. "We need to take her to the library. If she's to carry the connection to this creature, she needs to understand what truly happened during the Blood War."

"What if I can't stop it from waking?" I ask in a soft voice, feeling a pit of despair open in my stomach.

Serenath meets my gaze, unblinking. "Then the Blood War won't remain a distant piece of history."

CHAPTER TWENTY-FIVE

ELYSIA

Golden veins run through the polished white stone of the corridor, each one softly glowing as we pass on the way to the library. The air here feels different, still and reverent, as though the walls themselves are holding their breath.

At the end of the hall stands a massive set of arched double doors, taller than any I've seen in the castle. They're smooth, seamless, and etched with glowing glyphs in fluid golden script. Each one pulses faintly, alive with magic.

I stop just short of them, staring at them in confusion. "Who can even open these doors?"

Serenath steps beside me, her expression unreadable. "The doors open on their own for those the glyphs are made to recognize. Royalty, instructors, the sacred library staff." She lifts a hand and presses it against the nearest glyph. It brightens in response. "No one enters unless permitted by the magic itself."

The doors part without touch as she said they would, gliding open with a low, resonant hum. The sound sinks into my bones, as though the library has acknowledged me.

I step inside and my breath catches.

The space opens like a dream I'm experiencing while awake.

The main chamber stretches both upward and downward, spiraling in slow, perfect circles with endless stairs. Levels upon levels of white stone balconies curve around the massive interior, each one lined with towering shelves that rise to impossible heights. Gilded archways link one platform to the next, their gold trim glowing faintly beneath floating spheres of light.

My eyes trace the platforms connecting to different levels, jaw slightly agape as they rotate and change course. "It's a shame," I say softly, "that not everyone can see this. All this beauty and knowledge is locked behind those doors."

Serenath turns toward me with a faint smile that doesn't quite reach her eyes. "Spoken by someone who wouldn't weaponize the words that are housed here. Yet I find the most dangerous things in this realm are not blades, my Queen, they are ideas. Notions yet to come to fruition, or those that did and have proven catastrophic. I always say that we're only a step away from collapse if one soul discovers the ideal path to do so."

I'm not sure I agree, but as I'm about to voice it, she turns and whispers under her breath.

I couldn't have heard her correctly, because it sounded a lot like, "Not that that would be a bad idea at this point."

A breath falls from me and I shake my head, returning my focus to taking in the exquisite library.

Dozens of elven librarians move along the upper platforms, but none of them walk. Some hover just above the floor, their robes billowing gently as they drift. Others remain perfectly still, one arm outstretched as books slide from distant shelves into waiting hands. Scrolls and tomes float in midair, responding to silent gestures. A collection of six thick volumes lifts into the air and spirals downward in perfect formation before settling into a librarian's arms.

None of it is loud. None of it chaotic. It's magic as I always pictured it to be: fluid, serene, and impossibly enchanting.

I can't stop staring as a soft smile tugs at the corners of my lips.

This is the first time I've seen magic like this. It's not twisted with malice and it's not a glowing orb used to decide who lives and who breaks.

This is a wonder.

"It's strange," I say quietly, turning toward Serenath. "The only elven magic I've seen before this was . . . the High Priestess. The orb. That kind of power . . . it scared me. But this is beautiful."

Her eyes soften as her lips thin. "It should scare you. That magic was meant to judge. This," she sweeps her hand out toward the floating lights and floating texts, "was meant to preserve. There is a mixture of those with telekinesis and those with air magic here. They work together to air out and protect the knowledge here."

For a breath, I forget the eyes that stirred in the flame.

For a breath, I let myself feel only this wonder and excitement.

It's exactly the weightless and exhilarating feeling I imagined when I sat atop the hill with Pat and dreamed of this magical world.

We walk across a curved bridge toward a private alcove at the far end. As we pass, I reach out and graze my fingers along the rail. Gold inlays warm beneath my touch and I smile at it, as if the library itself is greeting me.

"This way," Serenath says gently, pulling my focus back.

She leads us to a curtained archway etched in glyphs, their glow dimmer, almost dusted with time. This part of the library feels different as we enter.

"The knowledge you need," she says, seeming to read my thoughts, "isn't public. It's buried where only a few know to look."

I nod, forcing myself to take one last glance at the magic dancing through the air behind us before Rhune pulls the curtain shut.

The awe hasn't left me as we continue forward, but the wonder no longer floats alone within me.

Fear of what occurred with the flame returns as I'm faced with reality again.

What might be waking because of me.

The air here carries a weight to it, like it doesn't circulate with movement often. Dust motes drift in the beams of filtered light spilling from the ceiling above.

Shelves line the back wall, carved directly into the white stone. Their spines are older here, worn and cracked. Some with bindings ripping at the edges.

Serenath walks to the center of the room and exhales. "Time to get to work. Rhune, if you will."

Before I can even process her words, Serenath begins pointing to titles in a language I don't recognize. Shadows spill from Rhune's fingertips like ink poured into water. They slither across the floor and rise with fluid grace, curling up the sides of the shelves until they find what they seek. Volume after volume slips from its place and lifts into the air, carried by ribbons of darkness that move with silent precision.

They fetch what she asks for without hesitation, and I can't stop staring. This is the power that concealed him in my dreams. The shadows that moved around him, cloaked him, held me back from seeing

too much . . . They weren't a coincidence. They weren't tricks of the mind.

They were his.

Nothing about this feels like the weak powers the High Priestess said he possesses.

I look at Rhune now, watching the shadows swirl at his feet, curling up his arms like loyal serpents. Somehow seeing the power used here makes it easier to reconcile the version of him I know here with the one from my sleeping mind.

She gives a satisfied nod and steps toward the dusty table where he directed all of her selected texts before muttering, "I trust you to shield us all, moving forward. We cannot be heard."

There's something in the way she says it, as if she knows he can make that happen. There's an obvious trust and understanding between the two, devoid of the half-truths it seems others know.

Rhune nods once and closes his eyes, and immediately the space around us shifts. I expect the shadows to shield us, but they disappear completely.

Whatever he is doing now is subtle at first, like a flicker in the air and a faint vibration beneath my feet. Then the light from the ceiling begins to pull inward. It collects into a dome overhead, a shimmering veil of reflective light that ripples like the surface of a pond. It curves downward until it seals around the edge of the alcove, dimming the world beyond.

Like the barrier that the High Priestess controlled.

A chill skates down my spine and I take a half step back.

The dome hums around us, curved in a way that feels too much like a cage with memories. The shimmer of light overhead pulses, steady and unrelenting, and I can feel something unraveling inside me.

It's too familiar.

The containment. The quiet. The forced stillness.

My chest tightens as the air thins around me. I know it's magic and know it's meant to protect us in this instance, but it presses in like the barrier that sealed us in the grove, cutting us off from the world and locking us in with death.

My breathing falters and my vision dims at the edges. Panic rises within my throat, gripping it tightly.

I press a hand to my chest, willing my heart to slow, but it only beats faster, echoing the rhythm I felt back then. The screaming, the searing light of the orb, the way my world shattered when I saw Thalia on the ground.

My legs threaten to give and I fold in on myself as the floor rushes up to greet me, trying to retreat from the memories flooding me.

Then a warm hand cups my cheek, followed by another.

"Elysia," Rhune says, his voice calming as it reaches the storm within my mind. "Breathe. Just look at me."

I don't know when he crossed the space between us. I only know that when I lift my gaze, he's already there kneeling in front of me, close enough to block out the light and the library and the memories pressing down on me.

"Stay with me," he says, softer now, thumb brushing beneath my eye, drawing my attention to the wetness gathering against my skin. "You're safe. You're with me. Nothing is going to touch you here, Little Dove. Breathe."

I try to speak, but my throat won't cooperate. Instead, I follow the command in his voice and begin to breathe again.

In. Out. In again.

My heartbeat slows, if only slightly.

"I know it's not the same," I whisper, "but it felt like the selection happening all over again."

His fingers tighten gently against my face, grounding me. "I should've warned you. I didn't think . . ."

He trails off, jaw working, guilt flickering behind his eyes.

The shimmer of the barrier reflects in his gaze, catching like a mirror. There's so much weight in his stillness, so much restraint in the way he doesn't move, like he's terrified to be anything but my anchor at this moment.

"I trust you," I murmur, the truth rising with the steadiness that his presence brings me.

At that, he closes his eyes for the briefest moment, and when they open again, the guilt haunting them has dulled. There is a heaviness in his silence, something fiercely protective.

"I won't break your trust," he says at last, voice low and sure, "even if I never get to keep you."

The words settle in my chest like a vow as his fingers tremble slightly against my cheeks.

Though the barrier still surrounds us, for the first time since stepping into this space, I don't feel trapped. I feel seen, and if only for this moment, safe.

Rhune doesn't move his hands from my face, and I don't ask him to.

The silence between us has settled into something softer. Not peace exactly, but stillness . . . the kind that follows a storm.

I swallow once, trying to find the right words to voice the question that's lingered in my mind since the dome began to build around us.

"Do you have the same power as she does?" I ask hesitantly, fearing his answer. "The High Priestess?"

His hands drop slowly from my cheeks, though he remains close. At the mention of the Priestess, his jaw clenches.

"No," he says, and his voice is rougher now. "Not even close."

I hesitate. "But the light . . . the barrier you just formed. It looked like hers. It felt like it."

Rhune shakes his head and sighs heavily. "The High Priestess doesn't wield that kind of power on her own. She has the ability to craft enchanted objects—rings, cuffs, charms—each one imbued with a specific magical energy. She drains them when she uses them, making it appear like she has multiple affinities."

He looks me straight in the eye. "But once each object is drained, she has no power left."

That revelation stills the bubbling fear I have of her inside me.

"She's not . . ." I pause, voice quieter. "She's not as powerful as she seems."

"No," he confirms. "But she's smart enough to make you believe she is."

It's one of the most reassuring things I've heard since ascending to this world.

Now I know the Priestess has limits.

Rhune shifts then, just slightly. "I'm the only one alive who can channel both without using an enchanted object. Sorryn wields the same light and Zayvin wields the same shadows, but I'm just as strong as them in their respective powers. Please do not share that, as it's a closely guarded secret only a handful know."

I nod and tuck that important information away.

The thought of Sorryn having that power aligns completely with the trapped sensation he already makes me feel.

His hand brushes mine as he shifts from his knees to his feet and the contact is so fleeting I might have imagined it if not for the tingles it leaves behind.

The sound of a tome slamming against the stone table cuts through the space like a crack of lightning.

We both jump and focus on where the sound came from.

Serenath stands beside the stack of texts, her expression neutral, though the speed of her hand slamming that volume shut says everything.

"I assumed," she says, voice light but unmistakably pointed, "you came here to flirt with ancient history, not each other."

My cheeks flare with heat as I look down.

Rhune exhales a quiet breath beside me, something between a scoff and a sigh. "We're ready."

He offers me a hand and Serenath raises a brow at me before opening the top tome, her fingers slow and deliberate.

"Good," she says. "Because the dead don't like to be kept waiting."

CHAPTER TWENTY-SIX

ELYSIA

The tome before us is thick, its blackened cover faded with age and wrapped in a violet ribbon that crumbles slightly as Serenath unties it. My heart aches as I think of Penelope's ribbon. I thought about twining it into my hair today, but an unease in my gut told me to keep it safely tucked away in my room where it can't be lost.

The spine of the tome groans in protest as Serenath opens it, revealing delicate parchment edged in gold, its ink handwritten in looping strokes. No one speaks as she turns the first page and suddenly the air feels even more stifling as I think about this being a direct glimpse into a dark past I know very little about.

She traces the first passage with her fingertip, then gestures toward the detailed illustration that blooms across the left side of the page. The image is drawn in swirling black and gold lines. There are two elves, one of the blue-skinned Dromin and one of the purple-skinned Nithrin, their hands clasped and their foreheads touching. Glyphs wind around them, glowing faintly against the aged page.

She looks up at me and our eyes meet. "This is where it all began. Unified between both dreams and nightmares."

"There weren't always two separate courts?" I ask quietly, even though the answer is obvious in the reverence of the image.

"No." Serenath speaks softly, like she's sorrowful about what has been lost. "The Dromin and the Nithrin lived as one . . . complements to each other. Dream and nightmare. Light and dark. Our magic flourished when they moved in balance together."

She turns the page and another illustration is revealed, this time a spiraling tree with two roots entwined beneath the surface, both dark

and light. My eyes widen as I recognize the tree I saw yesterday. It's the one the kings pressed their blood into for their vows.

"Soulmates between the two types of magic weren't rare," she continues. "They were expected. The joining of opposites didn't dilute our magic. It strengthened it."

I glance at Rhune, whose gaze is focused on the open book. His expression is unreadable, but there's a tension in his jaw. Like this is a truth he's known for a long time, yet it still hurts to hear.

Serenath's fingers rest on a line of text, and she recites it in a murmur, "When shadow meets light in truth, eternity blooms."

I let out a breath.

"As fewer soulmates appeared, something shifted in the flow of magic. Where once it came freely, it began to require intervention. The Goddess's blessing became necessary to maintain longevity and to sustain power."

"So the human queen choosing a king . . . that's what replaces the balance?" I ask, my thoughts muddied as I try to make sense of how it all fits together.

"No," Rhune says quietly. "It's a placeholder. A compromise."

His voice startles me. It's the first time he's spoken since the tome was opened, and his words settle heavy in the space between us.

"If the courts were whole again," he continues, "they wouldn't need the blessing. They wouldn't need the Queen."

I look at him fully, and he meets my gaze for a long, unblinking moment.

It's not an accusation. It's a truth . . . one that changes everything.

Serenath turns the page again, and the gentle grace of the earlier images vanishes.

This illustration is harsher, drawn in jagged lines. Dark shapes ripple across the page, tangled in thorny glyphs. Where the first pages glowed with harmony, this one bleeds with dissonance. A city in flames. A figure shrouded in shadows, but I recognize the heads snapped at unnatural angles, and their eight glowing eyes, before she says the words.

"The Valgys," Serenath says, her voice steadier now, almost detached as she recites the history. "An army of corrupted elves for the Dark God—the Goddess's brother. He fed on chaos, where she feeds on peace."

I stare at the image and murmur, "We're told of the Valgys, where I'm from. They're told as bedtime stories meant to scare children into

being good, but we learned that they were once real and not seen since the end of the Blood War."

"They were once like us," she continues with a nod. "But their bodies twisted to accommodate the power they took in. Their magic fractured and their souls cracked."

Rhune's arms are crossed now and his expression is as rigid as the castle's stone walls.

"The elves at the time of the war started fighting side by side to stop the Dark God's rise, but in war, division began to fester, which started to tear the Dromin and Nithrin apart."

She flips to the next page. "The humans played a part in this."

My spine straightens at that. We were never told of these details.

"They were allies," Serenath clarifies quickly as she sees my shock. "At least to the Nithrin, but to the Dromin, particularly those who were unmated and fighting on the front lines—humans were a means to an end."

I feel Rhune shift beside me.

"They began to overfeed," she continues. "To draw more and more dreams, hoping to bolster their magic for battle, not having the ever-flowing source like their soulmates did."

A sick feeling settles in my gut. "What happened to the humans?"

"Some recovered," Serenath answers with a grim set to her thin lips. "But others died from it, being kept in a constant state of dreaming."

I close my eyes for a moment, trying not to imagine rows of sleeping bodies, never stirring.

"What about the Nithrin?" I ask.

"They refused," she says simply. "They would not treat humans as an infinite resource. They considered them brothers-in-arms who aided in replenishing magic in a consenting manner."

"And that's what split the elves?" I ask in a hushed whisper.

She nods once. "That was the beginning of the fracture. Nithrin and Dromin fought side by side until the final day of the war, but afterward, the majority could no longer look each other in the eye. Mates were torn apart in the divide."

Rhune's jaw tightens at the same time my heart squeezes.

Serenath looks down at the book. "They signed a treaty that day. Divided our world into two courts and then split the humans' territory evenly between them. Dromin to the east. Nithrin to the west."

Serenath doesn't turn the page this time; instead she grabs a slip of parchment tucked carefully between its binding and the back cover. It's yellow and the corners are curled with age.

"This isn't part of the formal archive and not many know of its existence," she explains, laying the scroll on the table between us. "It was written by a scribe who witnessed firsthand the Goddess's decree after the end of the war. One of the few accounts believed to be unaltered."

My heart thuds at that and I begin to understand her notion that ideas and words kept here within the library are dangerous.

She smooths the parchment open, and I lean closer as she reads the scrawled ink aloud.

"If unity is no longer chosen, it will be forced. One queen. One bond. One blessing. So shall the cycle repeat until the realm remembers what it lost."

The words settle over the room.

"That's what all of this is for?" I ask slowly. "The selection. The blessing. The crown?"

Serenath nods. "It was never about the elevation of humans. The human queen's purpose isn't to rule. It's to act as a bridge between what's been broken."

"So I'm not a symbol of peace." My voice is quieter now. "I'm a punishment for the courts."

"No," Rhune interjects before Serenath can respond. "You're a chance."

I look at him and he holds my gaze as he continues. "The blessing isn't a reward. It's a leash. One designed to keep both courts tethered to a choice they were too proud to make."

"To each other," I say.

Rhune nods once.

"Without the Queen choosing," Serenath adds, "neither side receives the magic they've come to depend on. The blessing sustains their lifespan. It's conditional on the human queen's choice because the Goddess hoped it would make them remember how to stand together, in order to not need it."

"And if they don't?" I ask.

"We remain fractured and weaker the longer each court goes without her blessing. Since the creation of the two courts and this nuanced relationship with a human queen, there has somehow been a natural

balance, each queen alternating between the courts for her choice of king to bind herself to. Until recently. The last queen who passed broke the cycle. It was naturally supposed to be the Nithrin's turn, but she chose Sorryn."

The silence that follows is deeper than any I've known.

This has to be why the High Priestess forbade the kings, with their vow, from talking about the past queens.

I look down at the scroll, at the ancient lines penned by a hand that likely turned to dust long ago.

I stare at it, but the words blur.

One queen. One bond. One blessing.

A cycle. A condition. A correction for a choice that was never mine.

I sink back into a chair at the end of the table, the cushion offering no comfort.

This entire time, I thought the crown was a symbol of elevation. Of ascension. I thought being chosen meant something about who I was . . . my strength and my worth. But now, I see it for what it truly is: I'm a patch to cover a tear the elves refuse to mend.

"I was never meant to rule," I murmur, tucking a strand of hair behind my ear.

Rhune looks at me but says nothing.

Serenath closes the scroll and places a gentle hand over it, as if to tuck the words back into sleep. "You are meant to remind them," she says softly. "To remind us all."

My hands curl slightly in my lap. If I'm meant to be a reminder, then maybe I can be more than that too. Not just a symbol. Not just a patch. Maybe I can be the one who tears open the seams wide enough to force something new.

But I don't say that aloud . . . not yet.

Serenath reaches for another book, this one smaller, bound in cracked white leather with silver-edged pages. Its cover bears the mark of the Sacrum mountain range: two jagged lines split down the center by a single thread of gold.

Rhune steps closer, his gaze narrowing as a map unfolds across the inner page. It shows the Vothia Empire not as it is now, but as a land I don't recognize. A single, unbroken territory.

"These mountains," Serenath begins, her finger tracing the line where they are now, "were not always here."

I blink in surprise. "What do you mean?"

"They were raised," she explains. "Not by time or weather, but by choice. By force."

She flips to the next page, revealing an old etching.

"The final stand of the Blood War happened there on the ground," she explains. "The remnants of the Valgys were too many to destroy outright with Vayrith ripping through our magic. The lands were too saturated with the Dark God's magic. So the Dromin and Nithrin worked together to carve a prison from the ground itself."

She runs her palm across the page.

"It was one of the last acts of unity between our people, and one of the most powerful. They pulled the ground up around the valley, sealed the Valgys beneath it, and locked the soil with divine glyphs."

"The Goddess helped," Rhune adds, his voice low. "Or so the unofficial records say. She laced the seal with her power, so no magic, not even our own, could stir what slept below."

A chill whispers over my skin.

"What if something does stir?" I ask, the words leaving me before I can stop them.

Serenath pauses, but Rhune doesn't.

"Then we're not dealing with just Vayrith," he says.

My breath catches.

"The mountains were meant to divide the empire," Serenath says, "but its true purpose was always to bury the past. To keep what was made in darkness from rising again."

Serenath closes the tome with a soft snap, her fingers lingering over the cover.

When she speaks again, her voice has changed, this time quiet and laced with sorrow. "There's one more story you need to hear, with your connection to Vayrith."

She doesn't reach for a book this time. Just another slip of parchment, so thin it looks like it could tear from breathing on it. She places it on the table like it's something sacred.

"This isn't written in the official histories either, but those who were there, my own teachers who survived the Blood War, passed it down."

She unfolds the page. No drawings, no glyphs. Just words.

"There was a woman," she begins, "once revered among our people. A Nithrin with exceptional magical talent. She was gifted in illusion."

My stomach twists.

"She pledged herself to the Dark God near the war's end," Serenath continues. "No one knows why. Some say she believed she could control his power. Others say he twisted her from within."

She looks up at me. "She is the one who summoned Vayrith."

The words sit like lead sinking in my chest.

"The Dark God blessed her with blood magic for her commitment to him. She used this to bring her illusions to life. Bound the creature to her soul. As we said earlier, it answered only to her, and through her, it destroyed thousands."

She pauses.

"This elf . . . before the war, she had a Dromin mate."

I inhale sharply.

How could she bring destruction to her people, her family and friends, but also her soulmate?

"They were bonded before her defection. He refused to follow her. When no one else could stop her, when all other attempts to kill her failed, he was the only one who could get close."

Serenath's gaze drops to the final line on the parchment, and when she speaks, her voice is barely above a whisper.

"He used her weakness for him to end the war. He killed her and with her death, Vayrith disappeared."

A silence settles over the alcove.

My thoughts drift, not to the Nithrin woman, or the war, but to the eyes in the flame. To the way they stirred at my presence.

"Serenath?" I ask quietly, waiting for her hum of acknowledgment before continuing. "If the flame is to show what magical affinity I could have once I'm blessed, does that mean I have blood magic or illusion magic?"

She lets out a heavy breath before splaying her hands on the table. "That is a question I do not have the answer to. I could guess, but it would be mere conjecture."

My thoughts twist toward a different path as my gut churns. "Then tell me this . . . if I were to die and not be blessed by the Goddess, would that prevent Vayrith from rising?"

CHAPTER TWENTY-SEVEN

RHUNE

It starts with a ripple.

Not in the air, but in me. The kind of shift I've come to know by instinct—the drag of magic brushing against me, too polished and invasive.

Sorryn.

His power reaches me before he does, like it's announcing his arrival, demanding surrender in its presence.

I don't wait for Serenath's command, knowing this is far too big a display of my powers for him to see. My shadows uncoil before she even turns to me with wide eyes, clearly noticing the tremble in our protective barrier.

She trained all of us and is well adept at sensing our powers.

"Replace them all," she says sharply, but I'm already in motion.

My shadows pour from beneath my boots, cold and fast, wrapping around the forbidden texts and sweeping them from the table. They slither up the shelves, repositioning themselves where dust still clings.

Serenath's face pales as she reaches for a new set of books, whispering titles under her breath for me to pull simultaneously. I mirror her urgency, summoning the texts that are basic and boring enough to make Sorryn yawn, despite being in this restricted area.

She slides one toward the center of the table. "Surface theory. Passive affinities. Nothing volatile."

I nod, sending a final thread of shadow up to one of the tomes that slanted slightly on the top shelf, righting it to match the others.

All along Elysia stayed seated in the chair, mouth agape as she watched my shadows work. For once she didn't demand to know what

was going on, simply staring with curiosity and restraint that felt a lot like . . . trust.

The dome trembles again.

He's close now.

I close my eyes and collapse the light barrier, forcing it to retreat into nothing but dust. The second it fades, I slide into the shadows at the edge of the alcove, where I can watch without being the centerpiece of the room.

The curtain parts and there he is.

Sorryn steps into the alcove like a cat that has trapped mice he's been hunting. Light clings to his frame in a way that makes lesser people mistake him for something pure.

I know better.

His gaze sweeps the room once before it lands on Elysia, and he smiles.

It's not friendly or warm, if you truly know him. It's a smile that establishes his power over the room—that he's in control.

"Well," he says, voice smooth and sharp all at once as his gaze slithers over to me. "Quite the little hideout. Tell me, Rhune, what is the reason the Queen and her instructor are hiding away back here?"

I don't answer. My jaw stays clenched, the bite of my molars grounding me more than anything else in this room.

Anything I say will provoke him . . . we both know it.

So, I remain silent and watch, careful to keep my gaze off of Elysia.

Serenath doesn't blink, intervening smoothly. "For the Queen's safety," she replies coolly. "I've found the library less private than one might expect these days. I fear the workers may be too interested in the new queen."

A lie. Polished, perfect, and close enough to the truth to pass. Everyone is interested in the new queen. They all want a glimpse and a moment to know her.

Sorryn steps forward, slow and calculated. His magic brushes mine in challenge. I keep my shadows tight, coiled behind my spine. This isn't the time to display my strength to him. I've played weak for far too long in front of him to ruin my facade now.

He glances at the tomes on the table, fingertips grazing the nearest cover.

"Surface theory," he muses. "Harmless. Dull. Not the kind of thing that typically requires secrecy."

He looks at Serenath again. "Unless there's more to this than you're letting on."

Her expression doesn't change. "Only if you think your queen's safety and privacy aren't worth the extra caution."

A beat of silence follows, and just like that, she flips it back on him.

I almost smirk.

Sorryn doesn't flinch, but I see it, the smallest crack in his composure. He hates being challenged. Especially by women who are smarter and unimpressed by him.

His eyes flick to Elysia and that's when she moves.

I watch her posture soften as she steps around the table with an elegance that doesn't come from fear, but from confidence. Very quickly my little dove is beginning to blossom into the queen we need her to be. One who reads situations for what they truly are.

I know her strategy before she even speaks. She's going to play him and get him off of our trail.

As much as the thought makes me want to wrap my shadows around her to keep him away, I swallow my possessive urge. This is the best play for the situation.

Her hand lifts gently, trailing along his forearm as she meets his eyes. "You came all this way to check on me?"

My breath catches and it shouldn't.

Sorryn straightens, smile blooming into something smug and shining. "Of course I did. It's only right that I make time for my queen."

She smiles. It's perfect and measured.

She leans just a little closer, looking up at him beneath her lashes. "Do you have time to stay with me for a while or do you need to get back? I'd like to know more about the court . . . and you."

My hands curl into fists where they're hidden behind my back.

The flare in his expression is too bright to be anything but victorious. "Of course I have time for you."

He turns with her, already steering them toward the exit like he owns her. He pauses just before the curtain and tosses a look back at me, thin-lipped and taunting.

"Rhune," he says, "take the rest of the day off, won't you? No need to stalk the halls like a shadow with nothing better to do. You may join us at dinner to resume your post if you must."

I say nothing. I don't nod. I don't blink.

The hatred burning beneath my skin doesn't have a name right now. The way he looked at her and claimed her in front of me like she was already his.

Elysia's eyes find mine and it's like I sense her internal plea to take a breath. To trust her. It soothes the rippling anger undulating in waves within me.

Finally Sorryn's eyes melt away from me, abandoning his obvious quest to get a rise out of me.

My shadow is already slithering beneath her hem, curling quietly and invisibly beneath her steps. I will know if she's in danger.

The moment they vanish beyond the curtain, it's like the room itself exhales.

I stay frozen in the corner, eyes on the spot where they stood.

Serenath lets out a slow, shaking breath and lowers herself into the chair Elysia had occupied. Her composure fractures just slightly, but that's all it takes for the weight of what just occurred to truly settle in.

"That," she says, smoothing the front of her robes, "was far too close."

He wants her badly as it is, I think bitterly, *but if he knew . . .*

"I fear that if he had even a whisper of the power she may be able to wield," I murmur as a shudder rolls through my body, "that he wouldn't give her a choice of which king she binds herself to."

Serenath's fingers curl tightly against the table's edge. "He'd take that choice away the moment it no longer swung in his favor. While what occurred with the last queen is still hearsay . . . we must continue to treat the situation with unwavering faith that he has done such heinous things. We cannot falter."

The words sit between us, heavy and unspoken for too long.

Then she lifts her eyes, and this time there's something colder there . . . deeper than the fear of a manipulative king.

"Rhune," she says slowly, "Sorryn will be the least of our concerns if Vayrith is truly stirring."

I walk toward her, constructing another dome around us to speak freely.

She continues, voice low but firm. "We know blood magic is only given by the Dark God. How could Vayrith stir already if Elysia has no magic yet? Has his reach already extended to her somehow?"

I look down at my hands swirling with magic I swore never to wield in pride. Yet right now, all I want is to use it to shield her from every damned god and king who sees her as a means to their end.

"I don't have those answers," I say, "but we need to warn Zayvin."

She nods once. "You'll need to leave while he's occupied with Elysia. You know he watches your steps in this court. No one else can come and go as you do. The unknown variable in his world."

I don't like the thought of leaving her in this court without me for a moment, but she's right.

I turn away from the table and reach into the inner lining of my robes. My fingers close around the waystone, warm and pulsing, ready to take me wherever I desire within our world.

Turning my thoughts toward the shadow that follows her down the corridor, I whisper to them, "Stay with her. Watch her. Never let him see you."

The shadows respond, curling closer to her.

Please, I think, lifting my eyes to the ceiling as though our goddess might hear me. *Let her be safe.*

Then I close my fingers around the waystone and vanish. The shadows stretch around me as the magic in the waystone pulses once, then anchors.

When I step out, the air is colder here.

The sharp scent of rain lingers in the breeze, and for a moment, I simply stand at the edge of the courtyard.

The Nithrin Court is nothing like the Dromin.

Every edge is sharp. Every structure, precise. It doesn't gleam the way the Dromin Court does; instead it absorbs light and holds it.

It feels . . . honest. There's no beautiful facade. It simply is.

I make my way to the throne room without announcement and the guards don't stop me. They see the shadows trailing behind my boots and step aside. I may not be their king, but I wield the same power as theirs.

When the doors open, Zayvin is seated at the base of the raised dais—not on the throne but beside it. A circle of advisors stands nearby, speaking in hushed tones.

He sees me before I can call his name.

Zayvin stands immediately, the sharp silver detailing on his robes catching the low light. His dark brow furrows, and I catch the flicker of something deeper in his eyes. Concern.

"Rhune?" His voice is low, but urgent. "What's happened?"

I give him a tight nod. "We can't speak here."

He glances once at his advisors and gives a curt nod. "Clear the room."

The room empties without protest, leaving only the echo of boots walking outside and the weight of what I brought with me.

When the doors shut, Zayvin crosses the floor. "What is it?"

I hesitate.

I trust him. He's my brother. He's everything Sorryn pretends to be—measured, restrained, intelligent enough to fear the things he doesn't yet understand.

Still, I don't say her name.

"Vayrith stirred for someone within the Dromin Court," I say instead. "The Calling Flame reacted. Serenath confirmed it."

Zayvin stills, like the breath's been knocked from him. When he finally speaks, it's a whisper. "That's not possible."

He exhales slowly and runs a hand through his dark hair, tension bleeding into his features.

"If that creature rises again . . ." His eyes flick to the wall behind me, distant and haunted. "Do you think he could break the seal over the Sacrum Mountains? It's the only power we know of that can eat through magic."

I nod. "That's why I came."

He falls quiet for a moment, but when he looks at me again, his gaze is focused.

"Elysia needs to see Sorryn for what he is. For who he is. We both know what happens if she binds herself to him blind. The Nithrin Court must receive the Goddess's blessing if we have an impending war. We are too weak from the last two queens not choosing us."

"She's starting to see," I say quietly. "She's asking the right questions. Digging for answers."

Zayvin nods once, and after a long pause, his voice softens.

"I know this is difficult for you."

My throat tightens, but I don't respond. He watched as I fractured, seeing her brave the selection. He knows so little of exactly what she means to me. In truth, I still don't even know what she means to me. The curiosity that sparked the first time I visited her dreams has grown

and morphed into an infatuation. A relentless need to discover every facet of her.

He steps closer, his expression gentler now.

"If she chooses me . . . I will treat her with care. You have my word."

It's the right thing to say, yet it still feels like the worst thing I could hear.

Because everything in me recoils at the thought of her choosing anyone else. Even him. Even Zayvin. It doesn't feel right.

Not in my body. Not in my blood. Not in my damned soul.

Yet I say nothing, because it doesn't matter.

Zayvin studies me for a moment longer, then asks casually, "How's Maerel?"

I blink and jerk back, the shift in conversation so sudden it catches me off guard.

"She's the same," I answer carefully. "Guarded. Watching."

He nods but his eyes flicker, like he's trying not to ask something more.

I don't press, though. Some things can stay unspoken . . . for now. I, too, have my own secrets.

"I need to get back to Elysia," I say. "She created a diversion to get Sorryn off of our trail, but I must continue to watch over her."

He nods again, stepping aside as I pull the waystone back to my hand. "Don't hesitate to visit me again if you hear more, and be careful, brother."

I nod just before vanishing from sight, the weight of all we didn't say following me through the shadows.

CHAPTER TWENTY-EIGHT

ELYSIA

I'm already seated when the servers enter, an endless stream of beautiful Dromin elves with varying hues of blue to their skin. All have their hair slicked back into high ponytails and I'm entranced at the uniform swish of their long hair as they walk. Each one moves in complete silence as they place the dishes on the table in front of us with precision and care. I expect them to vanish as quickly as they arrived, but they remain silent and still along the edges of the room. Perhaps waiting for a command.

My gaze drops to the plate in front of me. Slices of something that looks like roasted fruit but shimmers faintly like it's been dusted with powdered glass. A rich purple sauce spills from its center like syrup. Next to it is a thin item in the shape of leaves. When I touch one it flakes apart, releasing a scent like cinnamon and firewood.

The food doesn't stop coming.

Another plate is placed before me, some kind of meat with a glaze that has faint wisps of steam curling into the air. The aroma is salty but with an underlying sweet scent. It makes my mouth water, even as my stomach coils tighter.

It's beautiful and it makes me feel entirely human.

The food I know doesn't glow. It doesn't hum. It doesn't look like carved art.

I glance across the table at Sorryn and wish with everything in me that it were my family across from me, eating root stew and discussing our routine days.

My eyes flutter shut as I imagine their table suddenly overflowing with meats, cheese, and anything else their hearts desire, once the blessing touches our village. I know they'd give it all up to have me back, but

it calms my own longing for home to know that they will be taken care of once I make my decision and receive the blessing from the Goddess.

A soft thud has my eyes opening again to a small silver bowl being placed at the edge of my large plate. I thank the server, but they step back without a response or even incline of their head in acknowledgment. The weight of eyes on me pulls my attention to Sorryn once more and a chill runs down my spine just as he glances away.

He hasn't said much since we left the library and we'd been together for hours already. We only parted briefly upon his request that I freshen up for our early dinner as he handled final preparations for it.

I thought I'd caught Rhune's scent in my chamber, but I still have yet to see him since I'd steered Sorryn away from the dangerous truth of my studies. Disappointment curls in my chest as nerves begin to blossom within my stomach.

Where is he?

Maybe I was beginning to become too dependent upon the safety his presence brings me.

During the walk through the royal gardens, Sorryn's usual cheery disposition had begun to melt away as we traveled the paths winding with silverleaf vines and bioluminescent blooms that closed when I touched them. He gave answers when I asked questions, but nothing more.

"You may leave us," he announces, startling me from my thoughts.

The servers obey instantly, robes whispering across the floor as they disappear through the side doors.

I reach for the glass beside my plate and take a small sip to steady myself at the weight of being alone with him now. Whatever's in it tastes like chilled fruit, sweet first, then sharp on the back of my tongue.

I try to break the increasingly uncomfortable silence. "The garden was beautiful. I've never seen plants that respond to movement like that."

He doesn't answer immediately, finishing the bite of food in his mouth. He dabs his lips with a napkin before setting it aside with careful precision.

His head tilts slightly to the side as he regards me. "Some magical plants respond to affinities, others depend upon the season and weather, what they will do. A few even respond to bloodline."

That wasn't what I expected. I shift in my seat, remembering the silver vines that had gleamed like small, polished dagger tips and curled

toward me like a friend. Had that meant something when they moved toward me?

I push the thought away and gesture toward the food. "Everything smells incredible. I'm still trying to figure out what I'm actually eating."

He hums once. "You'll adjust."

The smile he offers is thin. It's not cruel, but it isn't kind either.

I need to get him back on my side, at least until it's time to leave this court behind and journey to the Nithrin. The thought is sobering. I used to fear having to travel to the Court of Nightmares, and now I long for their shadows.

Even in such a short time in this Court of Dreams, it is easy to see there is something dangerous and corrupt beneath the beauty. I just need to survive it.

I try again to strike up a conversation. "Thank you for joining me. I know you have responsibilities—"

"What did you learn today?" he asks, cutting me off before spooning more food into his mouth.

I blink.

It's not the question that unsettles me, but the sharp precision of it. How it lands without a natural buildup to it.

I thought I'd done a decent job in distracting him, but it seems I overestimated my powers of persuasion.

I sit back slightly and soften my expression, preparing to enter a game of mental chess. "A lot. Honestly . . . most of it was overwhelming. It's hard to reconcile how much of your world humans were never told of."

His utensil stills and his eyes don't leave mine, waiting for more.

I press on with wonder in my tone, which isn't entirely made up. "We spent a while on the magical affinities. Serenath said some queens have an inclination for one, even before their blessing, and that I need to prepare for it by having an understanding of the different types."

If he asked me for details on any specific types, I'd be in trouble.

I let my shoulders sag just a little. "She said it can be really overwhelming if you don't know what to expect. Still . . . I guess I'm worried I might not have one. That I'll fall short and fail you."

It's a lie, but a carefully woven one. I let the insecurity sit in my voice. I let it make me look smaller to the king, who loves to feel large enough to swallow a room whole.

For a moment, he just looks at me like he's trying to peel the skin off my words to see what's underneath.

Then he leans forward. His hand rises slowly, cupping my cheek like he's about to say something soft and kind as he's done in the past.

His smile fades and his voice drops low.

"You're a liar."

My breath catches.

He doesn't raise his voice in his accusation. He doesn't snarl or shout. The words are soft, almost intimate.

You're a liar.

My heart punches against my ribs. I try to hold his gaze, keep my expression open, confused. Not afraid. Not confirming.

"I'm not sure what you mean," I whisper, playing the part of a mere stupid human.

A mistake, apparently.

His hand slides from my cheek to the back of my head, fingers tangling in my hair and knocking loose the crown from my head. It clatters across the floor as he grips the roots of my hair.

I gasp, the sound sharp and involuntary as he yanks me forward, dragging me from my chair. The feet scrape against the stone floor as my knees knock into the table, the pain white and sudden.

He stands as he pulls, and I'm forced to rise with him. My scalp burns. My spine arches from the pressure.

Fear blooms.

Where is Rhune?

Why hasn't he come?

He's always in the shadows, always watching. *He promised.*

I try to steady my voice, even as it trembles. "If this is about the tomes . . ."

Sorryn laughs, a sharp, guttural sound that cuts through the heavy tension in the room.

"You really thought you were clever," he says, voice thick with mockery. "Leading me away from the library like some master manipulator."

His grip tightens, and I cry out softly, the pain lancing through my skull.

"You thought I didn't notice how carefully you played that moment? Serenath feeding me those polished lies. Rhune doing everything he

could not to speak . . . He never does that. He *lives* to provoke me, but today he went still as stone at my questioning."

His head dips close, his breath warm against my ear.

"You think I wouldn't notice that shift?"

I whimper. My scalp feels like it's tearing, but I stay upright, legs shaking beneath me. I try to plead with my eyes, but he doesn't look at me like a queen to court. Not anymore. They're glassy and cold.

"Let go," I manage to whisper.

He doesn't.

Instead, he raises his free hand and snaps his fingers.

The dining hall doors swing open and Enari steps inside. A small gasp escapes me at the sight of her.

Her steps are stiff, unnatural. Her spine too straight and her arms too controlled, not swinging as they naturally would as one walks. The blue tattoos inked across her skin pulse with magic, glowing brighter with each breath she takes.

Her eyes flick toward mine, just for a second, and in that gaze is a thousand silent apologies.

"Bring in the prisoner," he says, voice light again, like we've returned to polite conversation.

Enari jerks forward, her body moving rigidly and reluctantly before disappearing down the corridor.

Footsteps return and my stomach lurches at the new figure.

"Serenath," I whisper.

Enari is dragging her.

Her head is bowed, the long braid of white hair trailing behind her like an afterthought. One of her eyes is nearly swollen shut, the other bloodshot and dazed. Fresh bruises are beginning to bloom across her cheek and jaw. Blood trickles from the corner of her mouth, a steady and quiet drip against the floor, leaving a trail.

I try to run to her. To help. To break us out of this wretched court.

Sorryn holds me firmly and pain flares through my scalp again as he yanks me back toward him.

I scream as the pain of his grip shoots down my spine.

Serenath groans as she's dropped beside the table next to us. Her head rolls against the stone floor, her breath shallow.

"What did you do to her?" I cry out, my body beginning to shake as I take in her wounds up close.

Sorryn doesn't even look at her, his gaze still on me.

"I didn't believe any of you," he murmurs, brushing a loose strand of hair away from my face like we're still at a dinner party in which he's trying to make me swoon. "But the gardens confirmed what I suspected after that odd interaction. You possess a magical inclination that requires the forbidden section."

His eyes narrow.

"I just haven't figured out yet how you have *that* bloodline."

My breath stalls in my throat as true confusion grips me. "I'm not sure what you mean," I murmur honestly, willing my voice to remain even.

He stares down at me with a glee in his wide eyes just before his lips peel back into a predatory smile.

I'm looking at a man who was always like this. I just hadn't seen beneath the mask yet.

He laughs, but it's not amusement that shakes through him. It's mockery.

The sound anchors the nerves inside me, letting loose my anger. It settles beneath my fear—not replacing it entirely, but becoming something I can wield alongside it.

I don't have magic, but I do hold power in this world.

I remember what Rhune said in the library and what Serenath warned. I remember the way every page of their history told me the same thing, again and again, in different ways.

I am the Queen and they *need* me.

This court and their king . . . this castle of fractured dreams—they're husks of what they could be, without the Goddess's blessing.

The only way Sorryn can secure that is through me and my choice.

My voice is raw, but even when I lift my chin and look him in the eyes. "If you want any chance of being chosen as my king," I say, "you'll let me go. Now."

He doesn't move, but I see the flicker of tension in his jaw. His grip remains tight.

"You made the wrong move," I continue, voice steadying with each word. "Hurting me. Hurting Serenath. Using Enari like a puppet. You don't win a queen by making her people bleed."

The silence that follows stretches, but then, without a word, he releases me.

I stumble back a step, breath caught in my throat. My head throbs where he gripped me, the echo of pain sharp and lingering. I don't look away from him, even as my legs scream to flee.

He begins to laugh as if he's just heard the best joke of his life. It rolls through the hall, echoing back, over and over.

I refuse to flinch despite the way the sound has my stomach churning.

"Run, my Queen."

The words are so soft they almost vanish beneath the sound of his laughter, but I hear them.

I glance at Enari, still standing with her glowing tattoos pulsing faintly along her skin.

"Please," she bites out. "She's coming."

Before I can react, a new voice answers the space with chilling clarity.

"She was supposed to be easy to mold," she continues, hands folded neatly in front of her. "I trusted the orb would guide her toward the same outcome as the last queen."

I freeze.

The High Priestess steps forward from behind a side door, gliding past the stone pillars with the kind of grace that doesn't match the destruction she leaves in her wake.

"The orb told me she had unwavering faith in the Dromin, my King."

My throat tightens as the memory slams into place. *"When you're tested, think of me. Only me,"* Rhune had whispered.

I thought he meant it as comfort, but he knew.

He knew what they did to the last queen. What they are now trying to do to me. Yet he's forbidden from talking poorly about Sorryn or the previous queen.

The room seems to tilt slightly, my stomach churning with the realization. They weren't looking for the true queen chosen by the Goddess, they were looking for a puppet. I wasn't chosen because of who I am, but because of who they thought they could bend.

Maggie's words haunt me. *"She chooses what bends. Not what breaks."*

Sorryn turns toward me with a grin that makes my skin crawl. His eyes gleam as he watches me try to stitch my horrified expression back

into one that doesn't belie just how much fear this situation has stirred within me.

"You failed, Adamaris," he says, voice almost playful. "But that's all right. It's not like I truly need her to choose me. We'll simply take the choice from her."

CHAPTER TWENTY-NINE

ELYSIA

"I apologize, my King," Adamaris says, her voice composed as ever, like the chaos in this room doesn't reach her. Maybe because she's always at the center of it, controlling it. "Are my enchanted marks at least working on her maid as we anticipated? It is the first living being I've used the magic on."

My body stiffens at her words as I take in the glow of Enari's tattoos once more.

She treated Enari like an object to enchant and have control over. A living, breathing soul.

The horror that grips my body is worse than anything I felt when Sorryn dragged me from my chair. I can't take my eyes off her, can't stop the swell of disbelief that thickens in my throat.

Suddenly I remember Rhune's voice in the library, explaining how those who craft magical items channel power into objects to simulate a strength they don't truly possess. That even the High Priestess, revered and feared as she is, relies on her creations to amplify her reach.

She's nothing without them.

Enari isn't a stone, a weapon, or a piece of jewelry, though. She's alive. I can't imagine the kind of energy it must take to continue to bend a living soul into a vessel with the enchantments etched into her skin.

The wheels in my head turn. There are vital differences, given that Enari has her own power, unlike an inanimate object. When the tattoos aren't glowing, her movements seem to be her own.

So, are there limits to how long Adamaris can control her?

I suddenly wish I had a better understanding of the different magics within this world. Countless questions flow through my mind, but I'm

unable to deduce which thought to follow that could actually lead to helping Enari.

Will Adamaris run out of magical energy to control Enari before the High Priestess has a chance to use all of the power within her?

I just don't know.

Sorryn lifts his hand as she opens her mouth again.

"Stop your apologies," he says, his tone no longer sharp, but weary. "I grow tired of them."

Adamaris falters mid-breath, lips parting just slightly as he turns to face her. The change in him is subtle but unmistakable. The rigidity in his posture softens and the sharp angles of his expression dull as he pulls his mask back into position.

"You know I appreciate you," he says, smoother now with warmth to his tone. "I need you by my side, Ada."

He says the name softly and reverently, and in the silence that follows, I see the truth unfold.

Her shoulders rise with a breath, and for a single heartbeat, her expression shifts, just enough for me to see it.

She loves him. It isn't magic that binds her here—it's devotion.

She's not just executing her own plan or following the whims of the Goddess. She's wrapped her will around his, twisting her power into a gift he never even had to ask for.

This wasn't about guidance or wisdom or divine instruction. This was about pleasing him and ensuring he and his court continued to stay powerful. Choosing queens that would choose him.

A shift runs through the air and the hovering lights flicker faintly.

I feel his presence before I see him, like the charged air of a brewing storm settling into the space around us.

For a single breath, I dare to believe I'm safe.

He's here.

"Don't move," Sorryn says softly into my ear, suddenly at my side, causing me to jerk.

A flicker of light hums to life in his palm raised in front of my chest. A blade made entirely of searing white energy coalesces in his grasp, and he lowers it slowly and deliberately, until the tip hovers just above my heart.

I can feel the heat of it already, hot and terrifying against my chest.

"Come any closer," Sorryn says, slowly turning us both to the right, "and I'll split her open before you can blink."

From the corner of my eye, I see him. There's no withholding the depth of his powers any longer.

He's standing in the massive doorway, shadows rippling like smoke pooling around his feet, eyes locked on the weapon Sorryn holds to me. His entire body is drawn tight, as though it takes everything in him not to rip the world in half.

Suddenly it's clear something or someone stopped him from getting to us earlier. There's a cut in one of his eyebrows, bleeding down to the tip and down his temple, and ash smeared across his cheek and neck.

He doesn't speak, but his silence is heavier than any threat.

His shadows draw higher until they wrap around him like armor, leaving his violet eyes piercing through the darkness as they drift up my face.

My heart stutters and my breath catches—not in fear, but in awe.

Adamaris moves closer to us with slow, graceful confidence, like she's already prepared for Rhune's arrival.

"I see the shadows brought you finally," she murmurs, her voice too calm for the tension thickening in the air. "Why'd it take you so long?"

She mockingly asks the question in a giddy, singsong voice, making my skin crawl.

Rhune's eyes don't leave mine as he answers in a low, menacing tone that makes his words seem to rumble. "You should have left more than the royal guard to stop me, if you wanted to keep me from her. But I suppose I have let you all think of me as weak, so I won't let it wound my pride."

The hair on my arms stands on end and it's like my heart sings a song meant only for him to hear.

"I suspected your intervention, Ada," he says as he takes one step forward. "Thank you for confirming it, so that I am free of the Goddess's judgment for what needs to be done now."

"Don't sound so perturbed," Sorryn says, smiling like he's savoring this. "It's not like any of this impacts your life. You are a king with no court. You aren't a choice. You don't belong, no matter the strength of powers you think you have."

I can't keep silent as Sorryn hurls insults at Rhune's deepest insecurities, in spite of the dagger of light at my chest.

"He's always been my choice!" I snap at Sorryn, "and he will always belong wherever I am."

Sorryn snarls at me and lowers the dagger an inch closer to my heart, the heat from the weapon of light beginning to sear bits of my dress away with its proximity. The burning smell wafts up between us and I stare Rhune down, unafraid of speaking my truth.

"As I said before," Sorryn purrs, leaning down to nuzzle his nose against my cheek. I grimace at his touch and breath on my skin. "We will be taking your choice away from you."

I see how Rhune's hands twitch at his sides and how his shadows stir around him with restraint.

I know he wants to fight, but he won't. Not while that weapon is pointed at me and not while Serenath is caught in the middle.

The elder elf stirs from the floor. A low groan, hoarse and broken, slips from her bloodied lips. Her one good eye finds Rhune, dazed but sharp with purpose.

"Take her," she breathes. "Leave me."

"No!" I counter, "we're not leaving you."

She shakes her head slowly.

"Go," she rasps. "Get her out. This court needs to burn."

Adamaris steps toward Serenath, slowly lifting her boot to rest atop her cheek. She presses down against her face, hissing, "I think that's enough out of you."

Rhune takes another step forward as my breaths come out in shallow gasps.

The light blade pulses brighter in front of me and the heat begins to make my exposed skin burn. "Don't tempt me, brother."

Brother.

He says it like a joke now, as if it's something that can be unmade with a single breath.

"Let her go," he says, voice quiet and deadly. "Or I will burn this palace to ash."

The air fractures with tension too thick to breathe before Sorryn answers, "So be it. Let us see this magic of yours, brother."

Rhune's shadows rush toward us along the floor and Sorryn doesn't move, as if he's anticipating this.

Then the air around me crackles just before the dagger at my chest is flung directly in Rhune's direction as he rushes toward us.

There's a crack of sound like lightning and I barely register the sound before Rhune is at my side, wrenching me backward with one

hand while the other slams a wall of shadow between us and the searing light rushing at us from Sorryn's palm. We crash to the ground as it scorches past, so close I feel the heat graze my shoulder.

I'm left blinking rapidly and trying to comprehend how he got to me so quickly. It has to be connected to the same powers Sorryn holds, with the way he seemed to appear next to me out of nowhere earlier.

The chamber erupts around us with light and shadow tearing through the air and clashing. Rhune launches to his feet to stand in front of me, summoning a wall of shadows that seems to consume Sorryn's beams of light. At the same time, a jolt of light is hurled directly at Adamaris, sending her flying into the air and crashing to the ground with a satisfying crunch.

I can't stay down and do nothing as Rhune fights them both.

As soon as I find my footing again, I stagger toward Serenath, who remains slumped just feet away.

"Hold on," I whisper, dropping to my knees beside her, trying to keep my voice calm despite the firestorm crashing around us. "I've got you. I'm here."

The magic above cracks again, casting the room into flickering hues of gold and black. A flash of light explodes across the ceiling, and the heat from a missed blast rolls over us in a searing wave. I press closer to Serenath, shielding her body with my own, but before I can speak again, something shifts around me.

Darkness presses in like a comforting blanket.

I glance up, and the world beyond blurs beneath a veil of shadow. We're enclosed now, Rhune's magic curling around us like a living barrier, weaving tendrils of darkness into a dome that shimmers faintly with silver strands. The chaos of the battle is still visible beyond its edge.

He's shielding us, encasing us in a pocket of safety, and I have to guess that it takes immense focus and energy to keep this going while fighting elsewhere.

Outside the veil, Adamaris rises from the ground with eerie composure as Rhune and Sorryn dance around the room. Her hands move with grace, her expression calm, but her voice slices through the air.

"Take him down."

Enari moves, her gaze locked on Rhune, and I see it—the horror in her eyes and her desperation.

She lifts her arm, and from her palm a stream of flame ignites. It flickers once, then roars like a beast toward its target.

The fire is wild, untamed, twisting into a serpentine column that surges across the room, aimed directly at Rhune. His shadows leap to intercept it, absorbing the flames in a cascade of dark smoke. The moment it takes for him to contain the fire is the same moment Sorryn uses to strike.

He charges through the smoke, light blazing in one hand, his expression sharpened by rage and the thrill of having the advantage. Rhune's head snaps in his direction just in time to leap backward with the slash of Sorryn's weapon driving toward his chest.

My hands tremble where they press against Serenath's arm.

"Enari," I whisper, watching as another ribbon of fire spills from her hands. "Please stop. Please break the control."

She rushes toward him, opposite Sorryn, and they attempt to box him in.

It becomes instantly clear that Rhune won't strike her. That truth lodges itself inside me as he only dodges her, never sending counterattacks her way unlike Sorryn. Because she's not the true enemy and she's being used.

Adamaris knows exactly what she's doing: weaponizing his heart against him.

My vision blurs with smoke as another wave of fire collides with Rhune's defenses, his shadows buckling briefly under the pressure. Sorryn doesn't relent. He drives forward, using the distraction to push harder, his blast of magic now finding its target.

"Rhune!" I shout, letting go of Serenath and banging my palms against the shadowed barricade. My eyes burn with tears as I strike over and over, but they don't relent.

Rhune staggers as another burst of light slams into his side. I see the moment his balance falters, the moment his shadows no longer rise fast enough to block the next strike. Sorryn's blade grazes his ribs and Rhune hits the floor with a choked gasp, blood blooming in sharp contrast against the silver of his tunic.

"No," I breathe out, my voice cracking.

My view is obstructed as Adamaris steps into view, blocking my sight of Rhune struggling to stand back up.

My hands shake as I reach for Serenath again, trying to shield her with what little strength I have, as if my body could somehow make up for the fact that I can't stop any of this.

Why couldn't this have happened after I was blessed by the Goddess? When I actually have magic to help. Why now when I'm helpless to watch innocent people used and broken?

Adamaris steps closer, fingers wrapped around an artifact, its glow pulsing in time with the flicker in Enari's veins. She raises it, her lips parting as she begins to murmur something I don't understand.

Light surges toward me and Serenath, and I throw myself over her as if I could make a difference. The light hits the shadows around us in a hiss of burning energy, and I don't scream, but I feel the heat bite across my shoulders.

I glance up quickly, finding our shadowed barricade gone, likely burned away by whatever artifact Adamaris wields.

Rhune lets out a roar that shakes the room, his magic snapping outward in a sudden burst that drives Sorryn back a step. Shadows lash from the floor like whips, crashing into stone and slicing into Sorryn's legs just before he can get out of range. Still, they don't touch Enari.

I quickly thread my arms under Serenath's, tears slipping quietly down my cheeks as I attempt to drag her away from Adamaris's advance. The battle rages and I'm left to retreat, weak and useless.

They keep saying there's power inside me and that I carry something rare, but what use is that if I can't reach it? What if all I can do is watch?

The walls of the dining hall blur through a haze of smoke and heat. I can barely hear Serenath's voice, broken and soft beneath me.

"Run," Serenath rasps again, voice brittle and fraying.

"I can't," I whisper back, breath shaking. "I can't leave you. I can't watch more people I care about die."

"You must," she says, sharper now despite the blood drying at the corner of her mouth. "We cannot afford to lose you. Listen to me, Elysia, there's a dagger. My ankle. Left side."

My hands tremble as I lower her to the ground and reach beneath the folds of her torn robe. My fingers close around the hilt, cool and small, and I pull it free.

Serenath's eyes flutter open again, pain cutting through the edge of her urgency. "Take it. Use it. Get out."

Instead of running, I rise. My breath steadies, if only barely. The blade stays in my grip, but I step toward Adamaris, placing myself between her and Serenath.

Serenath snarls behind me, the sound wet with blood. "What are you doing?"

"I'm tired of running," I say softly.

Adamaris tilts her head, eyes glinting with amusement.

"What," she croons, the word dripping with mockery, "you think you can stop me with that toothpick?"

I tighten my grip on the dagger. "Yes," I murmur, and then slowly lift the blade, not toward her, but to my own chest just as Sorryn had. "I think my life is what you all value most."

The blade presses just beneath my collarbone, angled toward my heart.

"And I will wield whatever I can."

CHAPTER THIRTY

ELYSIA

The world fractures around me.

Behind the High Priestess, war collides with shadow.

Rhune is still standing, but my heart tells me he won't be for much longer unless I do something to help.

He can't face this on his own much longer. Perhaps if his focus weren't split among five people—three of whom he doesn't want to hurt.

Blood drips from a new wound on his head, making violet bloom against his silver hair, dark against the pale gleam of his skin as it trickles down his face. His breath looks ragged, yet shadows still whip around him, fevered and violent, clawing at Sorryn's golden light and Enari's fire.

They strike against him in tandem, one after another.

I can feel the tremble of power even from where I stand. Each burst of fire and flash of magic crashes into Rhune's shadowed barrier, which seems to be growing thinner with each attack.

Still, his shadows never stop and my heart surges at his strength. They whip through the air in violent coils as Sorryn lunges again, a blade of light erupting from his hand, but Rhune deflects it with a column of darkness that splits the attack in two. Fire surges in from the left and Rhune spins, his cloak burning as he throws up another barrier, barely in time to hold the inferno at bay from his body.

He doesn't retreat or relent.

He fights, because he is all that's between us and them.

I take a deep breath as the floor beneath my knees pulses with the reverberation of their battle. Magic skitters through the air like a war of their wills and magic . . . all things I can't control.

But this . . . this I can.

I hold the dagger, firm and sure, even as my arms tremble and the roar in my ears crescendos into something deafening.

My voice doesn't tremble when I speak. "You forced me to be here," I say softly to Adamaris, whose shoulders are tight and her eyes trained on the dagger. "But you can't force me to remain here."

The air suddenly shifts as his gaze finds mine over her shoulder. For the briefest moment in time, everything else halts.

I see it hit him . . . the moment he realizes what I'm about to do.

I watch as his expression fractures. The fury that's carried him through the fight slips from his face, carved away by something raw and unfiltered. His mouth parts, lips shaping a word I don't hear but feel in the marrow of my bones.

Don't.

His body turns toward me without thinking. His shadows falter midair. One of them dissipates completely, struck by a wave of fire that he doesn't even attempt to deflect. It's as if the war he's been fighting vanishes beneath the weight of a single truth: that I might end it all with a single thrust of a blade.

In that fractured moment it's just us, the blade, and the breath between two hearts.

Enari's fire comes first as he forgets to guard himself.

It bursts across the floor like a snake loosed from a cage, its body coiling and splitting with every strike of her hands. Sorryn is already moving beside her, the light in his palm gathering sharp and deadly, condensed into a spear of pure white magic.

Together, they strike as my face morphs into one of horror, feeling like I'm watching this happening in slow-motion.

Rhune doesn't move because he's still looking at me.

Still watching the blade I've raised to my chest like it's the only threat in the room.

"Rhune!" I cry, the word ripped from my throat, but it's too late.

The fire wraps around him just as the spear of light slams into his side. His body lifts from the ground and then crashes into a stone wall, causing cracks to run through the area around him. His body slides down to the floor with a sickening thud that I'll never stop hearing.

I scream as he coughs up a pool of blood before stilling once more.

I rush forward, but I only get two steps before a blast of magic slams into my chest and sends me skidding backward, the dagger flying from my grip and vanishing into the chaos.

Adamaris steps in front of me once more, the magic she's channeling from an enchanted object crackling at her fingertips like lightning waiting for direction. Her lips curve into something twisted and pleased.

"Foolish girl," she says, her voice almost pitying. "You never understood your place."

She speaks, but I can't focus on her. All I can see is Rhune, crushed and motionless.

Blood glistens in the hollow of his throat. His shadows twitch like they're trying to lift him and put the broken pieces of him back together.

I'm in a trance as I stare at him, my eyes burning from the smoke in the room.

"No," I whisper, my mind in disbelief and shock. A hot tear runs down my cheek as my voice begins to quiver. "You . . . you have to get up. Please, Rhune."

I thought I was helping end this situation. Controlling what I thought was the most important thing to Adamaris and Sorryn. Yet all I did was allow Sorryn to remove one of his greatest opponents.

He knew all along that Rhune and I were the other's greatest weakness, while we tried to remain blind to it ourselves.

"Rhune!" I scream, my voice hoarse as I try to run for him once more.

Adamaris's magic coils instantly around my limbs. I'm dragged back across the floor, the world a blur of smoke and agony as I'm pulled farther and farther from him.

My hands try to claw the ground, to anchor me as my nails drag against the harsh stone, skin ripping off the tips of my fingers as I go. I barely recognize the pain as I try to thrash in her tight grip, desperate to break free and go to him.

He needs me.

It's all my fault.

Then, beyond the sound of my heart breaking, I hear a voice like thunder.

"Enough."

The word detonates behind me and the air surges.

I twist toward it and see Serenath's arm trembling beneath the weight of her upper body being held up by it. She has her other hand poised and open, palm out.

"You think yourself a sorceress with your little objects?" she snarls at Adamaris. "Let me show you what a true sorceress can do, even at the end of her life."

Amber-and-green energy that matches her eyes spins from her fingers, blinding in its brilliance. It grows and grows as Adamaris's eyes widen and her hands disappear into her robes, seeming to search for an item.

The spell slams into Adamaris midstep, knocking her backward with enough force to send her crashing against the far wall.

The room floods with Serenath's power, her hazel magic carving through the remnants of the Priestess's control like fire through ice. The air sizzles with it, pure, untamed, and righteous.

She doesn't stop even as I watch blood begin to run from her nose and eyes.

Another blast follows as she focuses on Sorryn, continuing as each one destroys her body, but she doesn't falter. Not once.

The magic cracks the very stone beneath our feet as she cries out in pain.

I cry out her name. "Serenath, stop!"

She's going to kill herself.

A smooth hand grips my arm tightly and my head whips up to find Enari as she yanks me to my feet. Her tattoos are flickering wildly, blue and unstable, her movements jerky like something inside her is resisting.

"Don't," I gasp, trying to twist away. "Fight this, Enari!"

Her grip is like iron.

She draws a dagger from under her robes and I don't have time to plead as it flies toward my head.

The object cracks against my temple. The world tilts around me and everything fades at the edges.

I groan, rolling onto my side, trying to blink away the blurriness in my vision as my eyes open. My wrists are bound in front of me, but my feet are free as I attempt to move them. My cheek is pressed to smooth stone, damp with condensation, and there's no light except for the faint symbols glowing on the metal bars all around me the beam of moonlight from a single window.

I hear the sound of breath, a rattling inhale that isn't mine. I push up slowly, a wave of dizziness washing over me as the room spins in front of me, but I spot her.

Enari sits crumpled by the far wall, knees pulled to her chest, her head against the glowing bars opposite me. The blue tattoos winding down her arms are flickering wildly, sometimes bright, sometimes dim, like dying embers that refuse to fully go out.

Her eyes are closed and her fingers twitch.

"Enari," I croak out.

She lifts her head slowly. Her eyes that I'd grown used to looking vacant and defeated under Adamaris's control now look almost like her own again.

"I didn't want to hurt you or him," she says, voice cracking. "I tried, my Queen."

My head throbs and my stomach rolls as I try to focus on her.

"You knocked me out," I whisper, the memories coming back slowly.

Rhune.

Hazel magic stirs in my mind's eye.

Serenath.

"She made me." Her voice trembles, and I swear I see tears rolling through soot-stained cheeks. "They turned me into an object to control after the last queen told them I tried to warn her of the King's evil. They gave me a choice to die or submit to the marks bestowed by the High Priestess."

Her distrust of me from the moment we met suddenly makes sense. The shock she seemed to feel when I was kind to her.

It seems the layers of deception in this world of clouds and dreams never end.

I once thought that humans were the ones trapped, bound to the ground with the scraps the elves give us and what we can harvest and trade. Perhaps we are the rich ones, after all, surrounded by simplicity and love, not magic and betrayals.

I groan as a fresh wave of pain thrums behind my eyes.

I have to get back to the dining hall. I have to find Rhune and Serenath.

The chains at my wrists clink as I shift closer. "Your marks aren't as bright or consistent. Is she still in control of you?"

"She's losing control with her own magical reserves depleting to keep the enchantment over me," she rasps as her head rolls back to rest

against the wall. "But she may kill me before that happens. I used all of the power I had in that fight and I haven't been able to feed on dreams to replenish any of my energy."

I search her face for any will to fight, to not surrender to the fate they've marked her with. "Can you free me so we can escape together?"

She shakes her head. "No, there are enchantments all over these bars that I can't break, but I can try to help with her hold over me fading. I'll find Rhune, or Serenath if she's still . . ."

Her voice trails off and suddenly what she was explaining clicks into place in my brain as the fog begins to clear.

"What happens if you are forced to use your magic with no source of power, Enari?" I ask sharply, tired of people coddling me from the truths of this world.

She hesitates for a moment before relenting. "Your soul is consumed to fuel the power, until it's burned out of your body. It's what I believe Serenath was pulling on at the end, and what the High Priestess will force me to do if this continues before I can feed."

Horror grips my mind as my eyes fall to the dirty floor.

Her hands curl against the barrier.

"I'm going to find someone. I'll come back for you."

I shake my head as she pushes to her feet. "Enari, you're in no shape to fight this battle anymore. If Adamaris forces you—"

She cuts me off with a heavy stare full of determination.

"You're not like the last queen . . ." Her voice trails off before it steadies, a fierce certainty slipping through her fear. "She didn't see. She didn't feel the way the world screamed for help around her. You do. I see it every time I look into your gaze. You know what it means to fight for something bigger than yourself. It's my turn to do that."

I don't speak—I can't—because if I do, the tears will start, and I'm not sure they'll ever stop.

Her voice breaks as her tattoos flare to life with the step she takes away from me. "We . . . we need you to change this. All of it."

She turns and casts one last glance over her shoulder. "If I don't see you again, thank you for seeing me despite my attempts to hide in the shadows of your life. Thank you for your kindness."

Then she disappears into the shadows, her flickering tattoos vanishing into the dark.

My hands press to my eyes, and I try not to sob.

Thank you for seeing me.

My body trembles with physical and emotional exhaustion. Pain blooms across my ribs from where Adamaris's power slammed into me. My head thrums with a steady flow of pressure, making me feel dizzy.

Yet it's the ache in my chest that threatens to undo me.

Rhune looked like he was dying the last I saw him.

Serenath might already be gone.

Enari's life is on the line and I'm locked behind a wall of magic I can't escape, and no powers to fight back, even if I did find a way out of here.

A frustrated scream builds in my chest before I let it explode out of me.

It echoes around me, reverberating against the walls and filling me with the energy to fight. I'm still breathing.

This isn't the end.

I won't let it be.

CHAPTER THIRTY-ONE

ELYSIA

There is no time in this place.

Only the steady, unwavering hum of enchantments pulsing against the bars of my enclosure. All I know is the stillness of the octagonal room, with its cold stone floor and high vaulted ceiling. I don't remember the last time I slept. Days must have passed since I saw Enari last.

I curl tighter into myself, knees pulled to my chest, arms wrapped around them, like that might keep the rest of me from unraveling in a place meant to trap me with my thoughts.

My skin is sticky with dried sweat, the soft dress clinging to me in places where the once silky material has crusted. My body aches with a hollowness, as if everything I am has been scooped out from inside me, leaving me to echo with nothingness.

I try not to think about what day it is. How long it's been. Whether Serenath is dead. Whether Enari made it back. Whether Rhune is breathing.

That last thought nearly undoes me. Every time it rises I push it down alongside the memories of his voice calling me Little Dove and the feel of his fingers brushing my cheek.

The door groans open for the first time since Enari left this room.

I scramble to my feet, heart hammering wildly within the confinement of my ribs.

Sorryn steps through the doorway first, followed by Adamaris, the hood of her robe draped low over her face.

My body trembles as she presses her hand to the bars, and the hum I'd grown accustomed to halts. I force myself to lift my chin as they open the door to my prison, stepping into it.

"Where are they?" I ask, voice raw from not having used it and the lack of water. "Rhune. Serenath. Enari. What did you do to them?"

Silence. Not even a flicker of reaction in their faces.

If they won't give me information, I need to forge a path forward with the mindset that I'm in this alone for now.

"You're breaking the laws of the Goddess," I say, forcing strength into my words that I don't quite feel. "*I'm* to choose the King. You are going against her will. Does that mean nothing to you?"

My words are pointed at Adamaris, considering she is their High Priestess and the one who should be closest and most attuned to the Goddess. Yet she claims her will as her own to twist for her desires.

For a moment, a sinking thought flickers through my mind. *Could this be the Goddess's will?*

"Do not speak of our laws like you understand them," Sorryn spits, cold amusement flickering in his eyes. "You may have been given the crown, but you are not one of her elves. You are not blessed by her."

Adamaris steps forward, her voice soft and lined with contempt. "You may have read restricted information in that library and think your small human brain understands our world, but these are the facts: *We* gave you that crown, and you will do what we demand."

I jump slightly as Sorryn tosses something forward, a glistening silver circle.

It rolls on the ground toward me before clattering to the ground at my feet.

My crown, twisted and bent.

"So tell me, my Queen," Sorryn murmurs while drawing a small vial from his pocket. A small silver-tipped vine gleams within. He holds it between two fingers, letting the water at the base catch the light from the lone window in this tower.

The one from the royal garden.

"Do you know why this responded to you?" he asks.

I don't answer. The truth is I don't know, but he won't believe me if I say that.

He answers for me after waiting a few breaths. "The roots of these vines were planted with a single drop of blood from the most powerful Nithrin in our history. Druids planted those veins to lie dormant unless someone of the same bloodline appeared near. They never intended

it as a path to power—more of a warning of sorts—but I'm not so shortsighted."

Dread fills my core as I blink rapidly, absorbing that information.

I can't let them know about Vayrith.

Adamaris speaks next, her tone eerily calm as she lowers her hood. "We've been waiting for a sign from the Goddess that she is aligned with our mission. She delivered you to us as a new weapon. Not to worship . . . but to wield."

I recoil and step back until I'm pressed against the wall, trapped as they step forward with wicked grins on their faces.

"I'm powerless," I argue weakly. "You think I would allow myself to be trapped in this prison if I were a weapon?"

"That will change when we have our formal joining ceremony," Sorryn says, his lips thinning to a smirk. "We've already sent word to the Elven Council that you wish to make your choice early."

Something cold slithers down my spine, setting my body on full alert as Adamaris runs a hand through the back of Sorryn's white hair and turns to admire his face. "The Nithrin Elders will take some time to placate, given their anger and pushback for you to still spend your three weeks with Zayvin."

Hope soars within me. *Zayvin.*

There's no chance he will roll over and accept this at face value. Not when everything I've learned points to his court suffering from the last queen's choice being twisted.

Her focus turns to me. "It's a good thing I know I can convince them to understand it is out of our control and in the hands of our queen, the same as the last one."

They've already pulled this off once. Why did I think for a second this time would be different?

My mind whirls as I try to think of anything that will give them pause.

"The last queen died far too early," I say, thinking back to our village's shock at her death. I should never have even been a candidate for another selection in my lifetime. "You think the Elven Council won't see through your treachery? The Queen is supposed to be granted an extended life alongside her king. How did you explain her death?"

I'm grasping at any details I can, but as the words leave my lips, they ring true.

Why would the Queen have died so young, as if she were still a human, if the Goddess had given her blessing upon choosing Sorryn?

Sorryn's lips curve into a smirk, as if he's enjoying this banter. Meanwhile, Adamaris's gaze turns thunderous.

"Tell us what you are," she demands, crossing over to me and yanking the chains between my hands toward her. My body is jerked forward and we come face-to-face. "Tell us what lies dormant in you and we may let you keep your mind intact. You know exactly what I can do with the orb if you disobey."

My knees begin to tremble at the memory, but this time I don't let them break me. I won't let them drag me down into the pits of despair.

Maybe they will break my mind at the end of this, but for now, with my mind still functioning and a desire to fight, I won't cower at *what-ifs.*

I straighten my spine and snarl at her, "I don't know anything."

There's a quiet pause before Sorryn steps forward and lifts his hand, drawing crackling light into his palm. I watch him morph it into several different weapons until settling on the dagger he seems so fond of.

"Back up, dear Ada," he murmurs while staring straight into my eyes. "I wouldn't want her blood to splatter upon you."

I watch her disgust of me dissipate as her eyes flutter and she steps back to his side.

Pain slices through me before I even recognize that he's sent the weapon toward me.

It starts as a burn in my cheek, slow and deliberate.

Another slice.

This time a gasp falls from my mouth as I yank my hands up to my neck on impulse. Warmth coats my hands and the shackles on them.

My knees hit the floor as the next strike bites into the front of my ankle.

I bite down hard on my lip to keep from screaming.

"I'll ask again," Sorryn says tightly with a forced smile. "What are you?"

I clench my jaw, refusing to give him the satisfaction of an answer or scream, even as he walks forward and the crack of his hand against my already bloodied cheek makes my head ring.

He crouches to my level, his voice suspiciously soft. "What were you researching in the library before I walked in? What tomes did you actually read?"

I don't speak. I narrow my eyes and feel blood seeping into my mouth as I smile and answer, "Surface theory."

His smile fades as mine grows.

I don't have a shred of knowledge on what that meant, but I recall Serenath asking Rhune for it.

His usual mask of warmth fades as I chirp, "Almost as interesting as the one on passive affinities."

A crack echoes again as my head snaps to the side.

Adamaris hisses something under her breath, elven words I don't understand, but the intent in her tone is clear. She's done with waiting for me to willingly give them information.

"Hold her," he snaps.

Hands wrap around my arms. I try to pull away, but with my hands shackled and the amount of blood soaking my dress from the wound in my neck, it's no use. Adamaris maneuvers herself to my back, holding me tightly against her.

"Heal her neck wound before she passes out from blood loss. I want her to be fully conscious for this."

Prickles break out along the side of my neck, as if I can feel the stitching of my skin occurring.

It reminds me of my mother's threadwork, and I hold onto her face and her love in my mind as I steel myself for whatever is coming next.

Sorryn steps forward again, inspecting my hands as if they're artifacts, not a part of me.

"This doesn't have to be complicated," he says gently. "Tell me what you know about your bloodline and we can avoid this."

I close my eyes and take a breath.

"I have nothing to give you."

Crack.

My scream shatters the air before I can stop it as he bends my pinky back until it breaks. Pain shoots like lightning through my hand.

I bite down on my lip, tears springing to my eyes against my will.

Crack.

Another finger.

I scream again, and this time the sound echoes off the stone walls.

Crack.

I begin to lose my sense of time. I may tremble and sob, but I don't speak the truth of Vayrith.

They try everything. Threats. Torture. Sweet promises of mercy. I feel none of it after hours of pain. Instead, I let myself drift to somewhere else. To when I was just a girl in my village, braiding my sister's hair after dinner with our parents.

To when Pat and I would run through the woods, racing to our spot on the hill.

To when I watched Rhune bleed for me, his shadows lashing like wild things to protect what he thought was worth saving.

I cling to those fragments like driftwood. If there's breath within me, there's still a fight inside me. However faint and fragile.

My breath scrapes shallow through my throat, barely enough to fuel my chest. My fingers throb like molten iron where they've been shattered. I cradle them close and let my eyes drift closed for the first time since being locked away.

Healing magic pulls me from the safety of unconsciousness. It's soft and warm, a false feeling of safety as it seeps into my skin and mends my body.

My eyes close . . . and they start over again.

Then again.

And again.

Sometimes it's Sorryn who asks. Sometimes Adamaris. Sometimes neither. Just the pain and the silence that follows.

I want to scream at the pain, but my voice is gone.

Still, I haven't told them anything.

You're not like the last queen . . .

Enari's voice echoes in the hollow of my heart where strength used to live.

I close my eyes and try to picture Rhune's face.

Not the broken version in the dining hall. Not the still, bloodied figure I was dragged away from.

The real Rhune.

The one who called me Little Dove in my sleep like I was a treasure to protect.

Little Dove, I hear him say. *Keep fighting.*

A small sob escapes before I can stop it.

I don't know if he's alive.

I don't know if any of them are.

"Please . . ." My voice cracks as I make a plea to their goddess. "If there's any power within me, let me have it."

Nothing answers.

No spark or divine warmth.

The faces of the women in the selection cross through my mind.

Virelle.

Lisbeth.

Thalia.

Tears trail down my cheeks as I try once more to let the Goddess hear me. "I can't let all of them down. I can't let their sacrifices be in vain. *Please.*"

The silence swallows me whole.

CHAPTER THIRTY-TWO

RHUNE

The world comes back to me in fragments.

Pain, first. Searing and deep, blooming just beneath my ribs and through my entire midsection.

The scent around me comes next, teasing my nostrils. Smoke curling in the air, antiseptic herbs steeped in tonic, and beneath it all, something faintly metallic.

Blood, maybe.

I hear voices, soft and urgent, but none of them hers as I try to filter through them all.

That's when the panic sets in and my eyes fly open.

Elysia.

The first thing I remember is her eyes.

Not the soft, defiant gaze she wore when she spoke of burning down this world in her chambers.

Not the haunted flicker that clung to her after we told her about Vayrith.

The sight of her eyes steady and sure as she held a dagger poised at the center of her chest. Those eyes were terrifying in their certainty. As if she'd already decided . . . as if she knew nothing else could save us at that moment.

I can still hear her voice, calm over the roar of chaos: *"You forced me to be here, but you can't force me to remain here."*

The image claws its way to the surface and I jolt.

My breath tears from my throat like it's been stolen. My heart pounds so hard I can hear it in my ears, drowning out everything else. I don't recognize the ceiling above me and don't know where I am, but it doesn't matter.

Because she's not here and I don't remember what happened after that.

Could she . . . could she be gone?

"Elysia," her name rips free from my throat, cracked and ragged.

I lurch upright, shadows reacting before I can think, flaring from beneath my skin in sharp, violent tendrils. The pain that follows is instant, white-hot and searing across my ribs and shoulder. My body's barely holding together, but I don't care.

The last image I have of her is with steel at her heart.

I wasn't enough for her to not feel driven to even think of doing such a thing. I wasn't strong enough, despite countless years hiding the depths of my powers and training in secret at Serenath's request.

For so long only she and Zayvin knew.

Everything I am would change our world if I let it be known. Never did I want the title or power of being king. I would have kept my strength hidden forever, if it weren't for Elysia being dragged into my world.

With her life on the line now, I don't care who knows.

Hands press down on me. Gentle words follow, but they barely pierce the haze. I throw them off and stumble out of the cot, searching the space around me.

Stone walls. Violet light slanting through the far window.

No trace of my dove.

None.

My shadows stretch outward in every direction, seeking her like they always do. A heartbeat. A flicker. Anything.

The threads come back cold, untethered from her.

She's gone from my reach.

A hollow ache opens inside me, deeper than any wound Sorryn gave me. This isn't just fear.

It's the unbearable knowledge that the one person who's ever seen through the mask—who looked at me and didn't see the broken, left-over king—is somewhere I can't reach.

I will tear apart the world to fix that.

You're safe. You're with me. Nothing is going to touch you here, Little Dove.

I told her those words—and not even a day later, she'd been harmed in my presence.

Rage swirls in my mind and I force my eyes shut as I take deep breaths, trying to center myself. I can't do anything for her if I can't pull my emotions together.

Instantly the image of my hands cupping her face reverently in her chamber surfaces. The brief moment I'd allowed myself to stop fighting against my need to touch her—to hold her and comfort her. How our breaths had mingled, so achingly close.

"You're the only soul atop these clouds I don't fear," she'd told me.

The storm in my heart and mind wanes and I realize my response to her hadn't been entirely true. My head hangs down.

Instead of telling her that hers is the only soul I do fear, I should have told her that her soul is the only one I fear not knowing—of not understanding every crevice of what makes her Elysia.

I fear not letting her see mine in return. Of being alone for eternity, when I know there's this woman who *sees* me and fights for me.

"He's always been my choice!" she yelled at Sorryn. *"And he will always belong wherever I am."*

I'm tired of fighting this. I'm tired of acting like I can stand on the sidelines and watch her with someone else at the end of these courtships, when I know where she belongs: hand in hand with me.

Perhaps there's a path in which she can be politically joined with Zayvin in their rule, but next to me outside of their throne room.

A hollow opens in my chest, dark and yearning. I barely hear the voices calling my name over the sound of my own heart breaking.

"Rhune."

I open my eyes at the sound of my brother's voice, lifting my head as resolve forms within me. It's time to find the woman I might have fallen for long before she knew I was even in the shadows of her dreams.

I refuse to believe she could be gone.

Zayvin steps into the chamber in a rush of shadows, his presence commanding enough that even my own shadows still.

I don't speak. I just look at him, waiting for the blow. Waiting for him to tell me she's gone and that my hope is for nothing.

"She's alive," he says with his hands up, and it's then I realize my shadows are still whirling around me. "But she's still in his court."

Relief hits me so hard I nearly choke on it as I call my shadows back into me.

She's alive. I can still save her.

With that news, I can truly take in the room I'm in for the first time. My focus is instantly on understanding my current situation with the hope of cultivating a plan to get to her quickly. I drag my gaze across it until my eyes land on the cot to my left.

Serenath.

Her chest rises in shallow breaths as her eyes remain closed. Her skin is gray, completely absent of the blue that marks her as a Dromin.

Her powers are gone.

"You both nearly didn't make it," Zayvin says, his gaze on her as he steps to my side. His tone is uncharacteristically tight. "It's been days, and even then, our healers could barely do anything. Her injuries . . . they were never meant to be survived. She gave too much and burned too hot. You know what it means when a soul fuels magic to that degree."

I nod slowly. The final reserve. The point of no return.

"How did I survive?" I ask, voice hoarse. "I felt the way his power seared through my body. It devoured me from the inside out, burning through me like a disease that took root."

Zayvin's jaw tics. "No one here could heal you, Rhune. You were too far gone. We tried everything."

My brow pinches at his answer—and the obvious, that someone clearly had, since I'm standing here. "Then why am I still breathing?"

He steps close until his lips are at my ear and his voice soft, not meant for others to hear. "Last night one healer was overseeing all patients. She summoned me, worried if anyone else had seen what your body was doing."

My hand rises to settle over my abdomen absentmindedly.

"Your shadows and light encapsulated you in a dome. She watched your shadows stitch your wounds together. And your light burned brightly in each wound after, searing them closed."

My head jerks back. "That's . . . not possible. I don't have healing magic."

Zayvin scans the room before leaning back in. "The healer said it looked like a miracle from the Goddess herself as the veins in your body seemed to pulsate bright silver, like when the Hearth Tree comes to life with connection to the Goddess."

I'm left feeling incredulous shock as my mouth opens and no words come out.

"Unfortunately the other elf that came through with you and Serenath didn't make it."

My shock shifts to utter confusion as he points to the back corner of the room.

A third cot.

The sheet is tucked neatly over a body. A gesture of dignity until the rites of passage over their soul can be performed.

I force myself forward, one step at a time, as I beg my mind to remember what happened. When I reach out, my hands hesitate for a moment before I pull the sheet back.

Enari lies still beneath the white linen. Her expression is softer than I've ever seen it in the short time I was in her presence. There's no more pain. No fury. No flicker of the battle that was always raging beneath her skin.

Just peace.

The tattoos that once flickered across her body are faint now. As if the magic has finally let her go. As if in death, she's finally free of it.

My knees hit the floor beside her cot.

The memories don't come gently. Images slam into me, one after another.

Adamaris and Sorryn were huddled together, hushed in their argument as she'd crept back into the room.

Her hands grabbed Serenath's body and dragged her toward me in the quiet aftermath of the battle.

The way her teeth clenched when the High Priestess's control pulsed in her tattoos and she moved anyway.

"Take her," she whispered to me, moving one of my arms to drape over my fallen teacher. *"Use your shadows and get out. If you don't, I fear what will happen to our queen."*

I'd found the last bit of energy locked deep within my body to find my waystone just as Sorryn and Adamaris turned to see her bending over us.

My eyes had widened and she jerked to face them, palms blazing with fire as her tattoos flickered over and over. Her knees had trembled as she screamed, *"I will not let you use me for your wicked plans anymore!"*

The way Sorryn and Adamaris had lifted hands wielding magic in unison. They sent blasts meant to kill.

Then, at the last second, I reached out for her. Just enough for the tip of my pointer finger to touch the back of her calf as my hand cradled the waystone.

That final, desperate touch to get us all out of there.

We had no plan and no time, but she made that one moment matter.

My throat burns. I don't realize I'm shaking until I reach for her hand and my fingers can barely hold steady.

"I thought I got us all out in time," I whisper. "I'm sorry."

She sacrificed herself for us.

I press my palm to her cool forehead and close my eyes.

"I swear I'll remember you as you were in the end. Brave. Brilliant. *Free.* Goddess, please wrap her soul into your welcoming embrace and rejoice her for the warrior she is."

Zayvin doesn't speak as I feel him come to my side and rest a hand on my shoulder.

There's reverence in the silence and comfort he offers. I'm grateful for it.

"I thought I could save us all."

"You tried," Zayvin says quietly. "You arrived tangled together and we did everything we could to save her, but she was already gone."

I rise, slow, trembling. My eyes scan the chamber again, restless now in my desire for justice.

"Where is it?" I ask quietly.

Zayvin lifts a brow. "Where is what?"

"My waystone."

He doesn't answer immediately—and that tells me everything.

"You took it," I say, the realization cold and sharp. "You took it from me."

"You would have gone back the moment you woke. Alone, enraged, and without a plan, which would have surely gotten you killed this time."

"I still will," I snarl. "I will go back there alone and right these wrongs and save Elysia."

"You won't," he replies calmly before taking a deep breath. "Because this time, you will have the backing of this court."

There's silence for a beat. Long. Heavy.

His voice softens as he says, "I need you to tell me what happened. Everything."

So I do. Every brutal detail. Every twisted manipulation. Every time Adamaris used her magic to serve Sorryn's desires. Sorryn's greatest weapon: her feelings for him.

When I finish, Zayvin exhales a breath like he's been holding it for years.

"I knew it," he growls out before shaking his head. "I knew she wasn't truly choosing him. They're trying to force the joining ceremony to occur in two days' time. Adamaris nearly has the Council convinced."

He walks toward the windows, staring out into the dark violet sky, streaked with lightning beyond the castle. His voice is low when he speaks again.

"We've gone through two queens in his favor already, Rhune. Two queens who chose him. Our magic's already fading as is, we can't . . ."

"The court can't afford for her to choose him," I finish for him, "because if she does, feeding on humans' dreams won't be enough."

He nods. "We could lose our connection to our magic permanently."

It's the first time I hear it spoken with such finality. Until now, it's only been whispered what-ifs between us over a glass of liquor late into the night.

The true cost that has kept me duty-bound for Elysia's choice to make a difference.

He turns back to me, his expression resolute. "Then we do what must be done. We will go to war against the Court of Dreams, before there is no Court of Nightmares to oppose them any longer."

The air shifts into something heavy and suffocating.

I'm coming for you, Little Dove.

CHAPTER THIRTY-THREE

ELYSIA

The ground beneath me is soft, almost spongy as my bare feet tentatively step through the forest. My nostrils flare as I scent something sweet and head toward it. The air is rich with moisture and a sheen of wetness quickly gathers on my brow.

I blink into the darkness and for a second I hesitate, wondering why I don't feel any fear here. I don't recognize where I am, but for some reason it's not the kind of darkness that suffocates and scares me.

It lives and breathes as I push through a dense bush and come into a clearing with the moon shining down on me and the magical world I've stepped into.

Above me, trees with obsidian bark stretch into a sky woven with violet and silver, their branches heavy with fruit that glows faintly like lanterns lighting the way. Awe threads through my body until it nestles into my heart, and my mouth falls open as I spin around. The air hums with energy, thick and warm against my skin. Blossoms the color of blood and moonlight sway on the branches, releasing threads of glittering pollen into the stillness.

This place . . . it feels like a spot occupied by the gods themselves. Wild. Untamed. Beautiful.

I reach out and brush my fingers along a vine spiraling up a tree's trunk. It pulses faintly beneath my touch, as if aware of me, responding in some secret language between the root and soil. Suddenly the soft grass beneath my feet lights up and follows me with each step I take.

I gasp as my eyes widen with wonder. My cheeks hurt from how wide my smile becomes as I begin to jump and dance around, testing if the light will continue to spread through the ground I touch.

It does, until I find myself dizzy and out of breath from my frolicking in the space. Contentment warms my chest as I come to a stop and stare up into the night sky. It was just clear and full of stars when I arrived, but now the light of the moon is beginning to become obstructed by clouds quickly rolling in.

A breeze stirs the undergrowth, carrying a scent that is sharp and clean. Rain is coming.

Suddenly a tingle runs down my neck and my gaze falls from the sky to the forest around me.

I have a gut-wrenching feeling that I'm no longer alone.

I stiffen, scanning the dense trees, heart hammering against my ribs. The vibrant colors seem to dim at the edges of my vision, as if something unseen drinks the light from the air itself.

A low rumble reverberates through the ground, vibrating up through the soles of my feet. I can't tell if it's thunder from the storm brewing above, or the being that has my senses on high alert.

The shadows thicken ahead, congealing into something massive moving toward me as the trees rustle and fruits drop to the ground from the disruption.

My breath catches as two slits of silver pierce the darkness, eyes watching me.

It steps closer, the shadows shaping into something both terrifying and beautiful as it comes fully into the clearing with me.

A creature forged of shadow and smoke, large wings folded tight against its sides. A long tail coiled low to the earth snakes around, swaying from left to right behind it. My eyes travel up its long neck to the head that cranes down to keep me in its view. Twin horns lift from the top of its head, curling back into a small spiral at the tips.

A dragon.

That can't be . . . it's not like any I've ever read of in the old tales. Where are its scales and gleaming teeth dripping with saliva? Surely fire can't exist in a belly of shadows if it chooses to attack me?

This one seems to be made of the night itself, every inch of it shifting and ethereal, as if it might dissolve into the forest if I blow on its shadows.

My legs refuse to obey my mind's frantic commands to run. Instead, I stumble backward, heart clawing at my ribs, until my heel catches on a root and I fall hard onto the mossy ground.

The creature lets out a rumble. A deep, resonant hum that rattles my bones.

I scramble backward on my hands, panic wild in my throat as it approaches.

One massive, clawed foot sinks into the ground, easily ripping through the very real and physical world. Then another.

So it is real. It's not just shadows that my mind is conjuring together to play a twisted joke.

I freeze as it lets out a large huff of hot air that blows against my face, taking my hair over my shoulders with it. Without warning, it lowers its massive head and shoves it against my chest with a rumbling sigh that nearly knocks me flat. On instinct, my hands fly to its large head to keep me from being flattened.

My eyes are wide and my body is gripped in terror and confusion as I realize I'm now touching the dragon. *What do I do?*

For a long, breathless moment, all I can feel is the cool ripple of shadows running along my hands as my fingers tremble on a very real and hard body that seems to lie beneath the shadows.

I don't move. I barely breathe as I wait to see what it does next.

Yet it simply stays there, leaning its enormous snout against me, waiting.

As if it needs something from me, but what could that possibly be?

I don't have any food on me—I *am* the food.

The creature lets out another low sound, a mix of a huff and a whine as it nudges harder against me, urging me to move, I think.

Could it be seeking . . . comfort?

I'm deranged for the thought, but slowly and cautiously I lift my hands and move one to the center of his nose.

My fingers hover inches from the dark mist of his skin, expecting them to pass through empty air as if the last time were a fluke.

Yet when I touch him, he is still solid beneath my palm.

I let out a shaky breath. "You're real," I whisper, the words seeming so stark against the hush of the forest.

He chirps, a short, sharp sound of approval, and nudges me more insistently. I move my hand up and down the part of his head that I can reach.

A laugh bubbles up my throat, shaky and disbelieving. I'm petting a dragon.

Suddenly he backs up and straightens his front leg and rests his head on the ground.

An invitation?

"I'm going to regret this," I murmur, my heart thundering with fear and wonder all at once.

The dragon waits, utterly still, silver eyes watching me with a strange, unblinking patience.

I gather my courage and move toward his foot. For a second I hesitate and glance at him.

"You're not going to eat me if I try to climb you?"

He lets out a chuff, as if I'm being ridiculous, and I take that as his approval to continue. Slowly I step up onto his leg and lower my hands to crawl up his limb until I cross over his shoulder and find a spot just behind his neck to settle into.

My heart is thudding wildly in my chest, but the fear has been swiftly replaced with excitement.

He is broad and solid beneath me as his wings unfurl with a whisper of movement, vast and glistening.

For a moment we remain still, but then suddenly he leaps into the air. The ground drops away beneath us in a rush of wind and weightlessness.

I clutch the thin tendrils of shadow that fall down his neck like the mane of a horse as we rise, the air turning colder, sharper, slicing against my cheeks.

The trees fall away, replaced by endless clouds around us.

A low rumble echoes from his chest, akin to exhilaration, and I laugh aloud as we ascend, the sound torn away by the wind.

"Same, buddy."

Clouds swirl around us, thick and silver-tinged, but a storm brews in the oncoming ones in front of us. They're dark gray and furious, lightning threading across the sky like veins of molten light.

He flies straight into it and I let out a scream and bury my face against his warm neck.

He's going to kill us both.

Then the first drops of rain kiss my skin, cool and refreshing as they trace paths down my bare arms. The air crackles with energy, the world alive in a way I've never felt before—dangerous, wild, and breathtaking.

Slowly I gather the courage to pull my head up and look around as we fly through the storm.

The dragon weaves through the worst of it with effortless grace, dodging forks of lightning that split the sky. His wings slice through the heavy mist, each beat carrying us higher, faster, as if he is daring the storm to try to touch us.

A giddy energy coils low in my stomach.

I bury my fingers deeper into his shifting mane, my heart soaring with a freedom I've never known.

I should be afraid.

I should be clinging on for dear life and begging him to take us back down.

Instead, I throw my head back and close my eyes, letting the rain soak me to the bone, letting the power of the sky and the creature beneath me burn away the fear.

A crack of thunder rumbles through the sky directly above us, accompanied by lightning that is sharp and blinding.

The dragon flinches mid-flight. I feel a ripple of tension through the shadows of his body, and for one terrible second, I feel the shift in his balance.

The world tilts and my fingers scramble for a hold, clutching at the wisps of his mane.

Then I'm falling.

The wind tears the breath from my lungs as the storm swallows me whole.

Rain lashes against my skin like needles. Lightning flashes, illuminating the sky in bursts of violent white, each glimpse showing me the dragon's form growing smaller above me. I see it reaching for me with outstretched claws of smoke that can't quite catch.

I tumble through the clouds, weightless and screaming, though no sound escapes my throat.

I close my eyes and let the storm rage around me. At least my life will end by daring to do something magical.

The air whips around me as I fall, until a searing pain explodes across my hand, yanking me back into my body with a violence that leaves me gasping. My eyes fly open.

I jolt upright from the stone ground in my prison, the breath tearing from my throat as the world tilts violently around me. Stone walls

shimmer and distort, the pulse of enchantments weaving through the air in broken, flickering patterns.

It was just a dream. A beautiful dream.

My stomach knots painfully, hollow and cramping from days of being fed only scraps of bread and sips of stale water.

The faint scent of blood and magic hangs heavy, saturating the damp air I drag into my lungs, but it's the burning pain on my hand that draws my focus. I glance down and find a mark seared into my hand glowing faintly, silver-edged and brutally raw in the soft flesh of my palm.

Was it real?

I press my hand against my chest, curling over it, and fight through the weakness trying to drag me back to the floor.

A shout cuts through the haze of my thoughts.

A clash of steel follows, the sharp crack of magic splitting the air.

Is the castle under attack?

The thought would terrify a normal person, but instead, it fills me with a trembling, reckless surge of strength.

Rhune.

If he's here, if he's fighting, then maybe . . . maybe Enari found him in time. Maybe Serenath fought harder than I even knew.

Hope stirs in my chest, fragile but insistent, daring to spread its wings, and I cling to it. To the image of them all alive and storming these cursed halls.

I cling to the belief that I am not forgotten and discarded, left to rot in this prison. I force myself upright, teeth gritted against the scream it rips from my fatigued muscles.

The dream of soaring through storm clouds atop a dragon fades from my mind, but the feeling it left behind remains—the memory of freedom in that sky.

I will not let that feeling die. Not now.

CHAPTER THIRTY-FOUR

ELYSIA

A low crackle threads through the silence of my prison, the sound much closer than the clash of magic I'd felt rocking the distant areas of the castle.

The soft hum of enchantments that line the bars pulses faintly in the dark of night, weaving blue-and-silver patterns that shimmer against the stone walls.

I walk over to a particularly shadowed area of my cell in an attempt to hide, as a sharp, splintering crack echoes off the walls.

As much as my heart wants it to be my allies, this world has proven that it loves nothing more than to test my strength when I'm down. If there were ever a time I felt too ragged to defend myself from whatever fate wants to send me now, it would be this moment.

The faint glow of the enchantments brightens for a heartbeat as the door to the tower bursts open.

My breath catches, the fragile hope I'd clung to flickering back to life.

The moonlight spills through the narrow window, and for a breathless moment, it feels like the world holds its breath with me as the figure steps into the light.

Rhune.

The sight of him cleaves through the haze of pain and hunger clinging to my bones.

I've always found him beautiful, but in this moment, he truly takes my breath away.

His skin, that dusky blend of deep blues and muted purples, looks almost celestial in the moon's pale embrace. His hair catches the light

like spun silver, the longer strands on top tousled imperfectly enough to make him seem untamed and wild as he breaks in.

He lifts his head, and the light catches those violet eyes I've come to crave seeing each day.

For a single, shuddering heartbeat, I don't feel the bruises, the chains, or the cold.

I feel only him.

I rush from the corner, my knees nearly buckling beneath me as a reminder that I'm not fit to run.

He's here.

He's alive.

Our eyes clash, and with one glance over my body, his face turns to one of fury.

His voice comes out in a rumble. "Stand back, Little Dove. I'm going to tear this prison to the fucking ground."

His hand presses flat against the enchantments and I stall in my approach as light magic crackles and sparks violently against his palm, casting wild flashes of light across his face. I see him grimace as the enchantments resist, the magic fighting to hold.

His other hand comes to the bars and his eyes close as his entire body lights up, pulsating and moving through him to his hands like a perfect conduit.

He grits his teeth as his jaw clenches and pours more of himself into the assault. His body shines like he's a star in the sky cast down to live with us.

With a final roar, the enchantments shatter in a cascade of silver sparks as the bars snap open with a deafening boom.

Then he's here, crossing the threshold between us in two strides. With a jolt of light magic, my shackles fall off my wrist, clattering to the ground with a resounding finality.

I crash into him so hard it nearly knocks the breath from my lungs.

His arms wrap around me instantly, pulling me tight against his chest, so tight I almost can't breathe, but I don't care. I press my face into his shoulder, trembling, the full weight of everything I've been carrying breaking open inside me.

For the first time since they took me, I feel safe.

I let out a soft, broken sound—raw and deep from my soul. His arms tighten even further, as if trying to shield me from the entire world.

From the atrocities he can only begin to imagine with the bruises on my body.

"I never want to feel that helpless again," I whisper against him, the words cracking under the weight of everything I cannot say. A shudder wracks my body. "I couldn't do anything except hope that all of you made it out alive. I . . . I'm so sorry I couldn't help you or the others."

"Stop it," he soothes before leaning back just enough to look down at me, his hands sliding up to cradle my face like I'm something precious. "You stayed alive. There's more strength in that than you give yourself credit for."

Pain flickers in his eyes and he hesitates as his mouth opens again to speak. I blink up at him as dread swirls in my stomach. I've never seen him choked up, and I prepare myself for the worst.

"Enari . . ." he says finally, voice rough. "She got us out. She gave everything to get Serenath and me away. She . . ."

His throat closes around the words and I know. She's gone.

I shake my head, tears spilling over even as I try to smile for the woman who changed our fate. "She was so brave," I whisper through them as my eyes close.

Her voice comes back to me. *"You know what it means to fight for something bigger than yourself. It's my turn to do that."*

"You did it, Enari," I murmur, hoping that somehow her soul hears me. "You fought like a warrior."

My eyes open and I steel myself.

"And Serenath?"

"She's alive," he says, and just as quickly as my heart soars, it comes crashing down, breaking into jagged pieces. "But she hasn't woken. We don't know if she will."

A soft, broken sound escapes me as I lean my forehead against his chest.

"We've lost too many," I breathe out, unsure if he can even hear me with the battle ensuing in the castle.

Life is so fragile in this world. Tomorrow truly is never promised for any of us.

It's a miracle we're both standing here now.

An aching urgency awakens within me to not leave things unsaid. To not go to my grave with my heart locked away in a prison even stronger than the one Sorryn built.

Rhune tilts my chin up, his thumb brushing a tear from my cheek with devastating tenderness.

"I'll always find you," he murmurs, his voice a low promise that cuts straight through me. "There's nowhere you could be lost to me."

My heart cracks wide open at that.

I bury my face in his shoulder again, my body trembling with everything I'm too afraid to say.

"What if I want to be lost *with* you?" I whisper. "What if I want to leave all of this behind and choose you?"

He goes utterly still against me. I hear his breath hitch as his hands fall to my hips, tightening like he wants to pull me even closer.

Slowly I tilt my head back, and when our eyes meet this time, it's like the rest of the world falls away.

There are no courts, no crowns, and no semblance of duty.

Only him.

Only me.

His hands slowly slide up the sides of my body until they caress my cheeks and gently thread into the hair at my temples. His movements are so soft and tender, a stark difference from the storm I see raging in his eyes and the way his jaw clenches like it's going to shatter.

For a moment, we just breathe each other in, our foreheads nearly brushing as he leans in, the space between us crackling with everything we've tried to deny.

I'm not sure who moves first, but suddenly his lips are on mine.

It's desperate and fierce. The kind of kiss that consumes your body and mind.

I gasp against him, my hands fisting in the front of his tunic, pulling him closer as his mouth slants over mine again, like he's trying to brand himself into my being.

His fingers tighten in my hair, angling my head, deepening the kiss until I'm dizzy from the hunger he pours into every searing touch.

I feel the way his chest shudders against mine as if he, too, is barely holding himself together.

When I open for him, he growls low in his throat, a sound of pure, ragged possession before his tongue sweeps into my mouth, stroking, claiming, and tasting.

It's two broken souls finding each other in the wreckage.

I drink him in like water after a lifetime without it, and he gives no mercy in return, devouring me with the kind of reckless, brutal need that leaves no room for caution.

Heat surges through me, curling low in my belly before spreading outward until I'm trembling from the force of it. My entire body presses against his, desperate to feel every inch of him, to convince myself that he's real. That he's here and I'm not alone anymore.

His hands leave my hair to grip my hips once more, hauling me against him so tightly there's no space left between us, only the pounding of our hearts pressed together.

I lose myself in him.

In the strength of his arms, the heat of his touch, the taste of him—salt and shadows and something fiercely, achingly Rhune.

When we finally break apart, we're both gasping, our foreheads pressed together, his thumb tracing slow, reverent circles against my waist as if he's trying to memorize the feel of me in his hands.

I keep my arms around his neck, unwilling to let him go, grounding myself in the feel of the way his body vibrates with restrained need beneath my touch.

He leans in again, slower this time, brushing his nose against mine. His breath is warm and unsteady across my lips.

His thumb comes up to drag along the curve of my lower lip, a featherlight caress that sends a shiver rippling down my spine.

"I almost lost you," he murmurs, so quietly I barely catch it over the pounding of my heart.

I tilt my head, pressing a kiss into the center of his palm that comes up to cup my cheek once more, savoring the way his hand trembles ever so slightly as he holds me.

This moment feels like we stole it from the beings above that tried to keep it from us, untouched by duty or fear . . . like we're defying fate.

I want to stay in it forever.

A sharp bang echoes down the corridor before I can even steady my breathing.

Rhune stiffens around me, his body going rigid in instinctive defense. His hands tighten against my hips, his chest vibrating with a low growl deep in his throat.

Heavy footsteps slam against the stone, accompanied by the shrill hum of power slicing through the air.

"Stop them at all costs!" Sorryn's voice bellows from beyond the doorway.

Rhune spins, shoving me behind him just as the High Priestess bursts into the room and lifts her hand. His shadows begin to rise just as the same thunderclap of energy she wielded in the grove during the selection erupts outward, spilling through the room.

It strikes Rhune with a crack of force that splits the air as he absorbs it all, preventing it from touching me.

He grunts, his body jerking as the magic wraps around him—thick cords of silver energy weaving into ropes that slam him back against the far wall, pinning him.

His teeth grit against the pain, but he doesn't cry out.

A fresh wave of horror slams through me, rooting me in place as Sorryn storms into the room.

A blade of searing white light forms in his hand and he stalks forward, his face twisted with rage.

"You will no longer interfere with what is mine!" he roars at Rhune, magic flaring wildly around him. "This ends now."

He raises the blade just as I watch Rhune's body begin to glow, as if he's trying to wield his powers to break through the magic around him like he did to the enchantments in the bars.

Rhune turns his head toward me, violet eyes locking onto mine, filled with something I can't bear to name.

Acceptance.

Like we know he's not going to be quick enough this time.

No.

A scream rips from my throat. I surge forward as Sorryn lifts his blade.

Something inside me breaks as time slows.

The world narrows to a single point of focus: *Not again*.

I will not watch him die.

Pain explodes across my back, sharp and molten, in the same spot as in the Valgys nightmare.

A wild and ancient magic surges free and it feels like home. It feels like *mine.*

Light erupts from my back in a flood of silver and purple that lights up the room.

I move without thinking, instinct carrying me as power spills from my veins like a predator unleashed.

Sorryn's arm jerks mid-strike as my invisible threads catch and coil around him. His sword clatters from his hand, useless, as I flex my fingers.

The blood in his body answers to *me* now.

I can feel the flow of life beneath his skin, the pounding rush of his heart, and with a simple, effortless tug, I throw him across the room like a discarded puppet.

He hits the stone wall with a crack of impact and slumps to the ground, unconscious.

I turn toward the High Priestess. She's already charging, her mouth twisted in fury, her hands gathering power in crackling spheres of silver.

I don't flinch. I remember the cold satisfaction in her eyes when she healed my wounds just to carve them open again.

I remember the way she used Enari against her will, as if she thought herself a god to do whatever she wanted with the lives around her.

I remember Virelle's strength as she stared this monster down.

I remember the way Thalia sought to give me comfort as the orb seared through my mind and she died for it.

A cold clarity settles over me as I raise my hand.

The blood inside her responds and she stumbles mid-step, her face contorting as she realizes too late. . . what I'm capable of now.

I draw on her blood as easily as breathing, willing it upward through her body, siphoning the life from her.

She screams shrilly as blood seeps from her nose and ears.

I allow her body to drop to the ground and she falls to her knees, eyes blazing with hatred.

"You will never be as powerful as *she* was," she spits, voice gurgling through blood that no longer obeys her as it pours from her mouth.

I step closer, my hand steady and my heart pounding for justice.

"I don't need to be," I whisper, not caring for a moment who she's referring to. "I only need to be enough to end you."

With a final pull, her heart ceases to beat. She crumples to the ground, lifeless at last.

I stand over her crumpled body, breathing hard with my hand still outstretched, like I'm half expecting her to jolt awake.

The room crackles with the fading remnants of magic, the metallic scent of blood suffocating the room. I hate the way I inhale it and feel . . . peace.

Taking her life shouldn't feel this intoxicating.

A broken sound draws my gaze to Rhune.

He's no longer struggling against the magic that bound him because it's gone, unraveled the moment the High Priestess fell. Yet now he's collapsed against the floor, his hands clawing at his chest, a ragged gasp tearing from his throat.

"Rhune," I breathe, stumbling toward him.

Was I too late?

The moment I reach for him, pain lances through my own body again—a sharp, burning ache radiating from the spot on my back. I stagger, clutching the wall for support as heat blazes up my spine and into my skull.

Once more the light that seems to come from my back flares, and as it does, I watch the same glow begin from the torn fabric of Rhune's tunic where he had clawed at it, pulsing just above his heart.

A mark.

Silver and violet, the same as the colors that seem to come from my back. The light from our marks spills outward, filling the chamber with a living glow that seems to pulse in rhythm with our heartbeats.

It hits me then, a flood of memories assaulting me.

My knees buckle as my consciousness twists.

The past claws at me, demanding to be remembered, and I feel myself slipping into it.

CHAPTER THIRTY-FIVE

ELYSIA

The world splits open inside me.

It starts with a tremor behind my eyes, a pressure that builds and builds until the ground itself seems to heave open beneath my feet, carrying me into the past.

Images crash through my mind like a blast of light magic, hot and blinding, each one cracking open the reality I thought I knew.

Steel clangs against steel, the reverberation racing up my arms until my bones ache. I stagger, my balance slipping before I dig my boots into the ground and summon an illusion of myself. I jerk to the side as my opponent watches the illusion of me falling to the ground. He takes the bait before his eyes can perceive what I've done. By then, it's too late, and my blade slashes across his neck.

The next memory races into my mind, jerking me into the sky.

Ash thickens the air around me, clogging my throat as I try to see through to the destruction below. I try to breathe, but every inhale tastes of fire and ruin. Tears run down my face. Pain erupts in my chest as if a sword cleaves through me, but I'm alone atop my creature.

The pain disappears as I'm pulled through to another moment in the sky. The wind whips around me, snapping my hair across my face, the strands damp with blood and sweat. Shadows bloom overhead, vast and monstrous, blocking out what little light seeps through the clouds.

My dragon roars, its sound splitting the skies open as purple flames blossom across the battlefield like poisoned flowers.

I recognize the shadows swirling atop the creature and that same echoing roar.

Vayrith.

He's the creature from my dream. He's no longer some distant, beautiful myth. *He's mine.*

The battlefield suddenly stretches out before me, my feet on the ground and not in the sky, or even the clouds. The human world. It's a broken wasteland of torn banners and shattered bones.

Through the carnage, I see him.

A figure cutting through the smoke, light clinging to him like a second skin.

A man with violet eyes and long silver hair, his hands stained red, his face twisted with grief.

Rhune, but not Rhune.

Castion.

The name burns across my mind with the force of a memory clawing its way out of the grave.

I run to him, my heart a frantic drumbeat, my body screaming warnings I refuse to heed. His arms open for me, and like a fool desperate for the comfort of a past already lost, I throw myself into them.

His warmth is real. His hands are firm and trembling against my back. His breath hitches in my ear as he says my name, "*Katalina.*"

It's so soft it cuts deeper than any blade. I've missed him.

For one stolen moment, I let myself believe we are still whole.

Then I feel it . . . the sharp, cold bite of a blade sliding between my ribs from the back.

I'd allowed myself to feel a semblance of tenderness again, just for it to be used against me. By him . . . by my soulmate.

My gasp is stolen by the storm as pain blossoms through my body, raw and all-consuming. I clutch at him, confused, terrified, feeling my blood hot and thick between us.

His hands don't let go, holding me through the betrayal. When my knees buckle, he follows me down, murmuring my name like an apology.

Rage and heartbreak ignite within me, twin infernos tearing through my soul.

With the last strength left in my failing body, I summon a blade of blood, plunging it into the heart I once trusted more than my own.

I see the shock flicker through his eyes as his life spills into my hands, but there's also relief.

We collapse together, tangled in ruin. Two souls cleaved apart by war and a fate we couldn't fight.

The sky cracks open above us, raining fire and ash as our blood soaks the ground, and everything we might have become burns away into the void as our souls leave this world together.

The battlefield tears away from me with a violence that leaves me gasping, my body jolted back into the broken reality of the stone prison that had become my home. I stagger, my hand clawing against the rough wall at my side, seeking something solid in a world that feels like it is crumbling beneath me.

The cold of the stone seeps through my palms, but it does little to steady the way the world tilts and reels around me. My brain struggles to know which life it belongs to—the one I live now or the one I remember from my past.

Pain throbs in my back, the wound that ended me remembered in this life. Each beat of its glow sinks deeper into my bones until it feels as if the mark has always been there, simply waiting for me to awaken.

The same spot Castion drove his blade into me.

I drag in a breath, the taste of iron and dust thick in the back of my throat as if the battle followed me to the present. As the haze of memory slowly ebbs, the weight of understanding slams into me harder than any blade ever could.

I'm not just a girl plucked from obscurity for the selection.

I'm the traitor that defected to the Dark God.

The Nithrin warrior who abandoned her court and soulmate and chose the path of ruin. I'm the catalyst for everything this broken realm still bleeds from.

Katalina.

The name surfaces from the ashes of my mind, carrying with it the crushing certainty of recognition. For a moment, I can't do anything but stand there, feeling it settle into my skin like a second soul waking inside me.

Dots begin to connect as unknowns become clear.

The Valgys in my nightmares weren't hunting me. They were trying to find me to follow me. I'd commanded them as the general of our army.

The Calling Flame didn't stir for a human queen desperate to prove herself, but for a soldier it once lived to serve. Vayrith felt my soul. He knew it was me calling for him.

The ground shudders beneath me, a low, resonant vibration that hums through the stone and into my bones. I lift my gaze toward the crumbling stones above as a sound splits the air.

A roar.

Deep and filled with fury.

Dust rains down from the crumbling ceiling, a haze of stone and ash swirling through the room, and I feel my connection to him burst to life.

Vayrith.

He's come for me.

I brace a hand against the wall, blinking hard against the grit stinging my eyes, forcing myself to scan the room as the last pieces of the world I knew slip through my fingers.

My gaze catches on the empty space where Sorryn's body should have been.

A bitter sound scrapes from my throat, low and raw.

Whether he fled or was dragged away by an ally, I don't know, but my gut tells me it won't be the last time our paths cross.

I press the heel of my hand hard against my chest, willing my heart to steady, willing the fire in my veins to burn away the rising tide of dread as I turn my gaze to the one I called my soulmate in our last life.

The same elf who had just consumed my lips and swore to find me in this life, always.

Through the settling dust and fractured moonlight, I watch his head shake and his brow crease, like he's coming out of the same trance I'd found myself in.

My lips open to speak, but as his gaze collides with mine, his body coils tightly and suddenly all words escape me.

The same violet eyes I was just relieved to see as he found me trapped in this prison are now the same ones that stare at me like I'm a dangerous unknown.

How had things changed so quickly?

He drags his hands down his face as if he could scrub the memories out of his skin, and for a fleeting moment, I wish we could. I wish we could forget and be those two souls who had embraced and felt safety and relief in each other's arms.

He stares at me and for a long, agonizing moment, neither of us speaks.

It is not just his distrustful gaze that weighs heavy on me . . . it's the crushing knowledge that we were soulmates. That we're here now, again, and I have to wonder: *That means we're soulmates in this life as well, right?*

Suddenly his earlier words hit hard and my heart squeezes. *There's nowhere you could be lost to me.*

"I . . ." I try to begin, but the word is a mere rasp that quickly dies on my tongue.

He flinches at the sound of my voice, just slightly, as if it strikes deeper than any blade.

How do I apologize for a betrayal that spans thousands of years?

The question makes me bristle. Do I even need to apologize, when it wasn't my hands from this life?

I take a cautious step forward, arms aching to reach for him, but he stiffens, the distance between us stretching wider than I ever thought possible.

The light from our marks still pulses faintly, casting eerie reflections on the broken stones around us. A constant reminder of where we'd struck each other down in our past lives.

I can see his struggle as his fingers twitch at his side before his hand lifts. I hold my breath as I think maybe he'll reach for me.

The part of him that knew me here, in this life. The Rhune who held me with reverence. The man who tore apart enchantments to reach me.

Layered over it now is the memory of the man who drove a blade into my back to end a war.

His hand falls back down to his side and I let mine do the same.

The same war rages inside of me, an aching confusion of longing and horror, love and betrayal, tangled so tightly I can't begin to separate where one ends and the other begins.

I try again, my voice barely above a whisper. "We're not them. We're not who we were."

A muscle spasms along Rhune's jaw as he drags his gaze away, his hands curling into fists at his sides.

"You say that," he murmurs, voice rough and hoarse, "but it feels like she's still inside you. It feels like I'm still him."

The pain in his voice tears something vital from my chest.

I take another trembling step toward him. "We don't have to be. We can choose something else. We can still—"

The stone wall behind him shudders violently, cutting me off with a blast of magic ripping through the castle with a deafening boom.

Chunks of rock and mortar rain down, forcing Rhune to pivot, shadows rising in a defensive shield around his body that quickly extends to encompass me.

With the wall gone, a massive form is revealed with the glow of the moon's light.

The head comes first, sleek and crowned with spiraling horns of black shadows. Wings beat up and down in deliberate sweeps, scattering rubble with each draft of air sent our way.

Vayrith.

Recognition and happiness erupts from within me. Not just from Katalina's memories, but from my own. From the dream I had where I met him in that beautiful forest of magic.

I ache to sit atop him and feel the wind along my body in this life.

A strangled curse tears from Rhune's throat as he summons his magic to his palms, light gathering in fierce, crackling bolts ready to be unleashed.

"No!" I cry out, instinct taking over as I throw myself between them, arms spread wide, my back to Vayrith's steady, humming presence.

Rhune's magic flickers midair, his hands trembling as he stares at me with a look of wounded disbelief.

The silence between us stretches taut as his shield of shadows slinks away from me, retreating back to him.

Our new reality settles heavily between us.

We aren't just Elysia and Rhune anymore.

We're two souls shaped by blood and war, by choices made long before we were born again.

The weight of it presses down on us, and I watch it suffocating any hope that might have lingered in the wreckage.

Rhune lowers his hands slowly, the light fading from his palms, but the betrayal in his eyes cuts deeper than any magic could.

"You defend him," Rhune says, his voice breaking apart like brittle glass.

I clutch my hands together at my chest, as if I can keep the cracks within my heart from splitting open completely.

"I have to," I whisper back, the words barely making it past the rawness in my throat. I feel something deep inside me tear free, a protectiveness so old and vast it feels like it was stitched into my bones long before this life. "I created him."

The admission hangs between us, thick and poisonous, bleeding into the ruined air around us until there's no space left to breathe.

Rhune closes his eyes, his entire body taut with the war raging inside him. His hands tremble at his sides, the shadows that cling to him flickering with each ragged breath.

When he finally lifts his gaze to me, the elf I knew—the one who kissed me like salvation, the one who broke every rule to reach me in my dreams—he's gone, swallowed whole by the shattering weight of everything we've remembered.

"I spent all these years wondering why I felt drawn to you," he mutters, the words scraping out of him like they hurt to say. His head shakes slowly, as if he still can't quite make peace with what he now knows. "Why I couldn't bear the thought of letting you go."

A dry, broken laugh huffs from his mouth, but there's no humor in it, only bitterness. A grief so profound it threatens to swallow us both whole.

His voice isn't tender anymore. It's hollow and vacant, like something beautiful inside him has died and left only the ruins behind.

The hot sting of tears blurs my vision before I can stop them, slipping free and carving silent tracks down my cheeks.

"Rhune, please," I choke out, reaching toward him without meaning to, the tips of my fingers trembling with the need to touch him, to remind him of what we still are.

His mouth twists into something that is almost a grimace, his hand lifting halfway toward me as if he might reach back, and then falls limply to his side again.

It still hurts him to see me like this, and that small mercy shatters something deeper in me.

"I understand it now," he says through clenched teeth, every syllable torn from his chest like a confession he would rather die than make.

The finality in his voice cleaves through me, sharp and merciless.

I stumble a step forward, unable to stop myself from reaching for him. "Rhune . . . ?"

His name on my lips is a whispered breath, a plea, and me desperately reaching across a distance that grows colder and wider with every heartbeat.

He takes a single, agonizing step back from me and the distance between us spreads open like the battlefield we once stood upon, on opposite sides of the Blood War.

He looks at me with devastation hollowed into the shape of his face, like he's already mourning what was, even though I am still standing right in front of him, wanting to fight for what we could have now.

He looks at me as if the decision has already been made. As if fate has been laughing at us all along for thinking we could find happiness in this life, together.

It's like he believes to the depths of his soul, that no matter what we do, we are doomed to repeat the same tragedy written into our blood.

His violet eyes, once filled with the fierce, trembling hope of a future together, are now empty voids. When he speaks, it's so soft and full of fear, yet the crack in his voice cuts through me deeper than any weapon ever could.

"Will we kill each other in this life as well, Elysia?"

ABOUT THE AUTHOR

R.L. Caulder is a *USA Today*–bestselling paranormal and fantasy romance author. She lives in her writing cave in Orlando, shielded from the intense heat of the Florida sun, with her husband and two furry writing assistants, MeowMeow and Winrey. Life is never boring for Caulder, who has hundreds of imaginary friends vying for her attention and begging for their stories to be told at all times.

Podium

FOR A GOOD TIME

follow us on our socials

podiumentertainment.com

@podiumentertainment

/podiumentertainment

@podium_ent

@podiumentertainment